To Pa

THE DIVISION

by
Ben Kennedy

fruity for sore

but not for you !?

Best wishes

Ben
xxx

About the Author

Ben Kennedy is English and spent almost two decades as an inspector in the Royal Hong Kong Police, both before and after the Handover in 1997, when the Force reverted to its original title of the Hong Kong Police.

Since returning to the UK, Ben has moved away from police work but has maintained close ties with Asia and visits Hong Kong regularly.

The Division is the first Sam Steadings story and will be followed in print by The District in 2023.

This novel is entirely a work of fiction. The names, characters and incidents portrayed in it are the work of the author's imagination. Any resemblance to actual persons, living or dead, events or localities is entirely coincidental.

First published by Thaumasios Publishing Ltd. in 2022

Author's Note

Over the years much has been written about the Royal Hong Kong Police and the author has taken the view that attempting to improve on the many fine factual works produced by ex-colleagues would be impossible. For that reason, a novel became the best way to capture the spirit of the times since Hong Kong was a very special place in the late 1980s.

This book describes the rites of passage that a young and newly fledged Royal Hong Kong Police inspector experienced in their first posting after completing 36 weeks of initial training at Police Training School. The story is in no sense autobiographical but inevitably personal experiences have moulded some of the stories in this book. Every inspector will have had different but similar experiences as they were posted to their first stations, some big, some small, some near, some far. Some loved that experience, and some hated it, and it is worth noting that for all the fond memories of expatriate colleagues, a large proportion of *gweilo* inspectors left after completing a single three-year tour of duty.

The structure and operation of the RHKP described are as the author remembers from when he completed his training in 1989. The organisational structure and chain of command had a significant impact on operational policing and the complex relationships between the various units and individuals was often a source of frustration. Detail that might at first glance seem trivial would have been highly relevant in any incident that crossed regional boundaries and involved multiple units. Internal politics was never far from the surface, and learning to play that game was a key part of a young inspector's journey.

The daily routine described is based on how the RHKP operated in the simpler days before mobile telephones and computers. The Force remained a paper-based organisation until well into the 1990s, and in many ways the equipment, tactics and uniforms were little changed from the 1950s, though certain units such as the Special Duties Unit were equipped with cutting edge equipment.

Characters described are fictional except where an individual is referenced for historical accuracy. All the places named in this book existed except for the two Sai Kung houses which are an amalgam of locations.

Events described are also entirely fictional, however they are inspired by actual events. It is a matter of fact that Hong Kong was on edge in mid-1989 after events in Tiananmen Square on 4th June 1989 and this had an impact on public confidence which was reflected by nervousness in the financial and property markets. There was a brief spate of rioting in Kowloon in June 1989 which has been left out of this book in order not to muddy the waters.

The history books record that serious crime was increasing in the late 1980s when Hong Kong experienced a wave of armed robberies involving the use of pistols, AK-47 assault rifles and grenades. Gangsters such as Yip Kai-foon and Cheung Tsz-keung became infamous for their exploits and a number of criminals, police and bystanders were killed or injured during shootouts. Incidents involving dozens of shots fired were not uncommon. Of particular note was a robbery on 9th June 1991, when a gang armed with AK-47s, and pistols simultaneously attacked five goldsmiths' shops on Mut Wah Street in Kwun Tong during which they fired 54 shots at Police and escaped with gold and jewellery worth HK$5.7 million.

I hope that you enjoy the book and join Sam Steadings for future adventures.

To Dad, for leaving me with a love of books and travel. RIP.

To Bernard for enthusiastic support from the beginning.

To Ian, BJ, Dave and John for being kind enough to offer gentle comment on an incomplete draft at an early stage.

To Valerie and Julian for your patience and advice, you made it all happen.

To Roger for your eagle eye.

To Andy for expert advice on intimate scenes.

To Ian and Bernice for their unfailing support for the project.

To Ric, Paul, Rick, Tommy and Cliff for all the laughs at Police Training School.

To the brave men and women of the RHKP who made this book possible.

CAST OF CHARACTERS

Tsim Sha Tsui Division
Brian McClintock, Divisional Commander
Ricky Ricardo, Assistant Divisional Commander, Operations
Alan Poon, Operations Support Sub-Unit Commander
Paul Wong, Sub-Unit Three Commander
Jenny Tsang, Sub-Unit Four Commander
Andrew Chan, ex-Sub-Unit Four Commander
Sam Steadings, Sub-Unit Four 2i/c
Station Sergeant Cheung, Sub-Unit Four
Station Sergeant Liu, Sub-Unit Four
A-Bo, Sergeant 2715, Duty Sergeant Sub-Unit Four
Eileen, Admin WPC, Sub-Unit Four
Sarah, Admin WPC, Sub-Unit Four

Police Headquarters
Peter Baldwin, Commissioner of Police
Roger Milner, Deputy Commissioner of Police

Other Units
Ronald 'Big Ronny' Brindley, Regional Commander, New Territories
Gerry Smithies, Assistant Commissioner, Operations
Gordon Bathgate, Regional Commander, Kowloon
Gerald Chan, Commandant Police Training School
'Lofty', Chief Inspector Dave Palmer, Police Training School
Patrick Koo, Acting District Commander Yau Tsim
Malcolm Wiggam, Duty Controller Kowloon Command and Control Centre
Steve Jameson, Officer Commanding, Special Duties Unit

Miles Foxton, Senior Superintendent Traffic Kowloon West
Station Sergeant Fung, Traffic Kowloon West
Mike Kelly, CID Reserve Team inspector, North Point
Terence Cheuk, Divisional Commander, Sai Kung
'Brawler', police constable, Sai Kung
Ralph Brooke, Sub-Unit Yau Ma Tei
Trudy Fang, Police Public Relations Bureau a.k.a. The Harlot

Other Departments
Phillip Tan, Legal Department
Derek Carlton, Independent Commission Against Corruption

Police Suspects
Silas Chu, Deputy Regional Commander, Hong Kong Island
A-Siu, detective sergeant
A-Ken, detective constable

Civilians
Dragon Wong, Silas Chu's brother-in-law, and gangster friend
Luen Ko, Silas Chu's gangster friend
Billy Lam, A-Ken's cousin

GLOSSARY OF TERMS

14K – a well-known triad society

A shift – the morning shift from 0700 to 1500

ACP OPS – the assistant commissioner commanding Operations Wing

ADVC – Assistant Divisional Commander – Operations, Crime or Administration

Assistant commissioner of police – a senior police officer, commanding a police region / major formation

AK-47 – a 7.62 mm Russian assault rifle

Auxiliary/Auxie – a part-time police officer

B shift – the evening shift from 1500 to 2300

Baton of Honour – a Training School award for achievement

Baai Kwan Daai – Cantonese expression for a celebration / offering with a semi-religious format

Black Star Pistol/Type 54– a common 7.62 mm Chinese military pistol

C shift – the night shift from 2300 to 0700

CBF – Commander British Forces, the officer commanding the military garrison

CIB – Criminal Intelligence Bureau

CID – Criminal Investigation Department

Chi sin – the Cantonese expression for crazy

Chief inspector – the rank below superintendent

Chief superintendent – the rank below assistant commissioner

Commissioner of Police – the most senior officer in the Royal Hong Kong Police

Console – the controller for each divisional radio channel

CP's Reserve – a platoon of Police Tactical Unit officers held in reserve on a 24-hour basis

Crime message – the initial police summary of a criminal offence

Cultural Revolution – a turbulent period in China that led to violent disturbances in Hong Kong in 1967

Daai fei – Cantonese expression for fast boat, used for smuggling

Daai lo – Cantonese slang meaning big brother and used with a boss or close associate/friend

Daai sik wooi – Cantonese expression for a formal dinner

Dim sum – a variety of Chinese breakfast or lunch dishes

District Commander/DC – the officer in command of a district

Diu Lei Lo Mo – Cantonese for fuck your mother

Divisional Commander/DVC - the officer in command of a division

EOD – the Explosive Ordnance Disposal Unit, part of Operations Wing

EU – Emergency Unit, a regional unit responding to serious incidents

EU KW – the Emergency Unit covering Kowloon West Region

Face – An expression meaning respect based on the Cantonese word *min*

Gweilo - Cantonese expression for a male Caucasian

Gweipoh – Cantonese expression for a female Caucasian

Hak jai – Cantonese expression for an unlucky man

Hakka – an ethnic Chinese group found along the south China coast with an associated dialect

Ham sap – a Cantonese expression for a dirty old man

HICOM – short for High Command, used for large operations

HMS Tamar – naval base containing headquarters British Forces

Horse / Little Horse – the English translation of *mah jai*, a derogatory expression for a follower

ICAC – Independent Commission Against Corruption

Inspector – the most numerous of the officer grades

JPO – Junior Police Officer (constables, sergeants and station sergeants)

Kai Fong – local community

Kowloon City District – a district within Kowloon West Region

Kowloon East – one of five police Land Regions

Kowloon West – one of five Police Land Regions

Kowloon Headquarters – headquarters for Kowloon West Region

Kowloon Regional Command and Control Centre- the radio control centre for Kowloon West and East

Lee Enfield Enforcer – a 7.62 mm rifle, primary sniper weapon of the Special Duties Unit

Macau – a small Portuguese colony close to Hong Kong

Mah jong – a Chinese game involving tiles

Marine Region – police region covering Hong Kong territorial waters

Mah jai – a follower – see horse

Mandarin – the official language of China, also known as *Putunghua*

Mong Kok District - a district within Kowloon West Region

Morning prayers – a daily morning meeting held by commanders

MP5 – a 9 mm Heckler & Koch submachinegun, primary weapon of the Special Duties Unit

MTR – Mass Transit Railway

NCO - Non-Commissioned Officer, Sergeants and Station Sergeants

NT – New Territories, the large area between Kowloon and the border with China

O-Gei – a Cantonese abbreviation for the Organised Crime and Triad Bureau

OP – Observation Post

Operation Condor – the name given in this book to the SDU operation in Tsim Sha Tsui

Operation Moorgate – the name given in this book to the Kowloon West anti-robbery operation

Orderly – a constable designated as the personal operational assistant to an inspector

Operations Support – the divisional unit comprising the Report Room, transport office and armoury

Operations Wing – the Police Headquarters formation comprising SDU, EOD and PTU HQ

Pai kau – a Chinese card game often involved in illegal gambling

Patrol Sub-Unit Commander – the inspector in charge of a sub-unit

PC – police constable

PCA – auxiliary police constable

PLO – the police acronym for Pistol Like Object, a suspected firearm

PolMil – abbreviation for the liaison office for police and military operations based in Police Headquarters

Potential Officer – a JPO qualified for promotion to the inspectorate

PTU – Police Tactical Unit, a unit dedicated to riot control and anti-crime duties

PTU company – each company consisted of four platoons, with one company per Land Region

PTU HQ – Police Tactical Unit Headquarters, the base for PTU training and SDU

PTU platoon – each platoon consisted of 41 officers, including four columns of 8 officers each

PTS – Police Training School

Regional Commander – the assistant commissioner commanding a Region

RAF Sek Kong – a small airfield in the New Territories, home to 28 Squadron's Wessex helicopters

Sham Shiu Po District – a district within Kowloon West Region

SBU – the Small Boat Unit, a unit equipped with high powered boats

SDU – Special Duties Unit, the Force's counter-terrorist unit, part of Operations Wing

SDU Boat Team – the SDU team responsible for maritime operations

SDS – Special Duties Squad or vice squad

Senior superintendent – a senior police rank, usually a Deputy District Commander

SGT – abbreviation for sergeant

Sherpa – a medium size van type used by the police

Sitrep – situation report, an operational update

Siu ye – a Cantonese expression for night snacks

SLR – the standard 7.62mm automatic rifle operated by the British military

SNAFU – an unofficial military acronym for a disaster – Situation Normal All Fucked Up

Snakehead – a people smuggler

Station sergeant – the most senior rank of Junior Police Officer

Superintendent – a rank usually commanding a division or other unit

Task Force – a divisional unit supporting sub-unit operations

The Hermitage – a hostel for expatriate officers

The Mainland – the name commonly used for the rest of China

Triads – a Chinese organised crime group, like the mafia

Tsim Sha Tsui Division – a division of Yau Tsim District

Typhoon signal – a graduated storm warning system with signals 1,3, 8, 9 and 10

Wessex HC2 – a Royal Air Force helicopter operated by 28 Squadron

Wo Shing Wo – a triad society

WPC – woman police constable

Yam booi – a Cantonese expression for cheers or bottoms up

Yat lap – a Cantonese expression meaning one pip Inspector

Yau Ma Tei Division – a division of Yau Tsim District

Yau Tsim District – one of the four districts of Kowloon West Region

Yellowed – Cantonese slang for an identity exposed or cover broken

28 Squadron – the RAF Squadron operating Wessex helicopters from Sek Kong airfield

Prologue

April 1989

It was just after midnight. The fibreglass hull was rubbing gently against the sand as the insistent waves lifted then pulled the boat. The grating noise was barely audible over the sound of the waves breaking on the shore. The beach was dark and deserted. In the distance, the glow of streetlights marked the concrete pathway they had left safely behind them.

The barefooted coxswain greeted them warmly. His rich tan, rippling biceps, and cut-off jeans marked him out as a fisherman.

"Great to see you, *daai-lo*," said the sailor, shaking their hands one by one.

"Evening A-Wai, right on time as always," Silas Chu said.

He affectionately slapped the sailor on the back and threw his bag onto the boat. A-Wai held the boat steady as Silas gingerly climbed aboard. The coarse wet sand was firm under his feet. He timed his movement carefully so that his expensive leather shoes stayed clear of the lapping waves. Silas's two companions silently followed him aboard. They sat behind, careful to show their respect by sitting apart from their master.

Silas had made the journey many times, yet the sea still frightened him, especially at night. Tonight the warm waters felt calm and benevolent. The boat journey was his own choice. He knew cheaper and more comfortable options for crossing the sea border were available. None offered the same level of discretion. Discomfort and risk came with the package. The clandestine service was worth every penny.

A-Wai had never let him down. He was a reassuring presence. His reputation was built on keeping passengers safe from storms and suspicion. Losing passengers was bad for business. It helped that he lived locally and knew the waters as well as anyone. He also knew the patterns of Hong Kong Police patrols, both ashore and at sea. He even drank with some of the off-duty cops. They knew him only as a friendly local fisherman who often donated part of his catch to the station cook.

A-Wai did not advertise his night-time service. The exclusive offer was reserved for a handpicked clientele who held the fisherman in high regard. The income it generated was helping to pay for construction of a grand new house on the island. His neighbours believed the money was being provided by his brother in Canada.

Strong hands heaved the boat off the sand and into the rippling waves. Taking one final look up the beach, A-Wai hauled himself up over the bow of the boat, steadied himself against the slight swell and moved to the stern. The small outboard motor started first time and a familiar smell of petrol and oil filled the air as he slowly backed them away from the beach. A-Wai gently turned to face south, and then accelerated towards Chinese waters and the islands sparkling in the distance.

Silas was excited. His plan was coming together. The lone constable at the pier had not even looked in their direction when they had alighted from the ferry from

Central an hour earlier. The walk across Cheung Chau island had taken the three men less than thirty minutes. An evening of Blue Girl beer and brothels awaited them. In the morning they were scheduled to conclude the arrangements that would make them all rich.

He glanced over his shoulder and saw A-Ken and A-Siu grinning. This was their first time: the thrill of illicitly crossing the border was palpable. In the distance, lights of fishing boats and freighters pockmarked the horizon as they carefully skirted the islands all around them. He could see no Marine Police. He speculated that the launch they had seen gently bobbing close to the pier would be the only one in the vicinity.

The trip marked a significant milestone. He was moving up a league, starting to play with the big boys. He wondered why it had taken him this long. With his position in Hong Kong and connections through his clan in Guangdong, all he needed to do was join up the dots. His contacts on both sides of the border were finally starting to come good.

His visits were always memorable. He was treated like royalty. The local ladies were a particular attraction. It was through these visits that he met his business partners, Luen Ko and Dragon Wong. They were kindred spirits, like brothers. They ran separate organisations but saw the opportunity to cooperate for mutual benefit. They would help Silas move up the food chain. Things had changed.

It helped that southern China was still so lawless. Ko and Dragon were just two of many local gangsters. Invisible strands connected the gangs. With the decadent wealth of Hong Kong so shamelessly displayed, it was inevitable they would occasionally venture over the porous border.

It was time to become the puppet master and make it pay.

1

Inspector Sam Steadings knew the station well. That didn't make him any less edgy as he walked through the gate. He had previously spent a week on attachment in Tsim Sha Tsui Division, but his duties had not extended beyond introductory briefings, drinking coffee, and trying not to get under people's feet. He had been a nobody with zero responsibility.

Today was his first posting after passing out from Training School. His first proper day of work, the real deal. Most of his familiarisation week had been spent marking time with a book in the canteen or the officers' mess. Though the daily programme required him to spend a full morning with all the unit commanders in turn, each of them had politely shown him the door after thirty minutes. His hosts had better things to do than mother some snotty-nosed *yat lap* Inspector, as the most junior one pip inspectors like Sam were known.

Sam felt fortunate. Tsim Sha Tsui was viewed as a plum posting. As the list of postings had been read out at Training School several weeks earlier, Sam had been tense. He was hoping to avoid a post in some dull backwoods division or worse still, a backwoods division surrounded by pig farmers at the arse end of the New Territories. He was delighted when their course instructor, Lofty, had informed him he was headed to Tsim Sha Tsui. Ralph Brooke, his friend and squad mate, being posted to next door Yau Ma Tei was a bonus.

The message from the Divisional Commander had come on the Thursday of the previous week, two days before their Passing Out Parade. He was directed to arrive at 2 p.m. He would meet his new boss prior to attending his first sub-unit briefing. His kit was already there, securely stowed in a metal locker in the inspectors' changing room on the eighth floor. He arrived carrying only his trusty battered orange coloured Berghaus backpack containing a few odds and ends.

Although the interview was to be conducted in uniform, he was taking no chances. He had dressed smartly in a pair of tailored beige chinos and blue shirt newly purchased from Harry Lee Tailors. He had had a batch of shirts and trousers made up for him when he first arrived at Training School. After nine months of incessant fitness, training exercises and marching, his body shape had changed so much that another batch was required.

He was pleased to be greeted warmly by a sergeant in the Report Room, who ignored the warrant card that Sam proffered in his right hand. What else would a suntanned expat with a severe haircut be doing in the station other than reporting for duty? Sam had arrived deliberately early, he wanted to make a good impression.

Already he could feel the sweat pooling under his arms. He wondered what the weather would be like at the height of the summer if it was already this hot in May. He had thought the weather during Saturday's parade was stifling. Patrolling in August heat was going to be a killer.

He had almost an hour before his meeting. A decision was required. Food or no food? Canteen or officers' mess? Now or later? He checked his watch. He worked out that he had time to grab a sandwich, get changed, and arrive at the DVC's door at 2 p.m. sharp. The mess it was.

He took the lift to the top floor. As he stepped out, he heard voices in the room beyond. He opened the mess door and saw what looked like a party in full swing. Everyone had a beer in hand. Most were drinking San Miguel, others Carlsberg and Tsing Tao.

He couldn't believe it was lunchtime on a Monday. Dozens of people were in the room, some in uniform, many in plainclothes. His first impression was that the entire officer cadre of the district was present. The District Commander and his Deputy were both there, along with the Divisional Commander. Even Ralph. He was standing at the back, chatting to a pretty young Chinese girl in a short skirt.

Sam wasn't ready for this on his first day. After a few ups and downs during training he aimed to get this posting off on the right foot. Without hesitation he turned on his heel.

Sam had aimed to beat a hasty retreat, but he was too late. As he turned, he was grabbed firmly by the elbow and hauled back into the mess. He was standing face to face with his Divisional Commander, Brian McClintock. The superintendent was grinning from ear to ear.

"Going somewhere?" McClintock asked in his thick Scottish brogue.

"Sorry sir," he responded. "I think I'm in the wrong place. I only came up for a sandwich. I need to prepare for my interview at 2.00 p.m."

McClintock continued to hold Sam's bicep firmly. It was as though he expected Sam to try to run off, which was exactly what Sam had in mind. "No laddie," he said. "Don't worry about that, you are in exactly the right place at the right time. Who is the interview with?"

"You, sir," Sam replied quietly.

"Ah, of course. Let's not worry about that just now. Come with me."

With that McClintock propelled Sam in the direction of the District Commander, Chief Superintendent 'Big Ronny' Brindley. He was deep in discussion with a coterie of attractive female officers.

"What do we have here, Brian?" Big Ronny boomed. He was an enormous man and was towering over the women competing for his attention. His immaculate uniform only added to the sense of power and authority.

"It's young Steadings, sir. It's his first day with us proper and I found him skulking near the door. Do you think he could be an ICAC agent sent to spy on us?"

He asked the question with a smirk. The ICAC reference seemed to be a private joke between McClintock and Big Ronny. If it was, it went straight over Sam's head. The female officers recoiled as though someone had messily broken wind nearby. Frowns replaced smiles. It was as though McClintock had suggested something abominable, like child rape or cannibalism. The Independent Commission Against Corruption was no laughing matter.

"I don't think so," Brindley replied seriously. "But we had better take no chances. Interrogate the lad and let me know how you get on," he directed.

Sam took a deep breath and tried to calm his racing heartbeat. This must surely be a misunderstanding that would blow over. He had heard about the ICAC at Training School. He knew nothing about them. He was racking his brains as to what the problem might be. Was the district a hotbed of corruption? Was the party illegal?

Had he stumbled into some enormous and illicit plot? In that case what was Ralph doing here? Nothing made sense.

"Follow me," McClintock said.

McClintock directed him towards one end of the long wooden-topped bar. Sam followed. Above the bar were hung row upon row of commemorative shields. Sam saw him reach for the gleaming mess bell that was hanging from the wall by a multi-coloured rope. McClintock turned and faced the room. Sam saw Big Ronny nod his approval before McClintock loudly rang the bell for several seconds. Silence descended on the mess and a space opened up around the bar. All eyes were on him and Sam.

"Ladies and gentlemen, can I have your attention please," he asked in his guttural Glaswegian accent. "Thank you, settle down, thank you, I will be brief."

He looked to be enjoying every moment of his performance. Sam suspected he was lying about brevity.

"The DC has entrusted me with an important duty. It involves a serious disciplinary matter."

He paused for effect and glanced in Sam's direction. A deathly hush had settled over the mess. Several of the local Chinese officers were looking distinctly uncomfortable. Some were already edging their way to the back of the crowd and nearer to the door. Sam felt like crapping himself. What type of lunatic asylum had he entered?

"The matter concerns an inspector who has arrived late for his first day of duty in the district."

Late? I was fucking early, Sam thought to himself. His accuser knew it. What a bastard.

"Sir, what time did you instruct the event to begin?" McClintock asked Big Ronny theatrically.

"12 o'clock, sharp," he boomed.

"By my reckoning, Inspector Steadings arrived precisely one hour late. How would you like me to deal with him, sir?"

Tension was building. Sam was sweating profusely. His testicles were seeking shelter in his abdomen. He was feeling distinctly queasy and he could taste bile at the back of his throat. His career was flashing in front of his eyes. All because of a quest for a sandwich.

Big Ronny had a maniacal look on his face. He had transformed into a sadistic ogre. Sam feared the worst.

"Get me the book," Big Ronny demanded.

Within moments a wizened and overweight expatriate chief inspector appeared at his side. He wore an extravagant moustache of Victorian design. He carried a large, ancient-looking, blue leather-backed tome and a black biro. Sam had seen similar books elsewhere. Every mess had one behind the bar. He had never seen one used for disciplinary matters.

Sam steeled himself for the verdict. Big Ronny scribbled in the book. There was complete silence in the room. The only noise came from the usual hubbub on the busy streets below.

"This is a most serious matter," the District Commander began. "In view of the circumstances, I am feeling lenient. Let this be a lesson to you. I fine you…"

Fine? What bloody fine? Where were the formal discipline proceedings that he had read about at Training School? Where were the charges, the Prosecuting Officer and more importantly the Defending Officer? What sort of kangaroo court was this? Inside, Sam was raging and it showed. His face had gone bright red as it often did when faced with embarrassment, or in this case, abject humiliation.

Big Ronny glanced in Sam's direction. The room maintained a respectful silence. Sam looked at some of the faces around him. The locals appeared equally uncomfortable with the proceedings.

" ...one round now, one round at 5 o'clock."

Sam said nothing. The expats erupted in a cacophony of cheers and hooting. They were the most likely beneficiaries of Sam's unwilling largesse.

Sam's shoulders relaxed as a wave of relief and understanding washed over him. So that's what this was all about. It was yet another of the many wind-ups that he'd experienced over the last nine months. The words "remember son, if you can't take a joke, you shouldn't have joined," suddenly sprang to mind. It was one of his training instructor's favourite expressions.

He took a deep breath. He realised that he had stopped breathing whilst Big Ronny spoke. The queasy feeling began to dissipate. A forceful slap on the back brought him back into the present.

"I got you going, you wee bastard." McClintock was standing in front of him and laughing like a drain. "Revenge is mine. That'll teach you to fire a cork up my arse. Follow me now," he instructed, "the mess chits are over here."

Sam suddenly recalled the first time he had met McClintock. It had been a heavy night in the Training School officers' mess. Not for the first time, things had got out of hand. He was now paying the price for that indiscretion. He dared not tell McClintock that Lofty had put him up to it.

Sam followed McClintock to the bar, like a lamb to the slaughter. He reluctantly signed two open ended mess chits that would cost him almost ten per cent of that month's paltry pay packet.

Lessons learned? Revenge was a dish best served cold, and don't fire a Champagne cork up a senior officer's backside when drunk. Sam had a feeling that

McClintock was far from finished with him. He was going to have to watch the devious bastard.

2

In contrast, the welcome from the Sub-Unit Four Commander was underwhelming.

"You should be briefing the sub-unit before they start their shift," she said. "But since you didn't appear yesterday and don't seem to give a damn about protocol, I've asked the station sergeants to do it instead. At least they know their responsibilities."

It was not a good start. He and Jenny Tsang were the only two inspectors in their unit. They were standing at either end of the cluttered office. Her disdain was palpable. The atmosphere was icy cold, like the air-conditioning. So much for the Chinese being inscrutable. She had not moved to shake his hand. Nor had she offered him a seat. He thought it tactful to continue standing.

Sam could not criticise her. After all, he was reporting for duty exactly 24 hours late. If he put himself in her shoes, he wouldn't have been impressed either.

"How did yesterday go, Sam?" she asked him coldly.

She said it through gritted teeth as she looked out of the window. She was refusing to even look at Sam, such was her contempt.

"It didn't exactly go to plan if I'm honest," he replied sheepishly.

It was the understatement of the year. His excuse sounded lame, even to him. The plan had not involved stumbling into Big Ronny's impromptu promotion party. Nor being bullied into buying two enormous rounds of drinks for everyone present. Nor being refused permission to re-join his sub-unit and being ordered to spend all afternoon drinking in the mess. The session had included a three-way drinking competition between District Headquarters, Tsim Sha Tsui Division and Yau Ma Tei Division. It had culminated with Sam being dragged stumbling around the bars of Tsim Sha Tsui until the early hours by McClintock along with a bemused Task Force team. McClintock had generously described the licensed premises checks as 'induction training.'

His head was thumping and he was struggling to think straight. He'd had the shits all afternoon, ever since he had emerged from his bed at lunchtime. The last thing he needed was to be hauled over the coals by an inspector of the same rank with only nine months seniority over him. He knew he deserved it though. He meekly acquiesced to her sarcastic bollocking and took it like a man, a very hungover man.

Sam glanced around the office, it was narrow and functional. The room was packed with three wooden desks, half a dozen battered wooden chairs, and a grey-painted metal filing cabinet. An ancient looking typewriter sat on the smallest desk. Above it, a wall-mounted white board described arrest cases. Atop the desk sat three dark brown trays marked In, Out and Pending. Each was stacked with piles of files and envelopes. These were mainly white, but some were pink or manila. The painted walls were chipped and grubby. Blue linoleum floor tiles were stained with coffee spillages and heavily marked by the constant traffic of rubber soled boots.

Jenny had turned to face him. Her arms were crossed defensively. Her stare was piercing. It felt like she could see right through him. His face was reddening. He guessed she had perfected her aggressive stance during her years as a woman police constable before she was promoted. He felt like a little boy in the headmistress's office. He was out of his depth, and about to get his arse thrashed.

"So, the DVC likes you", she observed caustically.

This was news to Sam. He suspected the opposite was true. McClintock was a classic bully and Sam thought he was a classic victim, the fly to the DVC's spider. "Like" seemed to be a farfetched concept at that moment.

"What makes you say that?" he asked.

"Don't you know? Really?" she snapped. She sounded genuinely angry. "We've heard all about you from the DVC. Sam this, Sam that, Sam the other," she mocked. "And that's before you'd even passed out."

Her voice was rising both in pitch and volume. He glanced uneasily over his shoulder to check that the office door was still closed. He did not want witnesses present to observe the latest assault on his dignity.

"I'm sorry" he said, "I don't know why he would say that."

It was the truth. McClintock had been away on leave during Sam's week-long familiarisation. He had only met him once before, at a Training School mess night months earlier.

"You *gweilos* make me sick," Jenny went on. "Do you know how hard it is for Force entry officers like me to work our way up through the Force? Imagine how we feel when some *gweilo* nobody turns up and starts kissing the DVC's arse on day one."

Sam was astonished by her outburst. Jenny hadn't been at the party but she seemed to have heard all about it. Sam didn't remember kissing anyone's arse. He didn't remember much about anything.

"Steady on Jenny," he said, as contritely as he could. "I'm sorry if I've upset you. Yesterday was nothing to do with me, honestly. I'd only met the DVC once before yesterday, I didn't ask to be posted here. I didn't have a clue about the party. What more can I say?" he pleaded. "I'm sorry."

Jenny seemed placated by his words. He could see her mind whirring, thinking through the implications of losing her cool. Getting off on the wrong foot with her new second in command was far from ideal for operational reasons. Pissing off the DVC's new 'horse', as she had referred to him, would not be helpful for career reasons.

"Fine. I'm sorry for losing my temper," she said finally. She shook her head at the disappointment. "It's very frustrating. You *gweilos* work so differently to local officers. I'm just going to have get used to it if we are going to work together."

She gave him a half-hearted smile and offered up her hand. "Welcome to Sub-Unit Four," she said. "You've got so much to learn. I hope you're up for the challenge and can help me run a good sub-unit?" It was delivered as a question. It was clear she had her doubts.

"Thank you," he said. He was relieved to be making progress towards a normal working relationship.

"I'll certainly do my best. I'm sorry about yesterday, it won't happen again," he promised.

"Glad to hear it. Let's talk about how we are going to work together," Jenny said seriously, pausing for effect. "At this stage, it's best if I manage the sub-unit whilst you get out on patrol. You need to familiarise yourself with the division and get to know the team."

It sounded suspiciously like the brief speech he had received from Ricky Ricardo, their immediate supervisor, half an hour earlier. Sam was delighted that they were all on the same page. He preferred to be out and about, and the two of them wanted him out on the streets. Happy days.

"Okay with you?" she asked.

"That sounds great," he said enthusiastically. "Where shall I start?"

"I'll take you up to meet the NCOs. They can show you the ropes. I've got a pile of Death Reports to work through. You can help me keep an eye on things outside whilst I catch up," she said flatly.

Sam tensed up. He worried that an avalanche of crappy jobs was likely to be heading downhill in his direction as he replaced Jenny as the official Sub-Unit Four dogsbody.

"Is that normal?" he asked with concern. "I mean a pile of Death Reports?" Death Reports were an inspectors' first experience of an investigation file and meant dealing with the Coroner's Office and a superintendent at District HQ. To Sam, giving him the responsibility for investigating an unexplained death so soon seemed premature.

Jenny paused before she responded. Sam could see her thinking carefully about her response. A dark look momentarily appeared on her face.

"Let's just say that the previous Sub-Unit Commander had an interesting approach to managing his workload," she said diplomatically. She was shaking her head as she said it. "I would love to pass some files to you, but don't worry about that just yet."

Sam knew she was referring to Andrew Chan, they had met briefly during his familiarisation. To Sam, he had seemed insipid and disinterested. Jenny explained that no one in the station had a good word to say about her predecessor. In a Force where there was always strong competition for the "Lazy Bastard of the Month" award, he was a shoo-in to win the divisional title, month in and month out. He perpetually complained that he was too busy as he was studying for his next set of professional examinations. Not that he had fooled anyone. The sub-unit had seen his type come and go many times before, Jenny explained.

"Andrew moved to a vice squad last week. After he left, I found a pile of overdue files stashed in the bottom drawer of his desk," she explained bitterly. She was pointing in the direction of a twelve-inch pile of paper in her pending tray. "What a wanker," she said unexpectedly. Sam couldn't help but laugh at her earthy language. Jenny shook her head and smiled, the ice between them now broken.

Sam's spirits rose. Not only was he being spared admin duties for the time being, it sounded very much like Jenny viewed him as the lesser of two evils. Although she was kind enough not to say it, they both knew he was as good as useless until he had been properly bedded in. About as much use as tits on a bull, as his grandad used to tell him. Their relationship might yet recover from a rocky start.

The door burst open with a brief accompanying knock and a surprised-looking woman constable entered. She took one glance at their meeting and promptly turned on her heel. She closed the door firmly behind her, probably not wanting to get involved in inspectorate-only business.

Jenny glanced at her watch. Sam realised that the second briefing must have finished.

"Time for a coffee," she announced. With that, Jenny escorted Sam upstairs to the canteen and the next serious business on the agenda – getting to know the NCOs.

3

Sam's transfer-in interview with McClintock had been re-scheduled for 4.00 p.m. As he loitered expectantly outside the DVC's office door, suitably early, Sam wondered what new surprises he could expect. He heard muffled conversations through the open doorway and decided to wait rather than interrupt.

Sam was taking no risks. He was giving the formal interview all necessary respect. He was wearing the shiny leather Sam Browne belt with its cross strap that he had worn at the Passing Out Parade just a few days earlier. His olive-green uniform still felt new and almost starchy. His best pair of uniform shoes were gleaming under the corridor strip lights. They contrasted with the scuffed grey linoleum flooring.

His whistle lanyard had been checked and adjusted and his cap was jammed tightly onto his head. Even the new police notebook in his breast pocket was up to date if McClintock tried to catch him out with a surprise inspection.

He felt sweaty and self-conscious as he stood in the 'at ease' position facing the wall opposite. Staff passing along the corridor eyed him with pity.

His throat was dry. He was surprised at how jumpy he felt. McClintock had been away when Sam completed his familiarisation week. This was their first formal meeting. So much had happened since then, Sam thought to himself. The events of Monday afternoon were still playing on his mind.

"Come in," McClintock shouted.

Somehow he was aware of Sam's presence even though he had not knocked. Sam marched crisply in, jammed his right foot into the tiled floor in his best imitation of a parade ground halt, and saluted energetically. Willie Fullerton would be proud of that one. The intimidating ex-Scots Guards RSM was responsible for the drill and musketry section at the Police Training School. Sam shivered at the memory of the many loud and creative parade ground bollockings he'd received from that larger-than-life personality.

"Good afternoon, sir," Sam said over-loudly. He ignored the seated McClintock completely and fixed his eyes on an invisible spot at head height, two feet above McClintock's head. He crisply brought his right arm back down to his side.

"Afternoon, Sam," McClintock said affably. "Relax, take a seat and take that hat off."

"Thank you, sir," he replied.

Sam spied a heavy wooden chair to the left of the desk and took a seat. He primly placed his cap on his lap, like a spinster gripping her handbag in front of the vicar.

Sam looked over at McClintock directly for the first time. He could see his new boss smiling contentedly, like a cat eying up a mouse as a new playmate.

"Coffee?" McClintock asked.

Before Sam could answer, McClintock ordered for both of them through the open side door into the General Registry.

Sam took his opportunity to eyeball the office. It was spacious and unremarkable. McClintock's large wooden desk was of standard government design. It was overlaid with a glass sheet covering a green felt base beneath. The desk was bare other than a pink A4 size folder with Sam's name on the cover, a sheet of blank paper, and a gleaming stainless steel Parker pen.

A side table held the obligatory brown plastic file trays marked In, Out and Pending. All three were completely empty. A separate side table held photos of his wife and children. A large Union flag stood on a longer wooden pole propped up in a corner of the office. The wall held a variety of framed commendation letters. A statue of *Gwan Daai* took pride of place on the windowsill. The Chinese god of war was a common feature of police offices.

"Welcome to Tsim Sha Tsui. It took a while, but I got you here in the end," McClintock smirked. "I always get my man. Remember that, my lad," he said emphatically.

Sam had always suspected dark powers were involved in the postings process. Here was the proof. It would explain why some of his squad mates had ended up with strange postings. One of his female contemporaries had skipped sub-unit and division altogether and was already deployed on so-called special duty with the Police Public Relations Bureau. Such high-level, almost world-class, string-pulling involved in an audacious move like that was of a different order to McClintock's influence. It had been heavily dependent on her father's rank and influence, Sam suspected.

"How are you settling in?" McClintock asked. "Has Jenny been showing you the ropes?"

"It's early days. Jenny has been very welcoming. There is a lot to learn but I'm really happy to be here," he said earnestly. He decided that reporting Jenny's initial reservations was unhelpful.

"Marvellous," beamed McClintock.

"You certainly made quite an entrance in the mess on Monday," McClintock noted, with a laugh. "Remember laddie, if you can't take a joke, you shouldn't have joined."

Sam said nothing, not wanting to re-visit the incident. He was hoping memories of his embarrassment would fade over time.

"So how was Training School? I've heard good things and this report confirms it," he said, tapping the file in front of him.

"I enjoyed most of it," Sam replied. "To be honest, after four years at university, I wish that I'd taken a longer break before joining the Force."

Starting 36 weeks of training less than two months after graduation had often felt like a mistake. He was glad to have finished Training School and its endless round of lessons, range courses, foot drill, law exams, leadership exercises, bollockings and wind-ups. It had been a tough nine months.

"You obviously enjoyed mess nights," McClintock said, mischievously. "It certainly made me remember you."

Sam blushed. He decided to take the bull by the horns and address McClintock's comment of the previous day.

"I'm sorry I hit you with that Champagne cork, sir," he mumbled.

It was at a Training School mess night where Sam had met McClintock for the first time. Mess nights were famously boisterous parties, major events in the Training School social calendar celebrating the passing out of the senior squad of probationary inspectors.

For some trainees it was an opportunity to let their hair down, especially the expats. Many of the locals were more wary of letting their guard slip. Although the principle espoused was "what goes on in the mess stays in the mess", many an inebriated trainee had come to grief at mess functions.

McClintock had been invited along as Lofty's guest. Sam had been introduced early in the evening in the ground floor bar before the formal dinner upstairs.

McClintock had greeted Sam warmly. "I've heard a lot about you," was his opening gambit. Sam quizzically raised an eyebrow and glanced over at his course instructor for guidance. "Lofty, tells you me you've done well in training."

It was nice that he thought so. It was hardly the impression that Sam had been given by the instructors. They had seemed fixated on exam marks to the exclusion of all other criteria. Sam had struggled to get to grips with some of the early law exams. Eventually he realised that he needed to adapt his style to incorporate rote learning if he was going to keep up with the locals. They scored ridiculously high marks every time despite operating in their second language.

Like a sprinter struggling from a poor start off the blocks, it had taken him time to catch up. His strengths were on the practical side of the syllabus. He felt that he was starting to come good, not that the instructors had seemed to appreciate that. He had started to wonder if their constant chiding was a deliberate tactic to motivate them.

"Chief Inspector Palmer if you don't mind, Brian," said Lofty mock-seriously, gently upbraiding his old friend for displaying excessive familiarity in front of a trainee. They all knew that he was secretly proud of his moniker. It was based on his limited height. He was barely taller than the top of the windshield of the Traffic bikes that he always talked about with such fondness. McClintock had used his nickname deliberately. It was typical of a Force that valued humour as much as the disciplined veneer.

"I'm the Divisional Commander of the best fucking division in the Force," McClintock bragged in an exaggerated Glaswegian accent. He leaned his red face aggressively towards Sam, breathing a potent mixture of beer, whisky, and cigar smoke towards him. "We need good men out there," he declared, prodding Sam's chest with a finger. "Not everyone is suited to life on the streets. So where do you want to be posted wee man?" McClintock continued.

Sam didn't know Hong Kong well. All he had seen were the main tourist traps and bar areas, together with some of the remote areas that they used for training exercises. He had not given much thought to his first posting. Most inspectors usually started off in a patrol sub-unit so that part of his career path was pre-ordained, unless you went onto Marine launches. Sam had no interest in that life. He aspired to be a proper copper, feeling collars. He had no intention of spending his life on the water, searching fishing boats and rescuing ungrateful yachtsman. In any case, he got very seasick.

"I don't know sir," he responded, "I was hoping for somewhere in Kowloon West, I've heard that's where all the action is."

"Good answer son, you'll go far," McClintock replied. He nodded sagely and winked towards Lofty. With that he was off, beer in hand. He worked the room aggressively, re-acquainting himself with friends and enemies alike. Sam noticed he focused more of his efforts on the dress-wearing variety of probationary inspector rather than the trouser-wearing kind. He never imagined that McClintock had treated the encounter as a job interview.

Sam remembered the incident with the Champagne cork vividly. It was much later in the evening and Sam had been 'belled' by Lofty for a rash complaint about some of the instructors telling tall stories repetitively. As the senior man remaining at that point, McClintock called the shots and fined Sam a bottle of Champagne. Launching the cork at McClintock's posterior had seemed a good idea at the time. Lofty had encouraged the foolishness, he thought it was hilarious.

"Apart from our encounter on mess night, which is now dealt with, you did well at Training School laddie," McClintock continued, perusing Sam's final report. "How close were you to winning the Baton of Honour?"

Sam hesitated before answering. It was a strange question. The Baton of Honour wasn't mentioned in the report, so why bring it up? Sam guessed that Lofty and McClintock must have been having words.

"I thought I did okay overall. By the end, I thought I'd done enough to win it," he said as calmly as he could. Sam had never been good at hiding his true feelings. He was striving to bottle in the anger and resentment that the episode brought.

"So I hear," McClintock said. "Go on. Honesty is the best policy and I like to know everything about my team."

"If I can speak frankly for a moment, sir, I was robbed of the Baton. Though others may see it differently," Sam said.

He was warming to his subject. He could feel his face starting to flush.

"An interesting view. In that case who robbed you? Anyone I might know?" McClintock asked with a serious look, cocking his head for emphasis as he did so.

"I don't want to start pointing fingers," Sam said.

"That's funny" McClintock said, "because I could have sworn that I heard you were on target for the Baton until some strings were pulled. Am I on the right track?

"In fact, I've heard that there was something of an uproar when the award winners were revealed. Does that ring any bells?" McClintock asked, the smile on his face replaced by a sudden scowl.

"I wouldn't know anything about that, sir, it's all above my pay grade," Sam lied.

"In that case I'll tell you what I've heard. You can tell me if you agree. Let me tell you son, I'm as angry about this as you are," McClintock said, pointing a finger aggressively in Sam's direction. "This has something to do with The Harlot I believe?"

Jesus, thought Sam, he even knows her nickname.

"And her useless fat fucking father, Bernard Fang," McClintock snarled. "Am I correct? Tell me about The Harlot."

Sam's mind suddenly flashed back to the first Monday morning at Training School and to his first encounter with her. The expats had landed on the Friday afternoon. Their local colleagues were yet to arrive. Trudy Fang, a.k.a. The Harlot, had stood out right from the off. Whereas her local colleagues had arrived dressed conservatively in suits and long skirts, The Harlot had arrived in what appeared to be a bright red cocktail dress. The hem was well above her knees while her arms were bare. Her long shiny black hair reached almost to her waist. Her matching bright red lip gloss made her look like she had just arrived from an all-nighter in a local club. Her expensive perfume was overpowering. The way she pouted and posed screamed 'attention-seeking hussy' to all present.

Sam had drawn the short straw. He'd been appointed as the first intake prefect with the task of collecting the local officers from the main gate and escorting them to a classroom. Sam saw the elderly-looking sergeant manning the whitewashed gate house and his weather-beaten assistant exchange amused glances. The sergeant was rolling his eyes and shaking his head in despair at the spectacle. Ralph lurked just behind Sam as he stood clip board in hand, ticking off names. It was he who first labelled the creature with a whispered comment of: "Jesus, Sam, this one looks like one of those harlots my grandma always warned me about."

"I've heard she's a bit of a handful," said McClintock with a smirk. He was enjoying Sam's discomfort.

"Yes sir," Sam replied. "She's special, in many ways." He allowed himself to smile, finally starting to relax.

"Drink your coffee," McClintock requested.

Sam sipped the tepid brew from the cup. The bitter canteen coffee and tinned milk combination was still not entirely to his taste. He knew it was the best on offer. Worse concoctions were available.

"How did you get on with her?" McClintock probed. Sam wondered if he already knew the answer.

He took his time to respond, wondering how it was possible to both like and dislike someone, how respect and disdain could sometimes be awkward bedfellows.

"We were in the same squad," Sam replied earnestly. "I like the girl, but she frustrates the hell out of me. She's like Teflon. No shit ever sticks to her. How can someone be so bright and so stupid at the same time? I suppose it's due to her upbringing. Who am I to say?"

"So, you don't think she deserved to win the Baton of Honour?" McClintock asked, fishing for further detail. There was plenty of that, including a memorable night when the Harlot had taken him home with her, but Sam had no intention of blurting that out to his superior officer. He decided to take the bull by the horns.

"Let's cut to the chase if you don't mind, sir," he said more firmly than he intended. "Whether I like her or not, most of my intake, myself included, believe she shagged her way to the Baton of Honour."

McClintock smiled and sat back, arms crossed, his mission accomplished.

"Don't worry about it, laddie," he said. "Missing out on the Baton is not going to hold you back. Everyone will find out what she's like soon enough. Take it from me, your paths will cross again one day. Keep your powder dry and your opinions to yourself. Complaining will do you no good. You know what they say about sympathy, don't you?" McClintock asked.

Sam was flummoxed. He knew that he should have the answer to this riddle. It was one he had heard from Lofty in the past. His mind was blank.

"If you're looking for sympathy, laddie, you'll find it in the dictionary between shit and syphilis," McClintock proclaimed triumphantly. He stood as he did so, as though to emphasise the point.

"Right then, that's enough for today. I need to get on with some paperwork," he said, glancing over at the empty trays.

Sam took his cue, stood up, straightened his Sam Browne, and put his cap back on.

"You seem like a good lad but watch it with the ladies," McClintock warned. "They'll see you coming a mile off. Welcome to the division and good luck. Dismissed."

"Thank you, sir," Sam said formally.

He was perplexed at the line of questioning and wondering why there had been barely any talk of police work. Nonetheless he was relieved to get it over with. He saluted smartly and marched out.

As he left the room, Sam thought he heard McClintock giggling to himself.

4

"Fall out," ordered Sam. The two ranks of officers standing in front of him in the compound quickly dispersed and headed out on patrol. Sam watched them go with some satisfaction: his first solo briefing and uniform inspection represented one more small milestone in his time in the sub-unit. As he looked around, Sam enjoyed the feeling of the afternoon sun on his arms and face. He allowed himself five minutes to savour the moment before heading back to the office.

With Jenny smoothing the way, Sam had quickly settled in to sub-unit life. There was so much to learn, so much that they had simply not covered during his nine long months at Training School, and he happily threw himself into the work.

Sam had discovered that the sub-unit's efficiency was largely due to the efforts of the small team around Jenny, especially the Duty Sergeant. A-Bo was a quiet individual in his mid-40s with thinning hair and thick black glasses dangling from a cord hung around his neck. A sallow complexion and dark bags under his eyes made him look ten years older, a common problem for veterans with years of irregular hours under their belt. A-Bo wielded power quietly and efficiently. With willing cooperation from his unit, he rarely needed to roll out the big stick brandished by the station sergeants and inspectors.

His accomplices were Eileen and Sarah, two junior woman police constables, who took it in turns running the office. Between them they oiled the sub-unit machine by processing the relentless admin, preparing duty lists, and running errands.

Eileen was cheerful and industrious; no request was ever too much trouble. Stocky and robust, she possessed saintly qualities and endeared herself by accommodating the leave demands of even the grumpiest officers. Like many of her colleagues she was a devout Christian. She had forsworn the smoking, drinking, and swearing common amongst her peers.

Sarah could not have been more different. She seemed shy, and hardly the police type. With slender arms and legs, she looked faintly ridiculous in her faded olive-green summer uniform which seemed cut for someone else. Her English was almost perfect, but she spoke in the briefest of sentences, and seemed incapable of looking Sam in the eye. Sam found her to be a closed book. Only later did he discover that she had spent several years at a liberal girls' boarding school in southern England before a change in family circumstances resulted in a painful re-integration into Hong Kong's stifling education system.

Shyness aside, Sarah was super-efficient. Sam wondered at the difference between the studious WPC on display in the office and the more sociable version he observed in the canteen. If they were alone in the office together an awkward tension was apparent, like sitting opposite a stuffy senior officer at a mess dinner. He escaped it by returning to patrol, something he never tired of.

The other two major cogs of the sub-unit team were the two station sergeants, Cheung and Liu. Cheung was old-school, a relic from the bad old days of the 60s and 70s when corruption was rife. Tall, overweight, with greasy hair and bad teeth, he was a loud and intimidating character. Cheung did not agree with the direction that the modern Force was taking and was happy to tell anyone willing to listen. Argumentative and foul-mouthed, he coped badly with orders from one pip inspectors. He barely concealed his disdain for Sam, and didn't bother to hide it at all with Jenny, whom he had known in her previous life as an Admin WPC in Sham Shui Po. His contempt often bordered on insubordination, and Jenny had briefed Sam about his idiosyncrasies in detail.

Sam viewed him as a dinosaur, and with just 18 months until retirement, he reckoned that extinction would be no bad thing in Cheung's case.

Liu on the other hand was short but athletic, fresh to the rank, and super keen. His background lay in the Criminal Intelligence Bureau's 'Hit Team' and the Special Duties Unit. Although he had limited recent frontline experience, what he lacked in procedural knowledge Liu made up for in enthusiasm and energy. Tough and committed, he spent most of the shift out on patrol, supporting, encouraging, and cajoling the team, especially the less experienced officers. An imminent return to counter-terrorist duties was rumoured. He seemed determined to enjoy his new rank and unit, even if he made clear that his stay was likely to be brief.

A typical eight hour shift for Sam started with the Sub-Unit Commanders' briefings. The briefings were separated by thirty minutes so that officers came on and off duty in two batches. Each shift lasted for a week at a time with the fourth week for change over and training.

Sam had heard the infamous 'C-B-A' shift system was a killer. One day off in seven and a 'short change' every two out of four Sundays quickly left cops old beyond their years. No wonder there was stiff competition for the few nine to five posts.

Having drawn weapons from the armoury, the commander briefed the team on their duties, current crime trends and notices. The briefing always followed the same pattern. After a while Sam followed it without difficulty, even with his basic Cantonese.

Sam was all too aware of his poor language skills. Understanding Cantonese was far from the same thing as speaking it. If he needed to comment during the briefing, he would make his speech in English and have it translated rather than risk mixing up his tones. With the pronunciation of many words sounding almost identical, he decided that confusing words like dog and penis was not a risk worth taking. Far better he thought, to allow the team to suspect that he was stupid rather than communicate in flawed schoolboy Cantonese and confirm their suspicions.

5

"Are you looking forward to tonight?" Jenny asked. The sub-unit were sheltering from the vicious heat of the early afternoon sun in the shadow of the Police Sports and Recreation Club. Like the rest of them, she was dressed in a running vest, shorts and training shoes. For Sam, the idea of energetic exercise after a large *dim sum* lunch in the restaurant upstairs was losing its attraction.

"I'm not sure what to expect," he replied. "I'm definitely looking forward to it though." He was grinning as he conspicuously stretched to touch his toes.

"Good clean fun," she advised. "The sub-unit will be interested to see how you perform."

"Perform? What, like one of the sea lions at Ocean Park?" he laughed.

"You know the score, Sam. You *gweilos* are infamous for your drinking. Tonight is your big opportunity to show them. And me," she added.

They both knew that teetotal *gweilos* were rare. Non-drinking expats were carefully weeded out at final interview at the Hong Kong Government's London office in Grafton Street.

Sam was all too aware that not all local officers drank, and for good reason. Many suffered a dramatic reaction to alcohol that left them with bright red faces after drinking even small quantities of alcohol. However, with persistence and training, this barrier could be overcome. He knew the Force contained many fine local drinkers, though few could match the expats in terms of commitment to their sport.

"Okay," said Sam. "I'll be warming up with a few quick ones in the mess beforehand. Just for you I'll make sure I take it easy and keep my powder dry for tonight."

"Madam, shall we start?" called Liu from behind mirrored lenses. His broad tanned shoulders were attracting admiring glances from other club users as he invited them to join the fifty other officers on the grass beyond the shade.

Jenny waved an acknowledgement and walked over to the head of the pack, Sam following along.

"Try not to embarrass me by coming last," she demanded slyly as she slowly led them off at a trot around the jogging track.

Sam shook his head in mock indignation and picked up pace to make his point.

"See you later," he laughed as he hared off with a bunch of younger officers sticking closely to him, seemingly eager to impress.

Sam deliberately set off at a furious pace, he wanted to put down a marker. Within 100 yards, he realised that the majority of the sub-unit were content to plod rather than make a race of it. Only three constables remained on his shoulder. They were already blowing hard and he was confident that he could beat them. He saw Liu and A-Bo tucked in just behind that group. Sam was surprised by how comfortable they were looking: their gait was almost effortless. It stayed like that until the final lap of the field. With 200 yards to go, Sam accelerated but A-Bo unexpectedly cruised past Sam just as he approached the finish line.

Sam smelled a rat. He had been completing the Force mile and a half fitness test regularly whilst under training. He usually completed the course in sub-nine-minutes and he never expected to be beaten by one of the oldest men in the unit.

"Better luck next time, A-sir," A-Bo told him cheerfully.

Liu was standing next to A-Bo and laughing. He looked barely out of breath. Sam realised that Liu had deliberately held himself back. Jenny arrived a minute later, sweating profusely but in a respectable position in the middle of the pack. He saw Jenny and A-Bo exchange knowing glances. It was another stitch up. He made a note to try harder next time.

A few hours later, Sam was back at the station and standing by the armoury hatch. A pair of B shift PCs were returning arms before their meal break, closely monitored by a hovering sergeant.

Sam was feeling relaxed after several hours of beer with Ralph in the mess. Ralph's posting in nearby Yau Ma Tei made him Sam's go-to drinking buddy whenever their shifts allowed. Sam had left him up there, receiving an unwanted lecture on the halcyon days of Hong Kong in the 1970s from a pair of old buffers.

Station Sergeant Liu was waiting for Sam, ready to escort him to the next stage of their training day.

"Perfect timing, Mr. Liu," Sam beamed. "I'm ready for something to eat, shall we go?" he said, heading for the rear gate.

"Is this your first *daai sik wooi*?" Liu asked as they commenced the short walk to the restaurant.

"The very first," Sam replied. "Is there anything I need to know?"

To Sam, a *daai sik wooi* had an air of mystery about it. He was intrigued. The Cantonese words translated simply as 'big eat gathering'. The word 'wooi' could also be interpreted as 'association' or even 'gang'. His instructors had repeatedly told Sam that Police General Orders should be considered as a written history of previous mistakes. Having an entire section dedicated to social events hinted at potential trouble. If the widely understood career pitfalls for inspectors were firearms, prisoners and property, then the risks associated with a *daai sik wooi* were gambling, gambling, and more gambling. It was not a coincidence that most *daai sik woois* took place after pay day.

"Just relax and enjoy yourself," Liu advised. "They are a good bunch and a lot happier now that you are here."

"Really?" asked Sam. He surprised by the comment. He wondered if he was just being buttered up, although that was unlike Liu.

"Anybody would be better than Andrew," the station sergeant said.

"But wouldn't they prefer to work with local inspectors who speak the same language?"

"It's very simple. They all hated Andrew. Most *gweilos* are easy to work with, it's well known. Even after a few weeks the boys can tell you are okay. Just relax and enjoy yourself," he said warmly, patting Sam on the back to emphasise the point.

"Thank you. In that case what are we waiting for?" he said.

The restaurant was on the upper floors of a tall but narrow Nathan Road building. It was festooned with billboards and bright lights, like every other structure on that stretch of road.

Liu ushered him through the restaurant doorway, past the astonished maître-d', and into a back room filled with circular tables. The party was well under way and they seemed to be the last to arrive. Jenny smiled, looked at her watch exaggeratedly, and directed Sam to a seat opposite her on the same table.

"A-Bo, can we get Sam-Sir a beer please?" Jenny instructed. A can of Carlberg instantaneously appeared, the wet aluminium skin pleasantly cool in his hand.

"*Yam booi*, A-sir," toasted Liu after Sam had filled his glass. Sam quickly drained it, gaining appreciative looks. Barely had it touched the table than willing hands re-filled it. It's going to be a long night, thought Sam, as Jenny caught his eye and raised her glass to salute the start of his initiation.

The food was a dazzling array of Cantonese dishes served in a series of ever larger courses. A constant procession of beer appeared in front of him. Then Jenny stood and made a brief speech. The room cheered exuberantly as she lauded the efforts of two popular young PCs transferring out to the Police Tactical Unit, presenting each of them with an inscribed tankard. Everyone's first posting was special. No one begrudged the attention briefly lavished on the two fresh-faced novices. Sam knew that Andrew being offered no such privilege was no mere oversight. The sub-unit had loathed the ground he walked on. Not inviting Andrew was a deliberate sleight.

Presentations complete, the gambling that had preceded the meal resumed. It burst suddenly into life like a grass fire re-ignited by a gust of wind. Sam watched on with interest at a group crowded around what was technically an illicit game of *pai kau* on a table at the back of the room. It was a fast-moving game using domino-like tiles. The rules dated back to the Song dynasty. As the game progressed and excitement built, Sam observed how usually quiet characters transformed into excited schoolboys in front of his eyes.

There could be only one winner. Station Sergeant Cheung took defeat at the hands of one of the drivers badly. The drivers were a law unto themselves, having all but declared their lack of interest in career advancement by entering the secret world of the Transport Office. Sam knew they needed careful handling.

After some perceived sleight from his opponent, Cheung lost his head. He suddenly went into bullying overdrive, wildly gesticulating and loudly deploying the foulest of foul language.

Sam felt uncomfortable and wondered if he should intervene. Looking around, no one else seemed concerned, and he decided to hold back. After a while he realised why nobody was upset by Cheung's behaviour. In the heat of the moment, Cheung had committed the foolish error of forgetting that the drivers were technically under the wing of the Operations Support Sub-Unit. His threats of retribution were toothless and everyone knew it. He was left humiliated by a nonchalant opponent who simply laughed in his face as he grandly flourished his winnings to loud cheers from all present.

Sam caught Jenny's eye and she gave an imperceptible shake of her head to warn him off. Cheung was an unpredictable hothead, and the risk of escalation outweighed the benefits of intervention. They both sat stock still, separated from the action by another table. Cooler heads amongst the NCO fraternity were trying to calm Cheung down and prevent him from following the driver as he skipped out of the door, giggling maniacally as he went.

Without warning the *daai sik wooi* was over, and everyone headed for the doors. It was almost as if the restaurant was being evacuated, such was the speed.

"What next?" Jenny asked. Not knowing what to expect, Sam had made no plans for the rest of the evening. He was considering a trip to Wanchai to see if any familiar faces were in the bars and discos along Lockhart Road. It was a plan with a high probability of success on any given night.

"No plans," he said, as they both stood up. "I might have another drink before I go home."

Jenny raised an eyebrow. "Really," she said. "Haven't you had enough?"

Sam shrugged. One for the road was a common temptation. There was always room for one more.

"Can you sing?" Jenny asked with a tempting smile.

The last time Sam had been asked that question was when auditioning for a school musical many years earlier. On that occasion he had managed to disguise his lack of ability by standing at the back of the group and letting others take the strain.

"No," he answered cautiously, "what did you have in mind?"

"Follow me," she replied with a knowing look, and with that she led him down the stairs and into the warm and sticky night air.

6

As they slowly walked down Nathan Road, Sam realised that he barely knew Jenny. So far, Jenny had made sure that time spent with Sam had been strictly business.

The past two weeks had been a whirlwind of briefings, patrols, meetings, and debriefs. He had spent much of his time accompanying different members of the team and he was starting to get to know a few of them. His introduction to sub-unit life had gone smoothly. He was appreciative of all the help. He knew it was all too easy to freeze out an inexperienced *gweilo*. Jenny seemed to have gone above and beyond in her welcoming and mentoring duties but their daily conversations had focused solely on work.

"Here we are." She led them up a steep dark circular stairway of stone steps to where a wooden lectern guarded a small landing. Two rough-looking bouncers dressed in cheap black suits eyed him suspiciously. A pretty and impossibly slim girl in her 20s dressed in a miniskirt and skimpy top greeted them. Her hair was tied up in a bun. Brightly painted nails matched her lipstick.

"Evening Madam," the girl said loudly in English, "how many tonight?"

"Hello Maggie, just two tonight, me and my friend Sam-Sir." That was his new nickname around the station, his surname being too much of a mouthful for the average Cantonese speaker.

The conversation switched briefly into Cantonese. Maggie giggled, grabbed two menus from an alcove, and smiled at Sam.

"Follow me please, Sam-Sir," she said coquettishly. With the bouncers nodding an unsmiling approval, the three of them entered deeper into the smoky and noisy recesses of one of the dozens of karaoke bars that had sprung up across Kowloon.

The narrow corridor led into a wood and leather-lined room. The room was surprisingly quiet despite the noise outside and it struck Sam that the room must be sound-proofed. The main feature was a large television screen on one wall. Opposite sat a long purple sofa, with a low black table between there and the screen. They settled at either end of the sofa. Jenny ordered drinks and savoury snacks, a large bottle of Tsing Tao for Sam, and a glass of red wine for her.

Jenny showed no urgency to practise her singing skills. Sam was relieved. He was all too aware that singing loudly was not the same as singing well. Years spent on the terraces at Elland Road had not prepared him for this moment. He knew local officers took great pride in their singing voices. Considered opinion had it that the tonal nature of the Cantonese language gave speakers a distinct advantage in the singing stakes.

Sam had watched Jenny closely during the meal. He was impressed by the natural way she interacted with the team. They responded to her well. She carried none of the airs and graces associated with many recently promoted officers. After several glasses of red wine, she started to relax, telling amusing anecdotes about life as a WPC and her inspector course at Training School. She handled her drink well and her cheeks were only slightly pink. A practised drinker, thought Sam.

They were chatting freely, for once uninhibited by the demands of duty. Jenny was interested in Sam's background. He gave her a brief synopsis of his life since school.

"And have you found a girlfriend yet?" she asked.

Sam was slightly startled by the question. After a moment of reflection, he decided that honesty was the best policy. Sort of.

"I had a girlfriend at university before I left," he lied, "but we're not together any more."

That's probably technically true, he told himself. Even if his relationship with Alice had never been formally ended, she was still in Scotland, and he was now 6,000 miles away. He knew that the arrangement was not satisfactory and the chances of her making good on promises of joining him in Hong Kong after graduation seemed slim. Nonetheless, he felt uncomfortable denying her existence. He had found Alice slipping further and further to the back of his mind. Writing weekly letters and making occasional phone calls was becoming a chore rather than the highlight of the week as they had been when he first arrived.

Jenny was staring at him, as though she seemed to know he had told a white lie, and he started to feel uncomfortable.

"Don't worry, I'm sure somebody will turn up before long," she said with a wry smile. Sam admitted to himself that he had secretly hoped he might have met someone by now who would give him the excuse to end things with Alice. But despite Hong Kong being widely considered by lotharios to be a target rich environment, he had so far failed dismally. His personal preferences were a big part of the problem. The lithe and friendly

Filipinas and Thai girls in the bars he frequented were attractive enough, but did not appeal to his tastes. His preference was for a tall and sophisticated *gweipoh,* but western women were in short supply. Those available aimed higher than the short-haired *gweilo* yobs emerging from Training School. That seemed fair enough after some of their off duty antics that he had seen in the bar areas of Wanchai and Lan Kwai Fong over the last nine months. He was open to a Chinese girl, but they tended not to frequent the same type of bars as he and his friends.

Keen to move off the subject, Sam decided attack was the best form of defence.

"What about you?" he said cheekily, "Surely Chinese girls are supposed to be married by your age? How old are you now, twenty-five?"

He wasn't sure of the etiquette involved in asking Chinese ladies about their age but since they were now friends, he figured he had nothing to lose in offering this guesstimate. If she had joined the Force at age 18, completed six years as a WPC and then one more as an inspector, she must be only a couple of years older than him.

"Way out, try again."

This was getting awkward, he thought, just how far away could he be? It must be higher was his conclusion.

"27?" he offered meekly.

She laughed loudly and rolled her eyes in contempt. She was enjoying this. "Last chance, otherwise you pay a penalty."

It's time to take this seriously he thought, and he re-appraised the woman sat in front of him. Slim, smart, good looking, well-dressed, confident, good English. Decidedly cute even with minimal make up applied. Her hair, usually tied up in a bun when in uniform, was hanging down to her shoulders and she flicked it out of her eyes whilst she waited for Sam to incriminate himself. What else did he know about her? Literally nothing. She was clever this one. They'd been talking for over an hour, and she had steered the focus on to him the whole time. She was a master interrogator and highly dangerous.

"Come on then, Sam-Sir," she joked. "No delaying."

Sam faced a dilemma. He had no idea how old she was and he worried about offending her. He decided to take no chances.

"29?" he asked quietly.

"Finish your drink loser, we're going," she said suddenly. She pushed the call button on the wall and downed her glass of wine. The same pretty hostess brought the bill through on a silver-coloured tray and Jenny directed him to settle it.

"*Doh je lei*, madam, Sam-Sir, see you next time," Maggie said gratefully as she thanked Sam for tipping her with the change from two red-coloured hundred-dollar notes. She bowed her head comically as she retreated to the door and held it open for them. Sam was more than happy to pay the bill, thinking that he had got off lightly and that the penalty could have been far worse.

As they walked out onto the street, still busy with traffic and pedestrians although it was nearly midnight, Sam was unclear what Jenny's plans were. Did she have another bar in mind or was she calling it a day? With a full 24 hours of free time before the start of the next shift, Sam was ready for a late night. Many of Hong Kong's bars were open until the early hours, the night was still young. He still had capacity for more drinks, despite the enormous eight course Chinese banquet that he had consumed earlier.

Jenny sensed his hesitation and took control. "Taxi," she shouted, raising her right hand to attract a red and silver cab touting for business by slowly cruising down the road with its light on.

"You first," she instructed, as the driver levered the rear door open. Sam did as he was told and climbed in, awkwardly shuffling his way across the rear seat until he was sitting directly behind the driver.

The taxi smelled of male body odour and smoke, so Sam wound down the window to escape the stench. Even the polluted air of Kowloon was better than the cabbage-like smell that had fermented over the course of the driver's 14-hour shift.

"Mei Foo Sun Chuen," Jenny directed. Without further words, the driver locked the doors and aggressively engaged the battered gear lever on the side of the steering column. The ancient Toyota moved off with a jolt.

Jenny had been perched on the edge of the seat as she spoke with the driver. The sudden move propelled her violently backwards and against Sam.

"Are you okay?" he asked in response to her squeak of discomfort, aware that his well-toned body was not a soft-landing zone for a woman with probably less than half of his body mass.

"I'm fine, thanks," she responded and shuffled slightly to make herself more comfortable on the hard bench-like seat. He noticed that she had made no effort to move across to her side of the taxi, and she remained close to him, her body heat warm against his leg and arm.

Sam had never heard of Mei Foo and didn't know to what or to where they were going. It could have been the name of a bar or a beach for all he knew.

"So where next?" he asked innocently. He was enjoying the ride north up Nathan Road through unfamiliar areas of Mong Kong and Sham Shui Po.

"I thought you might like to come back to my place for a drink and we could get to know each other a little better."

Sam was momentarily speechless. His mind was whirling and struggling to add things up but unless this was yet another wind-up, the signs were that his barren patch might well be coming to an end. He had not planned for this outcome, but he was not going to turn down the opportunity. Lofty's warning about the dangers of screwing subordinates suddenly came to mind again. After a rapid evaluation, he reminded himself that as he was technically the subordinate in this situation, no codes were being broken. Game on.

"Sounds good to me," Sam said cheerfully, trying to play it cool.

He started to relax, enjoying the thought that for the first time in his life a woman was doing all the running, and as yet nothing had gone wrong.

He noticed she had moved her right hand so that it lay flat and still on his thigh. In response he manoeuvred his left arm around her shoulders. They sat quietly for the remainder of the ten-minute journey, bracing themselves for the inevitable collision with the wild late-night traffic. Yet even several near misses with other members of the same kamikaze taxi squadron and gratuitous outbursts of foul language from the driver did not disturb their calm.

7

To Sam, Mei Foo Sun Chuen was bewildering. He had never seen so many identical buildings, each 20 stories high, lined up next to each other.

After further precise instructions the taxi halted just 50 yards from the entrance to Jenny's block. It was a drab building painted an unattractive dark green, festooned with air-conditioners and clothing racks, and streaked with rust marks. The balconies were large, with some enclosed to add living and storage space, and others open to the elements. To his inexpert eye it looked a mess, but Sam knew looks could be deceiving when it came to Hong Kong property, and he kept his thoughts to himself.

Jenny glanced at the meter, which flashed up the fare in red neon letters, and handed over a blue twenty dollar note. Sam was grateful to be released from the cab's toxic atmosphere and she led him by the hand to the entrance.

The aluminium-framed glass entrance door was wide open. Inside an elderly and frail-looking security guard sat fast asleep in a rattan chair, mouth gaping, just a few brown-stained teeth remaining. It was a typically humid summer evening and the man had invested in a small electric fan which sat on his battered wooden desk, slowly rotating backwards and forwards with an annoying squeak at the end of each arc.

The bright interior had attracted an impressive array of nocturnal insects. Moths had lived and died in their hundreds and were now a banquet for a posse of small dark lizards which darted hither and thither amongst the carnage.

Jenny walked purposefully past the rows of gleaming stainless steel letter boxes towards the lift doors. She punched the button for the 18th floor. As Sam followed, he could sense movement under his feet, and the small lift felt flimsy and claustrophobic. The doors closed with an annoying grating sound, and neither spoke during the slow and wobbly ascent.

As the doors opened, Sam heard televisions blaring from under the doors of neighbouring apartments and Jenny put her finger to her lips. They approached the gleaming wooden door in silence. Jenny expertly unlocked the three locks at the top, bottom and middle of her door before they entered undetected.

Jenny turned on the lights and air-conditioning and quietly bolted the door. "Welcome to Mei Foo. Can I get you a drink Sam-Sir?" she asked alluringly.

Sam didn't need asking twice. Whilst Jenny poured them both a glass of red wine, he followed her lead and took off his shoes. The floor was of highly polished wood, sealed with resin. It felt smooth and pleasantly cool through his black cotton socks.

She placed both glasses on a low teak coffee table and asked Sam to make himself comfortable. "I need to clean up, I'll be back in a minute," she promised, before clicking the start button on a slick Bang & Olufsen tape deck and disappearing down a short corridor. He didn't recognise the female voice singing Cantonese pop songs, but it was easy listening, even if he couldn't pick out the words.

Sam inspected the room and was relieved. After all the horror stories he had heard at Training School, the apartment was bigger than he expected. The lounge was longer than the kitchen-diner in his Hermitage apartment, but a similar arrangement, with a dining table at one end and a sofa and comfy chairs at the other.

The style was a mixture of classic Chinese and modern. The dining table, six chairs and drinks cabinet were made from gleaming rosewood, whilst the cream coloured fabric three seater sofa and two accompanying chairs were a more Western design. The rectangular table was overhung by a large crystal arrangement that poured out a dazzling quantity of light. The kitchen was clean and minimalist, and surprisingly Western in design. Whoever designed the interiors had taste. It was a warm and comfortable space.

A tall wooden white-painted bookcase covered one wall. Sam decided to investigate her choice in books, almost all of which were in English. Genres were varied and ranged from classics through to Orwell, DH Lawrence, and Tolkien, plus an assortment of racier titles by Jilly Cooper and Joan Collins. An eclectic mix, thought Sam, still unsure what this told him about Jenny.

"Anything you like?" asked the voice behind him, and he turned to find Jenny stood barefoot, posing provocatively. She was wrapped in a finely embroidered blue silk kimono, patterned with golden dragons, and was still towelling her damp hair.

Lady luck is smiling on me at last, he thought. The short kimono clung tightly to her slender frame and his mind started racing, speculating on whether her new outfit came with underwear. He tried to focus on her face and found his eyes being drawn back to her tanned bare legs.

Jenny appeared to be enjoying his discomfort. She walked a few steps to collect her glass from the coffee table. As she leaned over he gained a tantalising glimpse of what appeared to be a small but perfectly formed pair of breasts.

"To Sub-Unit Four," she said raising her glass and staring him in the eye. They drank a toast to their unit and their new friendship.

Jenny turned off the bright lights above the dinner table leaving only a small corner light behind the sofa. To Sam, the closed curtains, subdued lighting and soft music all added to the sexual tension.

She was in no rush and Sam was content to let Jenny set the pace. They spent several hours talking and drinking, and stopped only to top up their glasses and change the music. Their conversation was humorous, frank, and unhurried. As the wine loosened his tongue, Sam's secrets came tumbling out one by one.

Her own shocking admission came first; Jenny was actually aged thirty and had joined the Force later than most. After graduating from an American university she had tried several careers before choosing the police. After the initial disappointment of failing inspector selection, she decided to join as a constable, taking the longer and harder route to inspector rank. Since then she had excelled, but it had taken her five years to get back on track. She knew she would never be a high-flyer, but was determined to make the best of it.

A serious lady, thought Sam, as his respect for her grew. She knew what she wanted, and she knew how to get it, which was probably why he was sitting there.

Sam suddenly understood that Jenny was far more Western than she initially appeared. The impression she gave of being just another local girl who spoke great English was a deliberate misdirection designed to guard her privacy. The lack of openness was intentional, almost calculated. Sam knew how easy it was for women officers to be besmirched by the Force rumour mill. He was amazed at her new-found trust in him. The enigma was slowly being unravelled and he was enjoying the discovery process.

After Jenny concluded her story, she smoothly turned the spotlight back to Sam. Did he really have no girlfriend in the UK? Had he met any girls since arriving in Hong Kong? Did he like Chinese girls? What did the expats think of the local officers? Was he intending to stay on beyond his three-year contract? Jenny seemed intrigued by Sam and his *gweilo* compatriots.

His admission concerning his girlfriend made sense, he convinced himself. Although they had not formally finished, he was over here, she was over there, and the chances of the relationship going anywhere seemed remote. Disclosing a dysfunctional long distance non-relationship seemed sensible. The more he thought about it, the more he wondered why and how it had lasted this long when he hadn't seen Alice for over nine months.

His next confession was one he later regretted, though at the time it seemed an entirely natural if somewhat embarrassing thing to admit. No, he didn't have a girlfriend in Hong Kong, he told her, but he was open to the idea, now he had completed training and had his own place.

The follow up question exposed a local stereotype that reckoned all expats only cared about beer, sex, and sport in that order of priority. The local Chinese were direct, often too direct. If he didn't have a girlfriend locally, Jenny wondered, how had he managed without sex over that period?

He hesitated before answering but the cumulative effects of a long evening of alcohol had started to kick in, and his resistance crumbled.

"Well," he said cautiously, "although I've not had a girlfriend, to be honest I have met a couple of girls along the way." He had been deliberately vague with his answer. He hoped that his response would be enough to satisfy her curiosity, but the questions kept coming. The familiar feeling of a schoolboy standing in front of the headmistress returned.

Where had he met them, she wondered? In a bar? In a disco? At Training School? Were they local? The inquisition continued and she kept turning the screw.

"It's a bit embarrassing," he stumbled. His speed of thought was compromised by a long afternoon of Carlsberg and Heineken. She kept pushing him, wanting to know details.

Sam knew many locals took pride in the extent and use of their vocabulary, especially their use of English idioms. Jenny was no different, and she finished him off with one of her favourites, quickly and cleanly, like a freshly-sharpened executioner's axe.

"You know I'm not as green as I'm cabbage-looking you know," she stated in a matter-of-fact voice, like a nurse poised menacingly over a patient with a particularly large syringe in her hand.

Jesus, that's just the type of thing my mother would say, he thought to himself, as embarrassing incidents from puberty flashed through his mind. Sam could feel the pressure building and the ice under his position cracking. Whilst he welcomed the cathartic sensation a full and frank admission could bring, he was apprehensive about the possible consequences. What if the lady discovered that he was not actually a gentleman?

"I know what you guys are like," she said, "you are all equally *ham sap*, it's not a problem you know. Don't forget I was a WPC for five years. I completed two tours in Vice. I'm a woman of the world," she laughed.

Sam recognised *ham sap* as a Cantonese expression describing male lechery. He understood she was referring to the muckiness of the average Hong Kong working man, their interest in all things sexual, and a penchant for mistresses, prostitutes and erotic massages. Sam wasn't sure he was happy being compared with the infamous whoremongering truck drivers of Hong Kong. They were reputed to have a woman in every town, and often had both a Hong Kong and a Mainland wife. That was the direction of travel, and he was committed.

Seeing the conflict in his face, Jenny decided to help him along and put him out of his misery.

"So, what about the bar girls in Wanchai, don't you find them attractive?" The implication was clear: what's wrong with you, aren't you a real man. Are you gay?

It was time, he thought. He needed to put an end to this excruciating line of questioning even if it risked his prospects.

"Right," he said looking down at the floor and then pausing, as he tried to gather his thoughts and put across his version in the least incriminating way possible. "I love the bars, and the girls are nice, but they're just not my thing, does that make sense?" he asked his inquisitor.

"So?" she asked with raised eyebrows.

"So, we would sometimes go for a massage instead," he explained coyly.

"Ah ha, I knew it." Jenny seemed pleased with her detective work.

"But most of the time we only went there for just a massage," he pleaded, sensing that the end was near.

It was true. Sunday afternoons at Training School had often involved a *gweilo* excursion down to the Silver Springs spa and massage parlour in Causeway Bay. All daytime trips were sober affairs and completely kosher, with no suggestion of impropriety.

"And?" she persisted.

Unfortunately for Sam, on one or two occasions he had fallen into bad company on a Saturday night during a tour of Wanchai. The evening had ended with a trip to the Silver Springs to partake of their late-night menu which involved more than just a massage. A 'happy ending' had met his physical if not emotional needs, and in his mind, he could justify it because it was just like an advanced form of physiotherapy and did not classify as cheating.

Sam was not proud of his story. He was squirming like a bug about to be squashed underfoot, and unwilling to resume eye contact.

"I knew it!" Jenny exclaimed. She sounded as pleased as if she had detected a murder case, or was a proud shareholder of Silver Springs.

It was over. "Come on, it's time, I've embarrassed you enough," she chuckled, draining the dregs of her wine before leading Sam willingly by the hand into her bedroom.

Illumination came from a single dim bed side lamp. It was enough to confirm that Sam's speculation had been correct as Jenny untied her kimono and slipped it slowly off her shoulders to reveal she was naked underneath. Before he had an opportunity to fully appreciate her petite body she pulled him close, and then pushed him gently onto the bed.

"I don't know why, but I like you, Sam," she said softly. "Let's have some fun, but on the condition that it stays our little secret. How does that sound?" she asked.

Sam smiled and nodded in an exaggerated fashion to confirm acceptance of her terms and conditions. As he lay back he felt her fingers slowly undo his shirt buttons, and then his belt.

He was full of expectation as he arched his back to allow his trousers to be pulled down. Without warning, familiar feelings of panic suddenly set in and he realised he was starting to experience the first symptoms of room spin.

"Sam, are you okay?" she asked with concern. As her face began to blur he closed his eyes in a desperate attempt to regain control of a rapidly spiralling situation.

8

When Sam awoke, he was cold and lying in a strange bed. He was badly dehydrated and his head was pounding. The air-conditioner was loudly pumping frigid air into the room and his upper body was shivering. Blatantly disregarding his father's advice not to mix the grape and the grain was never going to end well, and it was his own stupid fault.

He realised he was naked, and he found his right arm was wrapped around the sleeping form of Jenny. She was also naked. Part of him wanted to stay put and enjoy the moment but his bladder was telling him that he needed to get to the bathroom.

His recollection of the night's events was hazy. As he waited for his headache to subside, pieces began to drop into place. His final memory was of coming to bed. Sam's experience was that alcohol had a depressive effect and his spirits fell predictably when he realised that he must have fallen unconscious just as things were about to get spicy. What an idiot, he thought, what a bloody idiot. But then again, he'd been drinking since mid-afternoon, so it wasn't entirely unexpected. Apart from that he hadn't disgraced himself too badly. Had he? He was struck by a sudden flashback about confessing the massage story, and he groaned at his own stupidity.

The effects of a long afternoon of drinking meant that lying in bed further was not an option. With Jenny still fast asleep it seemed like the right time. He carefully extracted himself from the clinch with his host and quietly padded into the en-suite bathroom. He found a small glass, filled it with cold water from the sink, and swallowed two extra strength paracetamol tablets from the mirrored bathroom cabinet. The water tasted rusty. It had a pale yellow shade.

After five minutes of staring into the mirror and another glass of water, Sam began to feel human. Remembering an old trick from home, he ran the shower above the bath to mask the sound of his potentially explosive ablutions, flushed the toilet and climbed under the powerful jet of water. A five-minute shower helped clear his head, and he towelled himself dry with a large towel which he wrapped around his waist.

Thinking about events from the previous night brought a smile to his face. He wondered what life had in store for the rest of the day.

Jenny was still asleep as he climbed back into bed. He resumed his position behind her, her warm body contrasting with the cold bed sheets. She smelled enticing, and he kissed her tenderly on the back of the neck, breathing in a lungful of her fragrant hair. He was always at his most horny first thing in a morning and he was not surprised to feel the beginnings of a physical reaction. She stirred slightly, moving her hand slowly behind her until it found his growing manhood under the towel, and then cupped his balls.

"How are you?" he whispered in her ear. "I'm sorry to wake you." She didn't answer for a moment and then she slowly rolled over to face him, keeping her hand locked in position.

She stared into his eyes and smiled. "I'm glad you're still here. Are you finally ready to fuck me now?" she asked.

This time he was ready on parade and required no prompting. "Yes madam," he replied as they began a passionate kiss.

Thinking about it afterwards, it seemed to Sam that he and Jenny were kindred spirits at that moment. Sam suspected she was holding some parts of her story back, but she certainly held nothing back when it came to lovemaking. He had heard that local girls were passive lovers, lacking in fun and spontaneity, but Jenny had no such problem. He put her enthusiasm down to her university years in America.

Their lovemaking was slow and sensual, and it became obvious that Jenny had far greater experience between the sheets. She guided and encouraged Sam then satisfied him in ways Alice never had.

Afterwards they slept, finally waking in the early afternoon. The room was still cool, and dark because of the blackout curtains, and it felt like they were cocooned from the outside world.

"Coffee, sir?" Jenny asked mischievously as she returned with two mugs on a small tray, still dressed only in her kimono.

She placed both mugs on the table next to the bed and kissed him on the forehead. "Thank you", she said, "that was wonderful. You were so gentle. You were good." She emphasised the final three words.

Sam felt himself blushing at the words every man craved to hear. He smiled coyly, before they both laughed. No girl had ever said that to him and he felt pleased and relieved. It was like he had overcome a major barrier, like breaking the four-minute mile or swimming the English Channel.

The rest of the day took on a relaxed pace. After showering Jenny suggested they go out for food. She had nothing in her cupboards and they had both built up an appetite.

Having looked through the door viewer to check the coast was clear, Jenny quietly opened the door, secured the three locks, and pressed the lift button. The elevator was empty, and she pressed the button for the first floor. When they got there, she gave Sam instructions to ride down alone and wait for her outside the main entrance. She was taking her privacy seriously it seemed, and she planned to delay her walk down to the ground floor long enough so the security guard would see them leaving separately.

Sam followed his instructions to the letter and met Jenny outside 30 seconds later, their eyes narrowing due to the bright sunlight as they emerged into the cloying afternoon heat.

"Follow me," she said, and they walked for several minutes until they came to a large Chinese restaurant containing dozens of circular tables. The lunchtime crowd was thinning as they walked in, and Jenny asked for a table for two at the back. "If anyone asks, we are just meeting for lunch," she instructed. It would be just his luck if they were seen by anyone they knew.

Sam stood out as the only *gweilo* in the restaurant, and Jenny carefully chose a table partially obscured by a large fish tank. The grimy tank contained various species of sad-looking fish floating listlessly in its murky waters.

The glossy menu showed colour photos of house dishes, few of which Sam recognised. Jenny asked for his preferences and ordered from a rotund manager who could not help but stare. His ill-fitting black suit was covered in stains and shiny through wear, and it gave him a comical appearance, like a Chinese Charlie Chaplin.

A pot of Chinese *heung pin* tea arrived within moments and Jenny rinsed out the tiny teacups with hot water, poured tea for them both, and made a light-hearted toast.

It struck Sam that Jenny was taking the whole privacy routine a little too seriously and he decided to ask her about it.

"Are we friends, Sam?" she said.

"Of course," he replied, taken aback by the strange question.

"Do you like me?" For one brief awful moment she sounded just like Alice.

"I wouldn't be here with you otherwise," he insisted.

He was starting to get confused. She reached over the table, took his hand, and looked him in the eye. "You realise that I'm too old for you?"

He was silent for a moment, thinking through his options, trying to appear neither clingy nor disinterested. He was trying to assess if this was another wind-up, but the girl was serious.

"Fair enough, but it's not as if I asked you to marry me. Yet," he joked.

"Good point, and yes my father would have a heart attack if I told him I was marrying a *gweilo*," she laughed. "Last night was great fun but as colleagues we need to be careful, don't you think?"

He nodded his agreement. The story of the new *yat lap* screwing his commander would cause quite a stir if it got out. He hated to think what McClintock might say, and that thought brought a smile to his face.

"What's so funny?" she demanded.

"I was just thinking about the look on the DVC's face if he found out. We would both be toast."

"Thanks, Sam," she said moodily, "But you know I will get the blame if this becomes public. You are his *horse* and he already dislikes me."

Sam was silent, her logic was inescapable. It was true that if there was a scandal, one or both would be moved. He could understand her concerns, but it was the final point that really got him thinking.

"I've recently come out of a relationship, Sam, and what happened last night was just what I needed," she said, with what sounded like genuine feeling. "But it's just too dangerous for us to carry on, I hope you understand? Please?" she pleaded, now holding both of his hands.

Sam did not understand at all, but he decided to keep his peace for the time being. It was her way of letting him down gently he thought. He needed to work with this girl. They should act like grown-ups, move on, and keep it friendly, he decided.

"Deal," he said with a forced smile. As they shook hands, he couldn't help noticing the relief on her face. And the look that had preceded it: abject fear.

9

Sam's first break in the routine came with the DVC's monthly conference two weeks later. It was a Tuesday morning. Since it was Sam's first conference, Jenny decided they would both attend. To Sam it felt strange to be in plain clothes. They had just started a week of afternoon shifts and were not on duty until 3 p.m. Uniforms were not required as they were free to leave afterwards.

The meeting in the district conference room started at 11.00 a.m. sharp with representatives from every unit present. Jenny had advised that minimal preparation was required, provided your name did not figure against one of the actions from the previous meeting. Low arrest figures were McClintock's personal bugbear. It paid to be aware of sub-unit productivity, and where necessary, to have prepared a suitably robust defence.

It was rumoured McClintock hated meetings. He tolerated the monthly conference because it was the only time he could get all of his team together in the same room. Sam was relieved to hear that public bollockings were not a regular occurrence. McClintock preferred to deliver those in private where he could better display the full range of his vernacular.

Jenny appeared nervous. The local officers dreaded the occasion, fearful of being on the end of one of McClintock's infamous barbs, misunderstanding his thick Glaswegian accent or some obscure Scottish expression. McClintock's ribald sense of humour and willingness to probe individual weaknesses was notorious. As Sam looked around at the other faces they returned wistful looks, like nervous sheep visiting the shearing shed for the first time.

McClintock started with a formal welcome for Sam and followed on with a briefing about local crime trends and detection rates. Commercial burglaries were up, pickpocketing was down and robbery was on the increase. More stop and search required, please. With McClintock and Ricky doing all the talking, Sam found himself relaxing.

When it came to the next agenda heading – 'Intelligence' – Sam became more attentive. McClintock's body language and facial expression changed, and he looked serious, almost pensive.

Force intelligence indicated, he told them seriously, that a large and heavily armed gang was on the way from China. They were suspected to be carrying AK-47 assault rifles and grenades. The DVC didn't have to tell the people around the table that Tsim Sha Tsui had one of the biggest concentrations of goldsmiths and jewellers in the Territory. They were a prime target.

The Regional Commander had published a plan detailing precautions for Kowloon West. Operation Moorgate, as the plan was designated, would be in effect until further notice and McClintock described how it applied to the division. Tsim Sha Tsui would be a priority tasking.

To Sam, this was music to his ears. His first few weeks in sub-unit had promised lots but resulted in precious little action. He felt almost gleeful and probably showed it. Ricky gave him a disapproving look.

With the meeting finished, McClintock caught his eye and called him over. Jenny left Sam to it and disappeared out of the door.

"How's it going, wee laddie?"

"Fine, sir, thank you. I'm loving the job," he replied cheerfully.

"Good lad, now two things for you." McClintock glanced around to make sure they were not overheard. "Firstly, don't take any chances with these bad bastards coming down from China, do you hear me? I know you're keen, but that's an EU and PTU job and I don't want any of your boys getting hurt," he said forcefully.

Sam knew the Region's Emergency Unit and Police Tactical Unit had officers better equipped and trained to handle serious crime. He didn't like to admit it was out of his team's league. Sub-unit were pushed to one side when it came to the big cases.

"Secondly," McClintock went on, more quietly this time, "how are you getting on with Jenny. How is she?"

At this Sam started to blush. For a moment he suspected that his recent sexual adventure had been revealed. He quickly recovered his composure.

"She's fine, sir, thank you," he replied. "She's a great mentor, really helpful. I've been very lucky." He meant that. In so many ways.

"Good, very good," McClintock said, "but between us, do me a favour and keep an eye on her. Let me know if you see or hear anything unusual. Do you follow?" He raised his eyebrows to emphasise the point.

Although entirely perplexed, Sam nodded his agreement and with that the DVC stomped off to his office.

10

Sam returned to his own office to file his meeting papers. His plan was to collect his backpack before heading over to the Police Officers' Club for exercise and lunch. It was just after 12.00 p.m. He had plenty of time to get to Causeway Bay and be back in good time for first briefing.

As he entered, the office light was off. Jenny was standing at the window. Something about her body language drew his attention. He watched for a few seconds to see if she would acknowledge his presence. Seemingly oblivious, she screwed up her fists and looked down at the floor. A tear rolled slowly down her cheek.

Sam was torn between leaving her to handle her emotions in private and offering support. With no idea of the cause, he was reticent. Certainly the meeting could not have caused this reaction. McClintock had been on good form. No one had come out licking their wounds and burning with humiliation.

"Penny for your thoughts?" he asked, not wanting her to think that he was ignoring her.

Since the Mei Foo Incident, as he tended to think of it, relations between them had been good. Their first shift back together the following night had been slightly awkward at first, especially with Sarah in the room. After the WPC had left, they spontaneously burst out laughing. That had broken the ice. It hadn't been mentioned since, but occasional glances and smiles from Jenny told him all he needed to know.

Over the following two weeks Jenny had seemed to be her normal friendly and professional self. Her tears were out of the blue. Although the office was unlikely to be invaded at that time of the day, Sam didn't want them to be disturbed. He locked the door.

He tried again. "Hi, are you okay?"

As she turned and looked up at him, he could see her eyes were red and puffy. She looked miserable. She took a tissue from a wooden box on the desk, wiped her face clean of tears and then blew her nose.

"That's better," she said, raising a wan smile for Sam, though he wasn't convinced by her feeble effort.

"A problem shared is a problem halved?" he ventured.

This comment seemed to strike home and she looked him intensely in the eye.

"Thank you, Sam, thank you so much," she said, and as the tears started rolling down her face again, she sobbed inconsolably. He held her tight for several minutes until her sadness passed. They parted shortly afterwards with Jenny encouraging him to head off as planned.

When they met outside the briefing room at 3.00 p.m., Jenny seemed back to her usual self. During a short business-like discussion, she delegated both briefings to him. The arrangement suited Sam. As he gained experience he was always happy to take the lead.

Following the briefings, Sam grabbed a quick snack in the canteen with the NCOs. His usual routine involved a local favourite, milk and cream soda. It came in a separate can and bottle before being mixed in a glass.

The concoction was on the sickly side, but was strangely refreshing. The French toast he ordered came as a thick slab of bread, deep fried and covered in butter. It was an acquired taste, and not especially healthy, but edible enough when liberally covered with syrup.

After updating his notebook, Sam headed out on patrol with Liu. Jenny was busy with annual reports. They agreed Sam would stay out whilst she got on top of the admin. McClintock always emphasised that he wanted his team on patrol. He discouraged inspectors hogging the office. Even he acknowledged that the wheels of Force bureaucracy rolled on remorselessly. It was best to stay ahead of those wheels rather than be caught under them.

Sam routinely walked the length and breadth of the division each shift. He rarely patrolled alone, which suited everyone. Sam knew the last thing anybody needed was to rescue a greenhorn *gweilo* with lousy Cantonese if he got out of his depth on the street.

He found long hours spent patrolling were the best way to get to know the team. With over 60 officers to manage, he knew it was going to take time. Sam was practising his Cantonese and learning the tricks of the trade. He could feel he was making progress. He was gradually becoming familiar with the Chinese street names and their layout, as well as developing an ear for chatter over the beat radio.

With the notable exception of Cantonese and paperwork, he felt confident in his abilities, and he was not frightened of getting his hands dirty. He was fit, strong and fast and believed he could handle himself if required. At Training School, he had proven himself to be a good shot. The .38 Smith & Wesson revolver at his side was reassuringly heavy, although it was secured in an antiquated cross-draw holster. It had a worrying habit of flapping open when he ran at any speed.

Whilst Training School had provided a sound foundation, he had learnt as much about the Force from banter with old hands in the mess. He heard some officers went through an entire career without seeing any action. Others were like magnets for mischief. Only time would tell if he was to be the type of officer who attracted or repelled trouble. His hunch was that his posting would be anything but dull.

Sam knew that serious violence against the police was rare. Suspects taking the cops on man to man was a tactic usually reserved for the pissed-up squaddies of the British garrison. Even they generally knew better.

He loved the sense of anticipation, the potential for excitement, and the buzz that came from patrolling Hong Kong's tourist mecca. As a *gweilo* cop, he was a rarity. He attracted curious glances and even an occasional request for a photo with a curious visitor. He was living the dream.

Nathan Road was the centre of his domain. As he patrolled past the multitude of jewellers, he saw brightly lit window displays packed with millions of dollars' worth of gold watches and jewellery. Tall Pakistani security guards armed with shotguns stood brooding in doorways, many with extravagant moustaches and brightly coloured turbans.

The pavements were busy with a mixture of foreign tourists, Mainland visitors and local shoppers. They meandered in and out of the boutiques, tailors and goldsmiths that stayed open until late. With all the nightlife that kicked in later, the division was only ever quiet for a few hours around dawn.

Towards the end of the shift Sam returned to the station and awaited the return of the first batch of patrols. The sub-unit had done its job: preventing, if not detecting, crime. No significant incidents had been reported. There were only two minor arrests to add to the board in the office.

Sam saw the Police Tactical Unit officers deployed as part of Operation Moorgate departing in their truck. High Risk Premises had closed for the night. All that remained was to count the team in and hand over to the C shift Sub-Unit.

He was standing in the compound. He chose a spot close to the loading area where he could keep an eye on things and chat to returning officers. It was a warm, balmy night. He preferred to be standing outside rather than freeze under the strong air-conditioning inside.

"Hi," Jenny said, appearing beside him and sounding very American for once. "All quiet?"

Sam realised it was her way of launching a conversation. He nodded accordingly and smiled.

"What are you doing after work?" she asked. "I was thinking of buying you *siu ye* to apologise for earlier." Her eyes looked sad. She seemed to be reaching out.

"Deal," he said. "No apology required though. Shall we meet down here at 11.45 p.m.?"

"Deal," she said smiling as they bumped fists. As she walked off to talk to the Duty Sergeant, Sam could not stop himself from grinning.

With the shift finished, he headed upstairs to shower and change. After hours of foot patrol, Sam's cotton summer uniform was soaked through with perspiration. He left it on the floor next to his locker, ready for the elderly room boy to collect and launder.

They met in the compound. Jenny suggested they leave by the rear gate. She was casually dressed in jeans, white Bossini trainers and a loose cotton top. She looked good. The night shift gate guard waved a cheery greeting as they walked out of the compound and headed to the MTR entrance.

They didn't speak during the short journey to Prince Edward station. He amused himself by people-watching. The train was quiet. Less than half of the metal bench-like seats were occupied. From their suntanned complexions and short haircuts, he guessed several passengers were fellow police officers travelling home after a B shift. He left Jenny to stare into space, deep in thought.

The station exit was next to Mong Kong Police Station. It was an area with a tough reputation, full of night clubs, triads and apartment houses where young lovers and prostitutes competed for rooms. They walked a short distance until Jenny found the section of road she was looking for.

The streets were closed to traffic. They were packed with a jumble of roughly made metal carts and tables. Gas burners on the carts acted as makeshift stoves. Crates of vegetables, seafood and meat were strewn around nearby. Plastic stools clustered around folding Formica-topped tables. Bare bulbs strung between lamp posts dangled precariously between lamp posts.

Packs of scruffy Urban Services teams, in brown safari-suit-like uniforms, maintained order from a distance, ensuring pitch boundaries and regulations were respected. To the untrained eye the *siu ye* experience appeared utilitarian, unhygienic, and uncomfortable. Sam knew the freshly cooked food was as good as anywhere. The open-air experience and narrow, congested streets gave it an exotic feel.

Sam had only tried it once before. He had loved the stripped back experience and the freshness of the food. The air smelled of raw seafood, chopped garlic, heated oil and boiling rice. Food odours mingled with vehicle fumes and the reek of sewers. He put the clammy evening heat and polluted Mong Kok air to the back of his mind as he scanned dishes served on nearby tables with keen anticipation.

The owner seemed to know Jenny. He allocated them a table to one side, away from the bulk of the other diners, and set back from pedestrian traffic.

"My shout", she told him as a friendly waiter approached. He was wearing a filthy white apron, black shorts, and flip flops. Within 15 minutes of her order they were presented with a variety of freshly cooked dishes of prawns, mussels and clams accompanied by vegetables and rice. It was preceded by a pot of Chinese tea and a large bottle of Blue Girl beer. After rinsing the glasses, bowls, and chopsticks with hot water, she poured each of them a small glass of beer.

"Cheers," she said. "Here's to teamwork." They drank thirstily before tucking in. Sam was comfortable with chopsticks. Other than occasional disasters with slippery button mushrooms, he could hold his own at the dinner table without the ultimate humiliation of resorting to a fork or spoon.

He flinched as something unexpectedly brushed his lower leg. He was fearful of rats, the sewers and back alleys were full of them. He was relieved to see only a mangy looking brown cat with an unnatural kink in its tail. It was begging for morsels. Jenny giggled at his nervy overreaction.

She appeared relaxed and they chatted light-heartedly. The previous week, thousands of protesting students had been reported killed in Beijing's Tiananmen Square. A chill had swept through Hong Kong. The stock market and property market were jittery. Newspapers were full of stories of horror and heroism. Sam was keen to avoid talking about Tiananmen. He didn't fully understand the background to it. He didn't want to depress them both by talking about a subject neither of them could influence.

"So", he ventured, "are you feeling better?"

She shrugged her shoulders in response. "Not really, if I'm honest," she replied.

He waited for her to resume but she didn't. She focused on re-filling their glasses, and then ordered another bottle. She looked at him seriously, seemingly hesitant. After a while she made her decision.

"If I tell you something," she said earnestly, "can I trust you to keep it to yourself?"

"Of course," he said without hesitation, "I'll do anything to help you," which sounded a vaguely foolish thing to say even to him. He thought it probably was what she expected from an English gentleman. He was at least one of those.

"Thank you, but we can't talk here," she said. "Let's drink up and go back to my place."

They shared a knowing look and a smile, and she put her hand on top of his. It was her first sign of physical affection since the Mei Foo Incident. Sam resolved to put in a better performance this time.

11

They were standing on Nathan Road. A procession of buses, mini-buses and taxis was passing in each direction, some at what seemed like reckless speeds.

"I've changed my mind," said Jenny. "I don't want to go back to Mei Foo."

Sam's heart sank. He turned to her with a confused frown. He was learning not to dive in with an immediate response. He sensed something else was coming.

"Can we go back to your place?" Jenny asked. She looked nervous. She was nibbling her thumb nail as she spoke.

Sam looked at her askance. Wanting to spend the night in a government hostel packed with over a hundred gweilos seemed strange. It was almost indiscreet when she knew many of them from Training School. A sudden vision of dozens of expats teasing him about their relationship over Sunday breakfast suddenly came to mind. He dismissed it rapidly and nodded assent.

"Let's go then," he replied as he flagged down a Hong Kong Island taxi slowly cruising past with its red flag covered. The driver was sceptical. Sam had to explain his destination twice through the window before the driver would open the door. His Cantonese might be lousy, he thought, but at least he could tell a taxi driver how to get to where he wanted. Usually.

Sam held the door open for her. As the taxi started its high-speed return journey to Hong Kong Island, she held on to him tightly all the way, silent with her thoughts.

The tall, nondescript building that was his home occupied a prime location on Kennedy Road. It was directly above Hong Kong Park, within convenient walking distance from the bars of Wan Chai and Lan Kwai Fong. With eleven floors of apartments for single *gweilo* cops, it was often rowdy and its occupants came and went at all hours.

It was just before 2.00 a.m. when their taxi pulled up outside. The entrance hall was quiet and there were no obvious witnesses to their arrival. An empty rattan chair and smouldering mosquito coil inside the basement garage indicated the recent presence of a security guard. The building was eerily silent as they walked hand in hand towards the lift.

As he unlocked his door, Sam felt pleased with himself for leaving the apartment tidy when he left for work that morning. It was dark and silent apart from the hum of the dehumidifier.

"Sorry, I'm not a red wine type. Will a beer do?" he asked.

Jenny laughed, and Sam was pleased to see her spirits restored. "Yes, please, after I use your bathroom."

Sam pointed Jenny in the direction of the bedroom and took two Heinekens out of the refrigerator. He heard the shower start and guessed Jenny was rinsing off the sticky grime of Mong Kok.

Turning the light off, he stood in the dark, by the window. The harbour vista entranced him and savouring the view was his favourite part of the day. He was rarely disappointed, unless mist and low cloud cloaked the island. He found it a catalyst for calm, and his vigil was usually accompanied by comforting music from home: Simply Red or Squeeze. Or the B52s if he needed a pick up.

Tonight the night sky was clear, with views up to Lion Rock on the other side of the narrow channel. Despite the late hour, a medley of freighters, ferries and police launches churned the murky harbour waters. The scene was illuminated by huge red neon signs clinging to the sides and rooftops of buildings.

The sounds of running water had ceased. He heard gentle footsteps. A pair of warm arms embraced him gently from behind.

"Penny for your thoughts" the voice whispered, echoing his earlier greeting.

"I'm just thinking I'm a lucky boy."

"And I'm a lucky girl," said Jenny, as he felt her slide his trouser zip down and unfasten his belt.

Jenny had taken Sam by surprise again. It was becoming a feature of their relationship. They then embarked on what was probably the best sex of his life. It wasn't just the duration or the wildness of the lovemaking. It was the feeling of being overwhelmed by her passion. It was as though she could read his thoughts and knew his desires. She embraced his inexperience and treated their union like a lesson, an opportunity to teach him what a woman really wanted.

He later guessed it was her insecurity kicking in, but she was relentless, seemingly never satisfied as she cajoled, demanded, and begged yet more from him. She drove him until he lay there spent and aching but content, and craving sleep. Now he realised what had been missing from his life, what Alice could never give him.

It was nearly noon when he heard a voice in his ear. "Hey sleepy head, are you awake?" she asked softly. "I'm hungry."

The room was dark. Only a sliver of light pierced a gap in the glass next to the humming air conditioner. Fighting a moment of panic he looked over at his alarm clock, heart racing. Still three hours until work, he realised with relief.

He lay back on the pillow. What a woman. He kissed her gently on the shoulder and neck. "Easy tiger," she protested. "Breakfast first. But there's nothing in your cupboards," she said with a pout. He realised he was overdue a trip to the ParknShop supermarket.

"Have you showered?" he asked. He received a shake of the head.

"Right, breakfast in bed coming right up, madam." He threw on a tee-shirt, tracksuit bottoms and flip flops. "I'll be back in five minutes," he promised.

Ten minutes later Jenny responded to Sam's knock and opened the door for him. He was carrying a brown plastic tray. Two large white ceramic bowls brimmed with steaming noodles, fried eggs and spam. The delivery came complete with disposable wooden chopsticks and a small bowl of her favourite chilli oil.

"Where did that come from?" she demanded, surprised by his endeavours.

"Didn't you know? Us *gweilos* live in luxury. We have our own restaurant upstairs. I must take you up to 'Dirty Dick's' for a romantic meal sometime," he laughed. The top floor establishment wasn't exactly cordon bleu, but it did the trick. He had rarely used it so far but it was handy and provided English-speaking company if nothing else. Dick was a legendary figure in his 60s, a welcoming character and fine host who was reputed to be batting for the other team at a time when homosexuality was yet to be decriminalised.

He had been lucky, the restaurant had been quiet, and no one had questioned why he was ordering brunch for two. He smiled as he realised Jenny was his first overnight visitor to use the facilities at 'Hotel Hermitage'. Female inspectors were especially rare sightings.

They ate greedily and sat back on the unyielding and dark brown government issue sofa, sipping the three-in-one coffees Jenny had located in the kitchenette.

"That was wonderful, Sam," she said sitting back and rubbing her stomach. "You're a great cook. And a good catch."

"But I'm still too young for you though?"

Jenny punched his bicep fiercely and he made a grab for her. She squirmed but there was no escape. Sam ended up on top, straddling her. Jenny's arms were pinned helplessly either side of her head, his face close to hers.

"There's two ways we can do this lady," he joked in his best Jimmy Cagney voice. "It's the easy way or the hard way."

"The hard way sounds good to me, officer," she responded coyly.

This time the lesson was short and sharp and Sam was almost relieved. Was it possible to get too much of a good thing he wondered?

Later Jenny took a shower. He went into the lounge and turned on the TV. Whilst he waited for the kettle to boil, he opened the door and placed the tray and dirty dishes on the floor outside as he had promised Dirty Dick. One of his Thai minions would collect them later.

The television was set to a Cantonese language channel. The lunchtime news bulletin had just started.

There had been a shooting. His interest was piqued. He moved closer to the screen, focusing intently on the images of police uniforms and vehicles, cordon tape, and spent cartridge cases. Under a white sheet lay what could only have been a body.

He was struggling to follow their more formal form of Cantonese, but he was able to get the gist. It was the aftermath of an armed robbery. Suddenly the camera shot panned out as they cut to images of senior police officers visiting the scene. He realised it was a familiar location, the bottom of Nathan Road. Sam recognised some of the officers. McClintock and Ricky Ricardo appeared, deep in conversation. Both looked grim, something bad had gone down. Jesus, he thought, they'd better get in early today, the shit had really hit the fan. The bosses would want all hands on deck.

He turned and saw Jenny standing in the doorway, towel hitched around her chest, tears once again rolling down her cheeks. He assumed she was upset by the news.

"What did they say?" he asked sharply.

"It's one of the Auxies. He's dead," she stuttered as she collapsed into Sam's arms in a flood of tears, sobbing uncontrollably, and muttering something unintelligible under her breath. The rest of the details could wait until he got to the station, he thought, zoning out the TV chatter.

After several minutes her tears subsided. He was eager to get going.

"Are you okay?" he asked. "I need a quick shower and then we'd better get to work."

Without waiting for her reply, Sam went into the bathroom. He showered and shaved as quickly as he could. He was ready in ten minutes flat, setting a new personal best turn-out time.

As he emerged from the bedroom, he was met by silence. The television was turned off. There was no sign of Jenny. Concerned, he looked out of the window. Below, he could see someone looking like her walking briskly through the park. I suppose she didn't want to us to leave together, Sam thought, as he grabbed his backpack and swiftly headed out of the door, but she could have said goodbye.

12

By 2.15 p.m. Sam was in the station. He had jogged the short distance from the MTR exit and found the rear gate under siege from the media. The compound was busier than usual, full of PTU and CID vehicles, and there was a definite feeling of tension in the air. He was desperate to know the case details but the CID crime message summarising the incident would not be circulated until the following morning. He needed a briefing and decided to change into uniform before showing his face.

Several minutes later he was back on the ground floor and drawing his weapon through the armoury hatch. He signed the register and drew his standard kit. Revolver, six rounds, handcuffs, and radio. More haste, less speed he told himself as he moved to the loading area and methodically checked his equipment.

Check both parts of the handcuffs for movement and place them in the pouch at the rear of the belt. Attach the handcuff key on to the whistle lanyard. Undo the belt and attach the radio on the right-hand side. Slide the leather radio clip holder on to the cross-strap. Draw the revolver and attach the lanyard to the bevel under the butt.

Check revolver for serviceability. Rotate chamber and check firing pin. Aim and dry fire. Load six rounds. Check handcuff pouch and holster buttoned down.

Check notebook and pen in top left pocket. Check nothing left on the counter. Job done.

He put his head through the office door and saw only Eileen. As usual she had arrived early and was getting ready for her shift. There were no messages and he headed along to Ricky Ricardo's office. The door was open but there was no sign of him. He could hear voices from further along the corridor and walked towards McClintock's office. He was about to knock before McClintock wagged a bony finger forcefully in his direction and he was summonsed inside.

"Have you heard?"

"Sorry, sir, I only know what I saw on the lunchtime news," he replied.

"We lost one Sam, we fucking lost one, and on my watch. I'm fucking gutted I tell you." He was shaking his head and kept muttering "the bastards" under his breath. He banged the desk loudly with a clenched fist.

Shame, disappointment, frustration and sadness were etched on his face. He looked furious; a malevolent, violent fury that might yet be meted out to those present.

"Ricky, you know what do," the DVC announced.

Ricky nodded and left the office accompanied by Paul Wong, the A shift Commander. Paul's eyes were puffy. He declined eye contact.

"Right, Sam, batten down the fucking hatches," McClintock said jabbing his finger in Sam's direction. "This is fucking personal, if anything like this happens again someone's for the chop, do you hear me?"

He was working himself into a frenzy and Sam didn't blame him one bit. He just wished it had been someone else who stood there facing his wrath.

"From now on we double up patrols close to the High-Risk beats, day and night while the goldsmiths are open. Fuck the other beats, they're no longer a priority. We're getting more PTU from tomorrow but just do what you need for now. Capiche?"

"Yes, sir." That's what every commander needs, Sam thought. Clear, decisive instructions. He felt like Montgomery in front of Churchill. Or on second thoughts, maybe more like Zhukov in front of Stalin.

The boss was done. "Are you still here, son?" barked McClintock.

Sam took the hint and scuttled out of the office. He was sweating, and his heart was pumping. He returned to the office and found it empty. Odd he thought, Jenny would normally be here by now but there was no sign she had been at her desk.

The door opened and Eileen returned.

"Message for you A-sir. Madam called and she's off sick for a week, I've just told Ricky-Sir."

Sam was speechless. It made no sense.

The faces in front of Sam were sombre. There was none of the usual banter and bonhomie. They had all heard about the shooting before coming to work. Sam guessed some would have faced difficult conversations with wives and parents before leaving home. There were several Auxiliary officers in the Briefing Room. They looked particularly downcast. It was bad enough risking your life as a regular officer, losing your life due to a part-time occupation seemed particularly unfair.

McClintock's instructions had caused the duty list to be drastically re-worked. A-Bo made the changes swiftly and efficiently and there was no complaining. The plan was to remove foot patrols on outlying beats and cover them with two motorcycles. In a division barely two miles wide and three miles long it was hardly the end of the world.

No one remarked on Jenny's absence. Not even Ricky Ricardo had raised an eyebrow. Let's see what McClintock says when he finds out, thought Sam.

Sam continued with his briefing. "I spoke with the DVC earlier and Mr. McClintock emphasised the importance of ensuring your safety," he said solemnly, taking liberties with the actual words.

"You all knew PCA Mok. Our thoughts are with his family." Too bloody right, he thought. It could have been any one in this room. He was sweating, and he could see their eyes locked on him. He was feeling more self-conscious than usual. He decided to keep it brief.

"Let's be careful out there, good luck," he concluded, unconcerned that anyone might accuse him of borrowing the cheesy line.

After the room had emptied, he re-convened with the two station sergeants. Liu was paired with Sam. Cheung was to take the MP car. Mobile patrol better suited his corpulent frame.

"Any news about Madam?" asked Liu.

"No", replied Sam, "I know as much as you."

"Ha," snorted Cheung with a leer. "She's probably in bed with Chu-sir," clearly delighted at the thought.

Sam was stunned by the unexpected comment. He said nothing. Cheung had a reputation for being outspoken and crude. This was base, even by his low standards.

Sam kept a straight face. He wondered if he was being tested. Did Cheung know something about them? It seemed unlikely but could he have put two and two together?

"Why do you say that, Mr. Cheung?" asked Sam flatly. He attempted to disguise his interest, but was intrigued by who Chu-sir might be. To ask the question would not seem unusually inquisitive.

"Madam was the station bike in Sham Shui Po. She was getting ridden by Silas Chu," Cheung replied enthusiastically. "He's a Crime guy and nasty. Super smart. Very well connected. And not just in the police. If you know what I mean?" he said with a wink.

Cheung walked away, looking pleased with himself, laughing as he went. There must be some old issue between Jenny and the station sergeant for him to speak so vindictively about her, Sam concluded.

"Do you know about that?" he asked Liu. "Who is this Silas Chu?"

"Of course, sir," Liu replied quietly, "everyone knows Silas Chu. He's the Deputy Commander Hong Kong Island."

Obviously not quite everybody, thought Sam. Fuck, what have I got myself into?

13

For the first time, Sam understood the loneliness of command. Jenny's absence felt strange. Sam realised he would be working on his own for a week.

He tried to rationalise the situation and that helped. It had been a terrible day for the division when the Auxie had died outside Chow Sang Sang goldsmiths. Losing the officer was traumatic but it was probably unlikely to be repeated. With a million dollars in jewellery and watches, the mainland gangsters would likely be long gone, spending the proceeds in Guangdong brothels.

Based on witness accounts and grainy CCTV footage, there were three in the gang, fewer than Force intelligence had suggested. They appeared to be carrying Black Star pistols. At least there were no grenades or AK-47s. Touch wood, he thought.

It seemed unlikely they would return to the same location, especially so soon. An increased police presence around High-Risk Premises could be expected. Every cop in the area would be on alert.

It was 6.00 p.m. and Nathan Road was returning to normal after forensics had been completed. Sam was patrolling with Liu and was keen to obtain his opinion. With his SDU and CIB contacts Liu might have some useful intelligence. Sam guessed both units would be on high alert. CIB would no doubt be tapping up their extensive network of informers to dig out useful information.

"Any thoughts Mr. Liu? You must have come across Mainland gangs before?"

Liu barely acknowledged the question. His eyes were focused on the crowds around them. He took his time to respond.

"Of course, A-Sir. There are many gangs on the Mainland. They've hit Hong Kong many times. But this is more than one group. I've heard several are working together."

That's interesting, thought Sam. That might explain their recent briefing.

They were standing on Nathan Road, near where the officer had died. Sam could see several pairs of officers dotted along the road. They were stationary for effect, deliberately high-profile. The cordon tape had gone, and traffic was back to normal. Faint blood stains were visible on the pavement.

"Can I give you some advice? If you don't mind?" Liu was staring at a taxi loitering opposite them. It suddenly moved off belching a cloud of black smoke. The driver gave them a contrite wave.

"Of course, please do," said Sam. He was eager to hear what Liu knew.

"If we hit trouble, stay behind me, and do as I say," he said firmly. Sam wasn't about to argue. He nodded.

"Secondly, count your shots. You only have six rounds. Lose count and lose your life." This had been drummed into them at Training School. Sam could not imagine firing one round never mind all six.

"Next, take your time. Accuracy is more important than speed. How is your shooting?"

"Pretty good. On the range I was one of the best."

"Very good."

Liu had not looked over at Sam once. His eyes were constantly raking the throng of shoppers and pedestrians. A look here. A movement there. A vehicle lingering a moment too long. Nothing escaped his gaze.

"If they strike again, we need to be aggressive, disrupt their plan and delay them until EU get here."

Liu was warming to his subject. Sam wondered if he should be taking notes.

"If it turns into a chase, pick a man and stick with him. Remember what he's wearing. Don't take your eyes off him. If you don't know where you are, look at street names. Update us through the radio. We'll follow you."

Good stuff so far, Sam thought. Common sense really, but how common is common sense when the bullets start flying?

"And one last thing A-sir" Liu said seriously, turning to face Sam for the first time. "If you get a chance, don't hesitate. Take the shot. Capiche?"

Jenny's home telephone number was in Sam's notebook. He'd copied it from the list in the office. He wondered if he should call her. He decided that was a decision for tomorrow, she would not appreciate a call so late. It would be past midnight by the time he returned home.

The shift had ended without incident, yet the atmosphere remained subdued. It was going to take time for the mood to return to normal. The fact that the gang was still on the loose only added to the gloom.

He was standing in his usual spot, in the compound close to the loading area. He didn't notice McClintock approaching. "Good shift, laddie?" the DVC asked gruffly.

"Quiet, sir, but then again lightning doesn't often strike twice. Does it?"

"Only time will tell." He was staring at Sam intently. "What about Jenny then?"

Sam assumed McClintock was referring to her sick leave, but he wasn't entirely sure.

"I've no idea sir, it came out of the blue," he said flatly, trying to mask his own frustration.

McClintock eyed him coldly. Sam felt like an impala seeing a lion about to pounce. He was in the presence of a killer and the chances of escape seemed slim at best. Running was out of the question.

"There are certain rumours that I'm privy to which make me wonder about that girl. And her fucking boyfriend." McClintock shook his head and stomped off in the direction of the C shift commander.

Sam felt like screaming. Jesus Christ, he thought, why did no one tell me this before? What have I done to deserve this? Fuck, fuck, fuck.

He gave himself a mental pep talk to control his angst until later and looked around to check the progress of the returning second batch officers.

"How are we doing Mr. Liu, is everyone back?" he asked more calmly than he felt.

"All good sir, these are the last ones." A pair of officers unloaded their weapons under his gaze and headed over to the armoury hatch to return stores.

Sam wondered again if he should try to call Jenny. He thought better of it and decided to take a shower and return home.

After changing out of his damp uniform and showering Sam felt considerably calmer. He decided to forego a late-night beer in Wanchai. It had been a tiring few days and he was looking forward to unwinding with a cup of tea and a good night's sleep. Jenny was on his mind, but he needed to do some thinking before he called her. He felt disappointed by her no-show. He was struggling to make sense of it all.

He remembered his food stocks were running low and picked up a few items from the 7-11 store on the cavernous MTR station concourse before jumping on the train. The tiny shop was empty other than the bored-looking lady shop attendant. Noodles and Heineken would keep him going until he had time for a proper shopping expedition.

Admiralty station had few other passengers when he alighted just after midnight. A group of chatty female contractors were busy emptying bins, washing down ticket machines and sweeping floors. The stainless steel fittings gleamed under the bright station lighting and looked almost brand new.

He was in no hurry to get home and decided to take a longer, meandering walk, through Hong Kong Park. He ambled along, deep in thought, and cracked open one of the cold tins of beer. The evening felt perfect, even with the lack of a breeze. The peak of the summer heat was yet to arrive. On a whim, he sat on a park bench under an ornamental streetlight. The park was quiet. All the tourists and pairs of lovers had departed and he was alone with his thoughts.

Sam was feeling confused. He liked to think of himself as a black and white type of guy. He wasn't keen on grey. He prided himself on his logic. Get on with it he told himself. Lay it all out, work out how the pieces fit together, and make necessary decisions. If you need advice, seek it. If decisive action is required, take it. Moping and feeling sorry for yourself will get you nowhere. You are paid to make decisions, he constantly reminded himself. He realised he needed more clarity.

He had spent most of the shift thinking about Jenny. He realised he was dealing with three different versions of Jenny. Outwardly she was a professional, determined, somewhat aloof Sub-Unit Commander. The private Jenny he had gradually come to know was a loving, sexual, even vulnerable being. But what or who was the third?

Jenny had told Sam she had come out of a relationship yet it seemed common knowledge she had a lover. Silas Chu, a man who Sam was rapidly coming to think of as 'the Boyfriend'. Was it just old gossip and had she told him the truth about breaking up with him? Or did she think that a *gweilo* wouldn't hear the stories? Did she even know she was the subject of gossip?

Why had she been so upset about the murdered constable? Was that just the natural reaction of a colleague or was there something else behind it? Why had she not reported for duty when she seemed fine an hour earlier? The whole sick leave story smelled fishy.

He wondered who he could depend on and who else seemed to be involved somehow. He made a mental list of likely players: 1. McClintock; 2. Liu; and 3. the Boyfriend.

What did he know about McClintock, he wondered? A hard bastard. Experienced. Spoke his mind. Knew what he wanted. Brought Sam into his division deliberately for some reason. Had a downer on Jenny. But why? What did McClintock know about her relationship with the Boyfriend?

What was McClintock's connection with Liu? It could not be a coincidence that they both used 'capiche' like that? It seemed strange. Had they worked together previously? Did McClintock bring Liu in? Why? He resolved to check Liu's record of service for previous connections to McClintock.

Sam violently crushed the empty first tin with this foot and placed it back in the plastic bag. He looked around furtively, feeling out of place, embarrassed at the noise he had just made. He opened another.

He realised he knew nothing at all about the Boyfriend. A senior cop with a bad reputation. Possibly with criminal or triad connections, from what Mr. Cheung said.

For now, the rest of the sub-unit seemed clear of complications. Station Sergeant Cheung was a pain but seemed well connected. He might yet be useful.

Sam was conscious that Ricky Ricardo, his immediate boss, had barely spoken to him. Ricky took a close interest in all the other sub-units but rarely troubled Sam and Jenny. Had McClintock warned him off?

Sam felt he had more questions than answers. It was time to start digging. He drained his second tin and walked slowly up through the silent park. Crossing Kennedy Road, he skipped up the flight of concrete steps leading to the deserted entrance of The Hermitage and took the lift to the third floor. The walls of the lift lobby were damp and his shoes left marks on the moist floor tiles. The battered wood-framed glass fire door was wedged open and he walked slowly down the long dimly-lit corridor to his room.

As he reached for his door keys he became aware of a figure that had appeared from the door well behind him. He turned quickly, dropping his keys. It was Jenny.

"Evening, Sam," she said. She was wearing the same white top and jeans he'd last seen her wearing, but now they were filthy. Her white trainers were scuffed, and dark streaks of dirt covered her jeans and shirt. Her shirt had a rip on one arm and buttons were missing. Her lip seemed swollen, as though she had taken a punch to the mouth.

He didn't immediately respond. He was trying to fathom what he was seeing, as though she was an apparition.

"Can we go inside," she insisted. "Please?"

Sam nodded his assent and retrieved his keys. He opened the door and let her enter.

"Back in a minute," she said as he locked the door. He heard the bathroom door close and the predictable sounds of the shower. The thought of tea passed, and he opened another can of beer. He flicked off his shoes and lay on his bed, propped up by an elbow. He watched the bathroom door intently. His mood alternated between relief and bewilderment.

She finally emerged 15 minutes later, with one of his large white towels wrapped tightly around her chest. Her neck and arms were covered in scratches and bruises. Her face was emotionless. She appeared drained. She reminded Sam of an athlete who had finished a race and come in last.

Jenny perched on the side of the bed but said nothing. She gently took the beer from his hand and took a deep swig before handing it back.

"I suppose you're wondering what's going on?" she said. "I need to tell you about Silas Chu and I only hope that, after I have, you will still respect me."

14

Sam and Jenny talked for hours. It was mainly just her, with occasional questions from Sam. She talked calmly, as though she were talking about someone else's case, or someone else's life.

"Silas Chu was my old boss in Sham Shui Po District when I was a WPC," Jenny said. "He was the deputy commander, fifteen years older than me. A Crime man. Smart, charming, ambitious. Considered a high-flyer. He was also dirty. In every way. But I didn't find that out until much later."

She stopped for an instant. Sam cracked open another Heineken and handed it to her. She realised how thirsty she was and drank down half a can greedily before continuing.

"I worked for him in one of the Vice squads and he took a shine to me, inviting me out for dinners and karaoke. He seemed so dashing and funny, and incredibly generous. Eventually I fell for his charms and became his lover."

For a while it seemed like she had met her Prince Charming. He had encouraged her dreams of becoming an inspector and promised to write up the necessary reports. She was smitten. Her own inspector eventually worked out what was going on but was in no position to intervene. Silas had inexorably reeled her in, like a fish on a long line. It was only as he grew more secure in their relationship that she learned how he was able to afford his generosity.

Sham Shui Po was an old area and riddled with triads fighting for control of vice and gambling activities. It was lucrative business, especially if the police could be kept at bay. Silas saw his opportunity. Late night dinners with local movers and shakers ensued. Silas controlled the Vice teams and aimed to report impressive results. The triads controlled the vice and needed to generate cash. It was a match made in heaven.

The arrangement led to a mutually beneficial series of tip-offs, in both directions. Failed raids became rare. Successful raids were mounted against competitors. Low level operatives were sacrificed and paid off. Everyone was happy. Triad profits were protected and Silas was receiving an amount more than his salary as a backhander every month. Police arrest, seizure and prosecution figures were commendably high.

By now Silas was generating so much cash that he was struggling to launder it without attracting ICAC attention.

Out of the blue he arranged to buy the Mei Foo property in her name. Naively she took it as a gift, presented to her as a token of affection by a grateful lover. It was also a convenient place for them to meet. Mei Foo sat within the district, not far from their office.

He had handled all the arrangements, and only told her afterwards. Her forged signature on the papers would be difficult to explain. She was trapped.

It had become increasingly hard for Jenny to deceive herself about Silas's behaviour when he was transferred to Wanchai after his promotion. Wanchai, with its multitude of nightclubs and bars, presented even juicier opportunities. With his background on Hong Kong Island Silas was soon able to build up a fresh network of willing police *mah jais* – the Cantonese term for 'small horses' or supporters - and replicated his operation.

Jenny had remained part of the picture but saw him less frequently. Things between them had started to sour when his replacement in Sham Shui Po smelled a rat and started to put his suspicions on paper. Silas, worried he would be reported to ICAC, started pressuring her for information, but she had refused.

The breaking point in their relationship had come with the shock news that Silas was getting married to a chief inspector, shortly after Jenny received notice of her promotion. She had already discovered he had a Mainland wife. She was feeling used, just a pawn in his money laundering operation. She felt disgusted, anxious and trapped, and feared a conviction for aiding and abetting, or worse. Silas insisted she sign over the flat, but Jenny refused. When she threatened to inform his new wife, he backed off.

Trouble came following Silas's sideways move to Deputy Regional Commander, a promotion post. Increased scrutiny was causing him problems and his activities were becoming riskier. Worse still, rash investments, the stalling property market and a stock market crash after Tiananmen Square had left him financially stressed. He was scratching around for assets to sell, and risked bankruptcy if he could not repay his loans. With insolvency he could kiss goodbye to his promotion chances, and probably his job altogether. Silas Chu had started to become desperate.

"How do you know all this?" Sam asked. "I thought you said that you haven't seen him?" His tone was brutal. Jenny realised that she must sound like an accomplice to a corrupt cop. Whatever feelings Sam had for her, she wasn't sure they could survive the revelation.

"I told you the truth," she insisted. "I broke off the relationship after he got married. But he kept on harassing me and it's gradually been getting worse. Sometimes he said he wanted me to continue as his mistress. Sometimes he wanted me to give him the flat back. And then yesterday I was kidnapped," she said with venom.

"Say that again," Sam said sceptically. "Kidnapped?"

"Yes, I was fucking kidnapped, Sam." She almost screamed it. Anger was in her voice. "Abducted, grabbed, taken. Call it what you fucking want. I was kidnapped before I went on duty."

"Tell me what happened. Everything." His face had reddened, whether his anger was directed at her or Silas, she couldn't tell. So she did.

She told him how she left Sam's apartment after suddenly feeling the need to get to work because of the robbery. Coming out of the MTR near the station she felt like she was being followed. As she left the MTR exit she was grabbed and pushed into a white van.

"But how did they find you?" Sam was confused. "You didn't go home after spending the night with me."

"Easy," she said bitterly. "It's obvious. They couldn't find me at home, so they waited for me on my way to work. All they had to do was know my shift and wait at the MTR exit closest to the station."

"Who was it?" She could see Sam's mind trying to work it out, wanting to believe her.

"The spotter was a cop. One of Silas's *mah jais* from Sham Shui Po, a detective sergeant. Named A-Siu."

"And the other two?" he demanded.

"The driver was another of his little horses, also from Sham Shui Po. A detective PC. A-Ken."

"And the last one?"

"A-Ko. He's a mainland guy. He was the one who murdered the Auxie." She paused, thinking about PCA Mok. He'd been a cheerful soul who had worked the day shift for years. Everyone in the station knew him. A-Ko had bragged about shooting him.

"It's an incredible story," Sam said, at last. "Abducting a police inspector in broad daylight…"

"And you know what else?" she said. "They used a police vehicle to grab me."

Sam looked stunned. "I need another drink," he said. It was approaching 2 a.m. The last of the four beers had gone. He retrieved a bottle of Bushmills Irish Whiskey from the kitchen. He brought the bottle and two small glass tumblers filled with ice into the bedroom.

"A Passing Out gift," he said. "From somebody in England I should have told you about sooner. She still thinks she's my girlfriend. I'm not sure I'm still her boyfriend. I'd been saving it for a special occasion. Not quite what I had in mind, but needs must."

Sam poured a large measure for himself and resumed his position on the bed.

Jenny smiled weakly at the sight of the bottle and at Sam's apologetic explanation. She'd guessed there was somebody back home he hadn't told her about. "I hate whiskey," she said. "Better pour me a big one." They both laughed.

Jenny added ice to her measure. They raised a silent toast and she emptied the entire glass. He poured her another.

"Take it easy. I've not finished interrogating you yet," he said.

She raised a half smile.

"How did they persuade you to call in sick?" he continued.

"A-Ko held a pistol to my head and told me he was going to kill me. I called the office and I told Eileen I would be off sick for a week. I did my best to alert her by calling her Sarah instead of Eileen but she didn't pick up on it."

"How could they abduct you in a busy public place?" he asked. She could tell he wasn't completely convinced by her story, so she tried harder.

"They identified themselves as police officers, with warrant cards, so people just ignored us. It looked like official business. A-Ko kept his mouth shut so they wouldn't realise he was a mainlander."

"Then what?"

"An apartment in Tai Kok Tsui. An old block next to the waterfront." That part of Kowloon had a seedy underbelly. It was a rabbit warren of old buildings.

"Could you identify it?" He spoke to her like a cop instead of a solicitous boyfriend.

"Absolutely. We need to find it. The whole gang is there. All eight of the bastards."

"Eight? Are you sure?" He was trying not to sound unbelieving.

"Eight Mainlanders. All armed to the teeth." When they had bundled her into their hideout in a third-floor apartment room her heart had sunk. Before it had been easy to think of Silas as just greedy and corrupt. Seeing triad types clutching weapons had forced her to confront the reality of his actions.

"How did you get away?" Sam asked.

"You're not going to believe this," she said, shaking her head. As she recounted it, it felt fantastic. She had been bound, gagged, blindfolded, and placed in a box room. She heard the men go out, but A-Ken had stayed behind to watch over her. He'd told her he had instructions to shoot her if she tried to escape.

Several hours passed and she heard a familiar voice outside. Her blindfold was removed. Standing in front of her was Silas Chu.

He was by himself. It seemed he had two things on his mind - sex and money. He instructed A-Ken the guard to put her in one of the bedrooms, untie her and leave them alone for thirty minutes. Silas was carrying a pistol.

She knew what he wanted: the Mei Foo apartment. He needed the money urgently. Faking her signature again during a sale or re-mortgage was impossible. If she disappeared, serious questions would be asked.

15

"Did you miss me?" Silas said in Cantonese with a grin on his face after A-Ken had left them.

He took his jacket off and put it over the back of a chair. Jenny noticed that he had put on weight. His late-night carousing was catching up with him.

"Of course not, you pig," she said. "What sort of fucking mess have you got me into?"

"You were always so naïve Jenny," Silas said with a disparaging laugh.

"What do you want?" she asked cautiously. She suspected she knew the answer and was wary.

"It's simple my dear. First, we are going to have some fun, for old times' sake. Then you are going to sign over your apartment to me."

"And if I don't?"

"I'm going to get the boys to kill you. And then your father. I'll lose out on the apartment but at least I'll be tidying up my affairs. Ko's already killed one cop this week. The boys might want some fun with you first." He laughed harshly.

Jenny had not expected the threat to her father. She realised Silas might not know he had recently moved back to Canada. The thought of being ravaged by a pack of Mainlander savages terrified her.

"Who are they?" she asked, looking at the pile of bags in the room beyond.

"Just some friends from the Mainland. Here to do a few jobs for me. Humping then dumping you in the harbour might be the first one." He stared at her malevolently.

She wondered where the other men had gone. Probably out for dinner.

Jenny was thinking frantically, weighing up her options, working out her chances. She was determined not to be a passive victim. There was more at stake than just her life, she thought. Images of her father and the dead Auxie entered her mind. Whatever happened, her career was in tatters. First and foremost she was still a cop, and she couldn't let her colleagues down. She realised Silas hadn't mentioned Sam. That meant he probably didn't know about him.

The other good news was that he was over-confident. He was alone in the apartment. He also thought he was dealing with the old Jenny. This is the new Jenny, she told herself defiantly. You are an inspector now. Think like one.

She decided that playing along was the best option. Buy some time. Lull him into a false sense of security and wait for an opportunity. Pounce when you can surprise him.

"Let's get it over with, you dirty old bastard," she sighed. She slowly stood up and started unbuttoning her white shirt. Silas smiled and placed his pistol on top of a chest of drawers.

"You will enjoy it, like the old days," Silas said. "The paperwork can wait."

He leered at her as she stripped down to her underwear and lay back on the single bed, bracing for the inevitable. Her bare arm felt the coldness of the wall. She was trying to look at the ceiling instead of his face or body.

Out of the corner of her eye she saw him drop his trousers and underwear. She felt herself tense up, recoiling from the approach of the man who now so repulsed her. She knew the moment for action was approaching.

"Suck it bitch," he said, inching his groin closer to the bed.

A plan suddenly formed in her head. She felt confident for the first time. You can do this, she told herself. Timing is everything, make it look good.

She sat up, shuffled closer to the edge and swung her legs over the side. The thought of what was to come was having the expected effect on his manhood. In anticipation, Silas started gently massaging it with his right hand. She artfully swept back the hair from her face and slowly edged towards his groin. She drew the moment out and placed her hands on the back of his thighs, moving them up and down, creating sensations that were starting to take over his brain. As she edged her mouth closer, she moved her right hand slowly and deliberately, tracing patterns on his skin with her fingers. She started around his buttocks and then gradually come closer to his balls.

The strike was fast and brutal. She viciously clamped her hand on his testicles and squeezed tight. Before he had a chance to react, her left hand pulled him towards her. As his cock neared her face, she put it in her mouth and bit down hard in one smooth motion. She kept her head in place for several seconds and an awful scream filled the room. He tried to pull away but it only increased the pain. He started striking her head. She had anticipated that and released her grip. Without warning she launched herself upwards and viciously head-butted him in the face.

Silas fell backwards and into the wall. She took a step across the room, grabbed the pistol from the table and brought the barrel down on his head. She struck him repeatedly, frenziedly. He desperately tried to shield himself. His flailing arms were useless. She saw gory indentations on his face and scalp and loud moans punctuated the awful sounds of impact. She was taking no chances. She struck him mercilessly until he offered no resistance. His hands dropped, leaving him slumped unconscious against the wall. He was bleeding profusely.

It was time to go. She quickly wiped her bloody hands on the bedding and slipped on her clothes. Her heart was pumping. Adrenaline was coursing through her body. She reminded herself to stay calm and think through the rest of her escape. She had come out of the encounter lightly. Apart from having to take his vile cock in her mouth one last time. Only a few of his blows had any effect. The side of her mouth hurt but that was all.

She checked he was still unconscious and looked around the apartment. She was disappointed to find no telephone. Locking the door and calling 999 would have been the easiest option she knew.

Jenny examined the old wooden door. She slid two rusty barrel bolts into place at the top and bottom. She quickly opened each of the bags, checked the contents and closed them again. They contained personal belongings. Shirts, underwear, and toiletries. Concealed underneath, white plastic bags held ammunition and grenades. She recognised the two long barrelled weapons with folding stocks as AK-47s.

In an envelope she found a series of photographs. For the first time in several hours she allowed herself a brief smile. She had seen enough. It was time to get out while she still could.

Silas was lying unconscious in a growing pool of blood in the bedroom. She regretted not having a camera to record evidence of her handiwork. It would have been a great crime scene photo. This once proud peacock lying dishevelled, covered in blood. His shrivelled manhood oozing blood onto the cold wooden floor, bite marks clearly visible.

She retrieved the heavy, black semi-automatic pistol. The foresight was matted with his blood. She guessed it was a Black Star and wondered whether she could work out how to fire it. It was unlike the revolvers she had fired at Training School, but it felt pleasingly solid.

The sounds of a key in the door made her heart freeze. She saw the heavily worn brass knob turn and the wooden door rattled slightly. Her heart was beating furiously. A voice came from outside. Jenny recognised it as A-Ken's. He was asking to be let in. He had returned quicker than she expected. She guessed he was hoping to get an eyeful. Even a piece of the action.

Jenny looked around and considered her options. The only way out was through the door in front of her. Or through one of the windows.

She peered through the window, grimy from years of neglect. It faced into a void surrounded by similar windows on all sides. The sun had already set and the occupants of other units had turned on their lights which cast shadows across the void.

The space stretched the full height of the building, to the rooftop a dozen stories above. It was dark and foul, littered with air-conditioners and detritus. The tangle of pipes offered salvation, she realised. If she had the nerve.

The window was open a few inches and she levered it higher. She climbed through head-first, then twisted to see her options. She was cheered by the number of possible footholds and handholds. The thought of the filth she would encounter repulsed her.

Sounds of hammering came from the door. She heard more voices. It was now or never. She tucked the pistol down the front of her jeans, and eased herself through the window backwards.

Only one other window was open, above her. To her left, less than ten yards away. She assessed possible routes and selected a vertical pipe.

The climbing was easier than expected. Rusty iron brackets were her footholds. She planned to follow a horizontal pipe along to her entry point. The pipe was covered in slime. Her passing disturbed cockroaches, and black spiders from their webs.

The traverse was more difficult. The pipes were thinner and flimsier. She carefully tested their strength before each move. It was agonisingly slow. Her time was running out. A-Ken and the others might break through the door at any moment.

Inch by inch, she edged closer to the windowsill. The interior was dark and foreboding. She could see nothing. She decided to take the risk. Pistol drawn, she climbed inside.

Jenny slowly and silently closed the window. Her eyes acclimatised to the gloom. A small white cat sat next to the open door, eying her suspiciously. It waved its tail in disapproval but was silent. Light and the sound of a television came from the adjoining room. She saw the apartment was clean and well maintained. The room was lined with classic rosewood furniture. A colourful patchwork divan covered a single bed.

The cat exited the room with a loud mewing sound. Jenny hesitated, listening for movement. She heard nothing except her racing heart. She edged silently closer to the door and nervously peeped around the corner. An old lady in a rocking chair was observing her, a blank look on her face, looking neither panicked nor surprised.

"I hope you brushed your teeth," ventured Sam uncouthly as Jenny concluded. His vulgar attempt at humour earned him a vicious punch to the arm.

He had picked his time well though and she knew it. The act of telling her story had been cathartic. It was as though a weight had been lifted from her shoulders. Though visibly exhausted, her smile had returned. Being able to share with him the imbroglio of lies and deception she'd become involved in had relieved part of the burden.

The final part of her escape had been less dramatic but equally nerve-racking. Her host had been calm and understanding after Jenny offered her a concocted yarn about a triad, a brothel, and a mistress. The old lady willingly provided Jenny a temporary place of refuge and a bathroom to wash off the grime. Chinese tea and snacks settled her nerves until she finally found the courage to leave.

She had considered calling 999 but suspected the gang would be long gone. Trying to hunt her in a building of that size made no sense. They would not want to take chances. The gang would have moved to another safe house already.

It was better for her to disappear into the night. Attracting attention to herself could be dangerous. Lives were at risk. Taking down Silas and the gang would take more than her calling the police.

By late evening she felt confident enough to leave. She left the hospitality of her elderly host just after 11.00 p.m. She crept down the staircase, one hand on the pistol in the back of her jeans. She encountered no one.

On the MTR she received strange looks but the journey from Mong Kok to Admiralty was uneventful. Then she had waited outside Sam's room from around midnight until his return.

"What next?" Sam asked. He looked out of his depth. Jenny was aware neither of them had been taught to deal with this type of situation at Training School.

"That depends," she said. I've not told you the best bit yet." She stood up and re-visited the bathroom, returning seconds later with both hands behind her back.

"I'll give you three guesses what I have in my hands," she said mischievously.

"The pistol?"

"Spot on." She produced it with a dramatic flourish.

"And the other?"

"The other," she said, "is the gang's plan for a raid in Tsim Sha Tsui."

She grinned like the cat with the cream. She waved a coloured foldout map of Kowloon marked with two sets of Chinese characters and other marks. She kept on grinning and put both items on the set of drawers at the back of the room.

"Now I need some sleep," she said. "But first, I have to brush my teeth."

16

Sam woke late the next morning to the pleasant sensation of a warm hand cupping his balls. Another hand gently traced fingers around his abdomen. Through a half-opened eye, he saw the bright light of the day intruding around the edge of the curtains. The usual rumble of traffic was barely audible over the sound of the air-conditioner. He lay still, enjoying a warm mouth tenderly kissing first his hip, then his thigh, then his abdomen.

He often woke up with a hard-on. This time he felt he was breaking new records. After what seemed an eternity, the hand finished its work. He groaned loudly, arched his back, and lay back, exhausted and content.

The hand remained on his groin, stroking him gently. His heart rate slowed and his breathing returned to normal. He felt the kisses moving up his torso, to a nipple, his neck, and finally his month.

"Thank you," a voice said.

'Thank you' was exactly what Sam was thinking. He was reluctant to say anything that might spoil the moment. It was the most memorable early morning experience of his life.

"You're amazing, you know. My knight in shining armour." Jenny was clutching him tight. A tear slid gently down her face. "My English gentleman."

He held her close, enjoying the glow of their love. Their eyes were locked, six inches apart. She wiped the tear away and smiled.

"I need to ask," she whispered. "Was that better or worse than the service you received at Silver Springs?"

He hesitated, then grinned. "That is the best I've ever had. You being so old and experienced really does have its benefits." Sam sprang out of bed to avoid the punch that he knew was on its way.

"Go and get us breakfast", she demanded. "I need a shower."

By 1 p.m. they were both washed and feeling ready for the day. Sam had repeated his noodle run to Dirty Dick's.

They were sitting on the slippery brown Government-issue faux leather sofa, sipping coffee. The lunchtime news was on, political and economic headlines dominated. Sam turned down the volume so they could talk.

"What next?" Sam asked. He was due at work in just under two hours. Returning to her own place in Mei Foo was out of the question. Jenny would be alone in his apartment. They needed a plan. He assumed Silas still knew nothing about their relationship, but taking anything for granted seemed dangerous. The pistol in his bedroom weighed heavily on his mind.

They agreed doing nothing was not an option. Silas might be out of circulation temporarily, but he would undoubtedly have unleashed his little horses to look for her. With such obvious injuries he would have to take sick leave and feign an accident. Unless he was already in hospital. There was no way of knowing how badly Jenny had injured him.

Jenny said, "I think you need to speak to Superintendent McClintock. This needs to become official. It's better to do it through him, even with that old bastard's vicious streak. You know he doesn't like me."

Sam had never mentioned McClintock's suspicions about Jenny. She seemed to have picked up on the DVC's not-so-subtle body language. He either liked you or he didn't. There was no middle ground. He thought it wise not to mention the comments from the two station sergeants.

"Fair enough, but what about you? You can't stay here, it's just too dangerous. You need to come in."

She said nothing. She stared pensively out of the window.

"It won't be easy getting you into the station. They might not be looking for me but they will certainly be looking for you. Even there you might not be safe. I'm sure Silas has plenty of other little horses and we only know two of them."

Jenny looked like she was going to argue yet the logic was undeniable. She needed to come with Sam, the question was how to do it safely. Time was of the essence if they were going to prevent the raid.

"There is a way," she said eventually. "It won't be comfortable, and I'll need your phone."

Sam guessed Liu had been involved in some dog shit operations in his time, but this one probably took the biscuit. He was standing next to a gleaming Toyota saloon in the dusty basement car park of the Hermitage. Liu had not asked too many questions on the phone. Now he raised his eyebrows at Jenny's dirty jeans and trainers. Her billowing tee-shirt was obviously also one of Sam's.

"When I attended the station sergeant promotion course they told us we could expect some difficult situations," Liu said.

He had kept his face straight whilst he said it. Sam could only smile at his understatement.

"It's a long story Mr. Liu. Even if I told you the whole tale, you probably wouldn't believe me," Sam told him.

Liu raised his eyebrows and smiled. He tactfully kept his thoughts to himself.

Involving Liu was a good call, thought Sam. If they could trust anyone in the sub-unit, it was him. It helped that he lived over the other side of Hong Kong Island, in Ap Lei Chau. The Hermitage was practically on his route to work.

Sam always carried a card with contact details of the sub-unit NCOs in his wallet, just in case. Sam reckoned that if this didn't class as an emergency, nothing would.

The short journey took them down through Central, along to Causeway Bay and through the Cross Harbour Tunnel. The car was on the small side, but he was able to push the seat back and stretch his legs. Air-conditioning would have been useful in the hot June weather. He obtained some relief by opening the window. He knew the boot, where Jenny was hiding, would be unbearably hot.

The two-lane tunnel under the harbour was quiet for the time of day. Within ten minutes of entering the tunnel portal they were turning off Austin Road into the station. The compound was as congested as usual. He saw several parked PTU vehicles from a platoon performing Operation Moorgate duties.

Liu spotted an empty space close to the building and parked up. "Wait here please," Sam said. He climbed out and walked up the rear steps into the station.

The main corridor was quiet. He saw only one of the Registry staff carrying several manila envelopes. She smiled as he passed. He felt nervous. He could feel his pulse starting to quicken. No matter, this can't be avoided, he told himself.

The office doors he passed were ajar. He scrupulously avoided looking into Ricky Ricardo's office. He did not want to risk being diverted from the task in hand. He decided he would feign deafness if he was called.

As he approached McClintock's office, he moved as quietly as possible, listening for sounds inside. If anyone was inside his plan was to walk away and try again later. This was not a conversation he could risk being overheard. The office was silent. He peeped around the corner to see McClintock stood at the window, surveying his kingdom. He hesitated for a moment, plucking up courage. The decision was made for him.

"Come in, Sam, we need to talk." Not for the first time Sam thought he must have eyes in the back of his head.

Sam entered the room and closed the door behind him. McClintock raised his eyebrows but said nothing. Sam walked over to the side door to the General Registry. He could see the civilian staff busy at their desks but none looked up. He gently pulled the door closed and turned.

He could see McClintock's curiosity was piqued. He seemed to be wearing the 'what the fuck is going on?' look beloved of superiors looking for an opportunity to jump on you from a great height.

Sam took up the usual position for supplicants in front of McClintock's desk.

"Good afternoon, sir," he said formally. "I'm sorry to bother you but I have something vitally important to tell you in private."

Before McClintock could respond Sam reached behind him and produced the pistol. He placed it gingerly on the desk. He was careful to face it away from both of them. McClintock inspected it from a distance. He didn't move to touch it.

"Is that the real thing?" he asked.

Sam nodded.

McClintock picked up the phone.

"Mr. Lung, please ensure that I am not disturbed until further notice. Not even the District Commander. Especially not the District Commander." He concluded the call and left the phone off the receiver.

"Go on, son. Tell me everything."

It took only minutes. Afterwards McClintock snatched up the phone.

"Ricky, we've got a situation here, I've got no time to explain. Grab Alan and a couple of his Report Room lads and all of you report to my office armed with shotguns. ASAP. Yes, I know it's unusual and yes, I also mean you too, you dozy bastard. Now move!" He slammed the phone down on its receiver.

"What a fucking mess," he shouted. "Someone's going to fucking pay for this, you mark my words."

17

It took Sam just five minutes to precis the situation before McClintock exploded into action. Whether one aspect of the situation irked him more than any other was unclear. A bent senior officer and an imminent armed robbery was enough to give any Divisional Commander heart palpitations.

McClintock shook his head in disbelief.

"Not today, not on my watch, not ever, no fucking way José," he announced loudly.

The cogs started churning in McClintock's head. He was an experienced policeman, but nobody climbed far up the promotion ladder in the Royal Hong Kong Police without realising that they needed to be a politician as well. Get this wrong and all the shit will be downhill, was his reading. Several minutes passed, during which he calculated who he could trust and which senior officers he needed to involve, while Sam stood at ease in front of him. Then there was a knock on the door.

"Come in," McClintock yelled.

The four officers stood outside, wide-eyed.

"You two," he said, pointing at Alan's two Report Room Reserves in turn. "Front entrance. Main gate. One each. No one enters this station without my approval until further notice. It's District and Divisional staff, EU and PTU on duty only. Check all warrant cards. No fucking CID from outside this station. Capiche? Go."

"Yes-sir," they responded in unison, moving off at the trot.

First things first. Double up the guard and strictly control access to the station. When your enemy had crooked cops working for him, security needed to be tighter and everything had to be 'need-to-know'.

"You two follow us," McClintock said sharply to Ricky and Alan. "We're going through the Report Room and out through the back door of the cells. There is a high value item in a vehicle to escort. You'll understand the job when we get there. This is top secret, not a fucking word to anyone. Understand?"

Ricky nodded though he didn't look like he understood at all. He wasn't the type to argue. McClintock liked Ricardo but was pretty sure he thought his boss was a lunatic.

McClintock stomped off down the corridor. Every head turned at the unusual sight of an armed team moving purposefully through the heart of the division. The most danger they usually faced in this part of the station was a nasty paper cut or lacerations from McClintock's tongue.

As they entered the Report Room, the Duty Officer swiftly hid his newspaper in his desk and stood up smartly.

"How many prisoners in the cells?" demanded McClintock.

"Just two, sir," he replied nervously.

"Empty the cells. Put them in the holding area. Right now."

The DO looked perplexed by the order. He barked out the instructions and his assistants jumped up.

Liu was standing by his car when the party burst out of the cell block rear entrance. Sam had gone up in McClintock's estimation by involving Liu. The DVC had his own reasons for trusting him implicitly. The station sergeant would be anxiously checking his watch. He should have been getting changed for B shift by now. The sub-unit would be wondering what was going on.

Ricky and Alan took up positions around the car. Sam motioned to Liu who quickly opened the boot of the vehicle. Curled up inside was Jenny, bathed in sweat. She was clutching a water bottle in either hand. She appeared close to collapsing. Sam felt relieved. It had taken longer than planned but she was safe now. All they had to do was get her inside without anyone seeing her.

"Get her covered up," barked McClintock.

Sam wrapped her with a rough cell blanket and helped her out of the car, too weak to stand. Sam swept up his consignment and carried it the 25 yards to the doorway.

As their escort entered, the Duty Officer closed and secured the thick door behind them, before returning to his duties. Sam carried Jenny into one of the cells. He lay her down on the long concrete bench and uncovered her. McClintock asked Alan to watch the entrance to the cells.

"What next, sir?" Sam asked.

"You need to stay here and look after Jenny," McClintock said. "I've got to send this up the chain of command."

"Will you be talking to District Headquarters about the raid?" To a new inspector like Sam, it would seem the obvious thing to do. McClintock wasn't so sure.

"Not if I can help it," he said. "Not with that plonker Patrick in charge. Talk about spineless and over-promoted." Relations with District had plummeted since Big Ronny's departure. McClintock held the acting

District Commander in disdain. Not his idea of a leader. Then he realised that the current situation was exactly the excuse he needed to do something really daring.

"Ricky, leave the shotgun with Sam and come with me," McClintock ordered. "Keep her safe," McClintock told Sam as he charged out, leaving quizzical looks from the Report Room staff in his wake.

Convention dictated McClintock's request for support should be routed through District, then Region. Out of courtesy if nothing else. McClintock knew that route would be too slow and leaky. Especially when he had no idea of possible connections between Patrick and Silas Chu.

It was an excuse McClintock could use to do it his way. The McClintock way. With Patrick rarely found in the station on an afternoon, McClintock had carte blanche to cut him out of the loop. But why stop there? If he called Kowloon Headquarters there would be difficult conversations with his chain of command. Why not just take it a step further and go straight to PHQ? If he could stop a series of armed robberies and catch a high-ranking dirty cop, the impudence would be worth it and a lot of senior coppers would owe him. He picked up the phone and dialled up Gerry Smithies, Assistant Commissioner, Operations. He was equivalent in rank to the Regional Commander, Kowloon but with the necessary power to bring the whole resources of the Force to bear on the problem.

"Gerry, Brian here, how are you?"

"Brian, long time no see, what can I do for you?"

"I'll not beat about the bush. I need the CP's Reserve Platoon here in Tsim Sha Tsui in an hour. The shit has hit the fan and we need urgent support."

"What shit? What fan?"

"I can't say, it's too sensitive. Walls have ears."

"Listen you cheeky Scottish twat. How dare you call me up, demand my Reserve Platoon and refuse to explain why. Sensitive my arse. And next time call me, sir."

"Gerry, for a start it's not your Platoon. All I can tell you is that it involves ICAC matters, a heavily armed Mainland gang, and a senior police officer involved in a conspiracy to mount the biggest armed robbery in history in my fucking division. If the raid goes down tonight and I've got no PTU cover because you refused me, then you know what will fucking happen. Sir. Capiche?"

"Are you serious?"

"Deadly."

"They're on their way."

When McClintock returned to the cell block corridor, Sam, clutching the shotgun tightly, was barring the way.

"Is everything okay, sir?" he said.

"Okay, verging on perfect," he said.

"Anything I should know?" Sam persisted.

McClintock was laughing to himself and rubbing his hands together gleefully, like a miser who had discovered a lost penny.

"Let's just say that things are coming together nicely young Sam," he said with a wink. "Now's not a time to stand on protocol."

McClintock could keep it to himself no longer. He described his conversation with Smithies verbatim and explained his reasoning. This had the potential to become a legendary anecdote. The type endlessly repeated over many beers. The best stories were like fine wine, slowly gaining potency as they quietly re-circulated, often for decades. He knew the best anecdotes needed no witnesses. A good story developed a life of its own. They could be taken as the Gospel truth without inconvenient facts tripping up the storyteller. The difference was, this one was completely true.

McClintock was still chuckling as he followed Sam the ten yards to Jenny's cell. The gate was wide open, like all the others. He hated the cells. The bars reminded him of a zoo. The gloom and fetid odours were more like a medieval dungeon.

"How are you, my dear? I hear you've had a tough time?" he asked solicitously. He was surprising himself by demonstrating a touching level of concern. He'd need to watch that. He had a reputation to maintain.

"I'm fine thank you, sir," she replied quietly. "I'm so sorry to cause you problems. I know I'm in big trouble. I just want to help."

Big trouble was correct, thought McClintock. Getting tangled up in this web of corruption was a career-ending scenario. Now did not seem the time for examination of the whys and wherefores. There would be plenty of time for all that later. Once the enquiry launched, he would have very little control of the process but if she had behaved as Sam said, he would do his best to help her. First, though, she needed her life protecting.

McClintock knew the risks. He had earlier despatched Alan to prowl the station and listen for gossip. He wanted to know if anyone had seen Jenny covertly transported into the station. Alan was a long serving officer. McClintock considered him a safe pair of hands. They could rely on him to be discreet.

There was just the three of them in the cell. McClintock had placed her in the most secure part of the station.

"Tell me what you know about this gang," McClintock said, "and why you think they are going to hit Tsim Sha Tsui? I want to know when and how." His friendly bedside manner had evaporated. He had become all business.

Jenny explained how she had got involved with Silas. How he had tricked her into owning the Mei Foo apartment. How she had been first pressurised and then threatened. She described her abduction. Where she was detained. Her observations of the gang and premises. Her escape. The return to Sam's apartment and the journey into the station.

Jenny ended her report. She had delivered it clearly and professionally, just as she had been trained. McClintock thought she told the story well. She had tried to avoid eye contact with Sam, but McClintock wasn't a fool and could see something was going on between them. Why not? he thought to himself. Sam was young and good-looking, and if Jenny had broken up with Silas, she was single. He'd keep that out of his report though. He had marked Sam down as an officer with potential. The young laddie couldn't afford a note on his record associating him with a disgraced copper.

The pistol Sam had brought him was safely locked away in his safe, pending examination. That weapon alone gave her account a sheen of authenticity. Especially if the weapon was connected to the Auxie's death.

"You did well," the DVC said. "Now I need to know what they are planning."

Jenny resumed her story. She included several pieces of information and supposition left out the first time. Individually those elements were worthless. Joined together in a logical and reasoned argument, and set against the known facts, they were dynamite. The clincher was the map that McClintock examined closely. It tied in with photographs she had found in the bags.

Pictures of six goldsmiths and jewellers along a hundred yard section of Nathan Road close to the Hyatt Hotel.

McClintock was thoughtful. There was a lot to consider. A lot to decide and plan. And not much time.

"Let me get this straight. There will be an armed robbery in Sham Shui Po tonight. It will be a distraction. The real threat is to six targets down here shortly afterwards. The escape will be on foot and by sea."

"Yes, sir. That's what I believe."

"Right, good. Thank you very much. Very good indeed." McClintock's smile was back. He turned to leave the cell. "Sam come with me. Jenny, stay here. We'll be back shortly."

McClintock checked his watch. It was approaching 5 p.m.

"Shut the door Sam, I need to make another call to my friend Smithies," he ordered as they entered his office.

"Hello, sir," McClintock said politely. "I'm glad I caught you."

"Bloody good of you to call me sir for once. Before you ask, the Reserve Platoon is on its way from Kowloon East and should be with you shortly. Now what do you want this time?" Smithies asked sharply, sounding exasperated.

"Very much appreciated, sir, that will be a great help. It's a good start. Unfortunately, it doesn't completely solve my problem," McClintock continued gently.

"Really?"

"Do you still live in Kowloon Tong?" asked McClintock.

There was a pause. There was caution in the voice at the other end.

"Yes, I've lived there for 15 years. As you damned well know."

"Excellent. How would you like to pop in here on your way home and have a little chat? Can I expect you in say 30 minutes? By the way, would you put SDU on standby? Oh, and Boat Team and an RAF Wessex too. If you wouldn't mind? Sir."

There was a short pause at the other end and then a distinctly different tone as realisation dawned. "I'll see you shortly."

McClintock put the phone down and grinned. He gave Sam a firm thumbs up signal.

"Game on, Sam," he declared confidently. "I knew our Assistant Commissioner friend would play ball if I buttered him up. Me and him go way back. His Highness Gerry Smithies and I used to play football together years ago. Between you and me he's fucking shite." McClintock chuckled. "He can be a plonker, but you just need to know how to handle him." McClintock was grinning and rubbing his hands by way of celebration.

"Sir, can I get changed and draw arms?" asked Sam.

McClintock looked at his watch and realised Sam's shift had started two hours earlier. "Good idea, laddie. Get your arse back in here in ten minutes and we can put our heads together with Smithies."

Ten minutes later Sam was back in the DVC's office, now wearing his full uniform and service revolver.

"First things first," the DVC said, with a glint in his eye. "Ask Ricky to join us. Secondly, since an army marches on its stomach, do me a favour and ask your Admin lassie to sort out refreshments. Sandwiches and coffee for four in here ASAP. Arrange a rice box for Jenny. Then we've got work to do."

18

Assistant Commissioner Gerry Smithies stormed into McClintock's office in full uniform shortly after Sam had returned from his errands. Getting from Police Headquarters to Tsim Sha Tsui so quickly in rush hour traffic was no mean feat. Even with blue lights and siren.

"Right," he said aggressively. "Are you going to tell me what the blazes is going on or do you want to be running the Police Driving School for the rest of your career?"

Sam had never heard a superintendent spoken to like that.

"Thanks for coming, Gerry." McClintock smiled serenely, as though he hadn't heard the threat. "Let me make the introductions. Coffee?"

"Yes, thank you. Get on with it," retorted Smithies.

"Gerry, this is Ricky Ricardo, and Sam Steadings, my B shift Sub-Unit Commander."

Smithies eyed each of them coolly in turn. He made no attempt to shake hands but nodded curtly. He was an intimidating character, 6'4" tall with wide shoulders and a large nose that seemed to take up most of his face. A dark five o'clock shadow gave him a thuggish look. His square jaw gave him a Desperate Dan-like appearance. To Sam he seemed to have the frame of a sportsman. He imagined Smithies hurtling down the pitch and mercilessly bowling a cricket ball towards his face. He looked like the type who took no prisoners.

"Sam, shut the door please," McClintock requested. "Before we start, can I clarify if SDU, Boat Team and a helicopter are on standby?"

"Yes, yes," Smithies answered tersely. "This is most irregular. You should have gone through Region. This had better be good. Otherwise I'll have your balls on a plate. And the Commissioner will have mine."

Sam stood timidly to one side. He had never even spoken to an assistant commissioner before and was looking forward to the next few minutes.

"SDU are at high readiness and can be here from Fanling in 45 minutes," Smithies went on. "Boat Team can get to this side of the harbour in 20 minutes. I've requested a chopper from PolMil. An RAF Wessex is on standby. Now tell me what the devil is going on and why you need me here personally."

"It's a long story. It's best if you take a seat first," McClintock advised as he started to explain.

Twenty minutes later Smithies was left shaking his head in disbelief. Ricky looked like he was about to have a heart attack. Sam imagined he had visions of his pension disappearing down the toilet.

"I can see why you've come directly to me," Smithies said sympathetically. "Of course you know Region and District are going to go up the wall. We can worry about that later."

In front of them lay the pistol and the map.

"Ricky, tell me," the assistant commissioner asked, "what those Chinese characters mean?"

"Yes-sir." Ricky leaned closer to the map. "From north to south they are marked as 'Target One' for the star marking the spot in Sham Shui Po. 'Target Two' marks a spot in Tsim Sha Tsui. 'Pick up point' marks Kowloon Pier."

"And what would you deduce from all this?"

"I concur with the DVC, sir," Ricky said. "The aim of the first raid is to drag EU and PTU out of position. They then hit their main target and escape."

"Escape how?"

"The map indicates a route on foot from the bottom of Nathan Road, along Salisbury Road to Kowloon Pier. Its only about 400 yards. It would take less than five minutes. Even if they are loaded down with bags. That's the last thing we would expect. Usually they disappear into the MTR or use a vehicle."

"And then what?" Smithies asked suspiciously.

Daai fei," McClintock interrupted. "That's the only thing that makes sense. Get out of there in a fast boat."

"There is one more thing, sir", Ricky interjected. "These characters at the top. It's today's date. 9.30 p.m."

"So that's why I'm here," Smithies said with a sigh.

There was a moment of silence. All eyes were on Smithies. He bought himself time by draining his coffee.

"Right then," he finally said through gritted teeth. "We need a plan and we've got less than three hours. Thoughts gentlemen?"

"Two choices in my opinion," said McClintock. "We flood the area with PTU or we catch them in the act. If we frighten them off today, they will hit somewhere else tomorrow."

He paused and looked at each of them in turn. Smithies said nothing as he waited for the rest of McClintock's pitch. Sam could already guess his preferred option.

"We will never have a better opportunity to catch them red handed," McClintock said forcefully. "It's not going to be easy but with SDU we can handle it."

"And the plan?" Smithies asked.

"We let them go ahead then spring the trap. When the raid in Sham Shui Po is reported we withdraw duties from Tsim Sha Tsui and give them a free run. In the meantime, we covertly deploy SDU near Kowloon Pier. As they escape, we roll them up. Before they reach the *daai fei* and well away from the crowds. We can use PTU as backup."

Sam could see Smithies thinking it through. He was the one who would be calling the shots. So far, the assistant commissioner was keeping his cards close to his chest.

"Surprise, speed and SDU are the key," Smithies agreed. "To avoid leaks we must keep this need-to-know only. If we make a decision now we have plenty of time to deploy SDU and get ready." He took out a small pad and started making some notes.

"It's worth a try," Smithies said. "But before I make a final decision let's get into the details."

Sam could see the relief on McClintock's face. The DVC sat down and started sketching a diagram on a blank sheet of A4. He drew four circles in a line and linked each with an arrow.

"My guess is that they will not actually rob somewhere in Sham Shui Po. I think they will stage a show and make it look good, possibly with a couple of shots fired." He wrote 'SSPO' into the first circle.

"Agreed," Smithies said.

"They will expect an immediate response from EU. We get the radio console to deploy EU as normal. Every car. The gang will be hoping for the Operation Moorgate platoon to be re-deployed in response so we send them as well. That leaves only sub-unit."

McClintock looked at Sam and smiled. Sam tried to hold his boss's stare and to appear unperturbed.

"We saw what happened with the poor Auxie so we need to get sub-unit well out of the way. We can do that easily enough by organising a beat conference away from the target area."

Smithies and Ricky both nodded.

"After that we leave it to SDU. They will want OPs overlooking the target area and leave the bulk of their team closer to the pier." Sam saw McClintock write 'OP' in the next circle and 'SDU' in the third.

"What about the *daai fei*?" Smithies asked.

Sam was puzzled yet reluctant to say anything. He was racking his brains. He was sure it was not an expression *Hung Tai-Tai* had included in her Cantonese lessons.

"Sorry, sir. I don't want to sound ignorant. What exactly is a *daai fei*?"

"A fair question," McClintock said, more reasonably than Sam had expected. "Bloody fast boat is the shorthand version. Bloody fast and bloody dangerous. Smugglers' boat. Several big engines on the back. I'll explain later. Suffice it to say we are going to need Marine assistance to deal with it. We take the same approach. We let it enter the harbour unmolested then pounce."

Smithies nodded. It seemed he was starting to like the plan. "Command and control?" he asked.

"We need Region and High Command," McClintock said. "Can I ask you to grease the wheels on that one, sir?"

Smithies smiled and raised his eyebrows suggestively. He seemed to derive some pleasure from having McClintock eat humble pie.

"Leave the rest to me," the assistant commissioner said. "I'll sort out District, Region, and Marine. You will be the field commander on Nathan Road. Let me use your phone. I'll shout if I need anything."

"Ricky, let's head to your office," McClintock instructed. He cheerfully slapped Sam on the back as they stepped into the corridor. Their plan had been accepted.

The DVC's office door closed on Smithies who was shaking his head in exasperation as he reached for the receiver of the grey desk phone.

19

It was 8.00 p.m. Smithies, McClintock and Sam were in the High Command suite within the Regional Command and Control Centre at Kowloon Headquarters. Sam was finding it a most uncomfortable experience, and not just because of the fierce air-conditioning. The windowless room was a hive of activity. Already three SDU officers were setting up their radios and paraphernalia on one of several rows of desks. Blue-coated civilian communications officers fussed about, logging into computers and testing radio systems. Black and white television screens showed views of key traffic junctions.

The senior officers in front of Sam displayed various degrees of agitation. The Regional Commander and his team looked furious. Smithies was playing his hand with a straight face. At times he appeared to be enjoying the discomfort of his colleagues.

Sam sympathised with their anger and frustration. The Regional Commander, Assistant Commissioner Bathgate, loudly complained that his wife's birthday dinner had been ruined when Smithies unexpectedly called and requested him to return to his Argyle Street headquarters. He had already fought his way through the Cross Harbour Tunnel twice that day he reminded them. Only his initiative in calling police transport had allowed him to finish his pork chops and potatoes and still get there in time.

As the most junior officer, Sam felt out of place. He had already questioned McClintock on whether he should come at all. McClintock had insisted Sam accompany him to add authenticity to the tale. With Jenny safely under guard, Sam was the closest thing they had to a witness. Smithies had made arrangements for Jenny to be moved to the PTU base at Fanling temporarily. The pistol was in McClintock's safe, but the map was still in Sam's pocket, just in case. He intended to stay in the background and say as little as possible.

The other officers present decided this was a heavyweight turf battle they were best staying out of. They stood quietly to one side as the two assistant commissioners slugged it out, marking their territories and battling for dominance. McClintock's contribution made it a three-way battle of egos.

"Gentlemen enough," Smithies said, trying to draw a line under matters. "We have a major operation to manage. Recriminations are going to have to wait for another day."

McClintock looked ready to resume battle, like an angry bulldog straining at his chain. The others said nothing. Sam guessed they would prefer to bide their time. Payback might be years in the making.

"Does anyone have any more questions before the DVC and Steadings depart?" Smithies said. "They will both be needed on the ground later."

"Yes I do," Bathgate announced, looking in Sam's direction. "Well done so far Inspector. That's good work from you and the girl. But, and this is the 64,000-dollar question, will they miss that map and take fright?"

It was a fair point and it had been preying on Sam's mind.

Sam said: "All I know from Jenny was that she was very careful to leave the bags as she found them. She told me that there were a number of maps in there. I doubt they will miss one."

"Here it is," he said, pulling it out of his tunic pocket with a flourish then unfolding it. They came closer and scrutinised it minutely. Sam was pleased with his answer. The map seemed to have done the trick.

"Gerry," Bathgate said. "You are absolutely right. Let's put this operation to bed first and we can then sort out any issues later." He stared in McClintock's direction. "Let me tell you now though…" He paused for effect and jabbed a finger at McClintock, "…if you nail those bastards tonight, I'll be buying the beers. You can tell that to SDU and PTU and whoever."

"I'll drink to that, sir," McClintock said.

Five minutes later Sam and McClintock were in their Sherpa van on the way back to Tsim Sha Tsui. McClintock was in the front passenger seat, Sam in the rear. It was a warm night and with no air conditioning they had only the breeze through the open windows and the small hatches in the roof to keep them cool. The metal grilles on the side windows rattled noisily as they hurtled down Waterloo Road. The driver was using blue lights to ease through the traffic.

Sam was running through the plan in his mind, visualising the phases in sequence. He was trying to understand his role in the operation and anticipate where things might go wrong. He considered himself fortunate. This might be a once in a lifetime experience, he realised. He was appreciative of how McClintock had taken him into his confidence and not excluded him from discussions.

Several issues still bothered him. He decided it was time to share his doubts with McClintock, whose greater experience might provide the answers.

McClintock appeared deep in thought. "Excuse me, sir," he asked. "Can I run something past you?"

"Go ahead son, what is it?" McClintock replied amiably.

"There's a couple of things concerning me." He wondered if he was about to make a fool of himself. McClintock turned his head to face Sam.

"If you were Silas, would you risk splitting up the gang between the first and second raids?" he asked.

"What do you mean exactly? I'm not following you?"

"How likely is it that the whole eight-man gang would go to Sham Shui Po to mount a raid and then travel straight to Tsim Sha Tsui?"

"I suppose they could all jump on the MTR or travel in a van or two taxis. But yes, it would be taking an unnecessary risk. I'd say not likely at all."

"In that case, where and how would they meet?"

McClintock was quiet for several moments as he analysed the implications of what Sam was asking.

"Now I'm with you," the DVC said. "If they separate, they will have to arrange a meeting point before the second raid."

"That could be risky for them," Sam suggested.

"Yes, a meeting point could be agreed in advance, but it might not be safe to join up if police are in the vicinity," McClintock said nodding.

"Exactly," Sam said.

The DVC said, "I would agree an alternate meeting point," Sam realised that his boss was starting to understand his concerns. He hadn't wanted to spell it out in case it sounded foolish.

"But can they risk the delay that an alternate meeting point might involve?" Sam suggested.

"No, of course not," the DVC said. "They are on a tight schedule. If they are going to board that *daai fei* it must arrive within minutes of the raid being over. Unless they are using radios, which is unlikely because they could be intercepted. They will have no way of communicating with the *daai fei*. Which means......."

Sam finished the sentence for him "......that the best way is not to separate the gang in the first place. Is that right, sir?"

They were both quiet for a moment, thinking through the consequences of their reasoning. The pieces were still circulating in Sam's mind as he reached the obvious conclusion and hoped McClintock would agree with him.

"So, if they are all together in Tsim Sha Tsui," Sam asked, "who is doing the raid in Sham Shui Po?"

"Our dirty cops more likely than not," the DVC said grimly.

20

Steve Jameson had been about to leave the office when the call came. He was looking forward to a serious night of drinking with Delta Force. Their visitors were waiting in the mess. The Special Duties Unit was the best job in the Force. As officer commanding, he needed to lead the charge. It was a tough job but someone had to do it. He smiled at the thought of the night ahead of them.

The Yanks were obviously professionals. They all looked like American football linebackers: huge men, not one was less than 6'2". All gym bunnies and properly ripped. They talked a good game. He would have expected nothing less. They were nice guys but that didn't mean Jameson was dazzled by them.

They looked nothing like his boys, who were more like runners. Small, lean and wiry, most of the local lads had grown up scrapping around the rough, run-down housing estates of Kowloon. If they hadn't joined the RHKP they would have become triads.

Jameson was rarely impressed by anyone who drank Yankee beer. Bud and Coors were like cat's piss. Hardly beer at all. Nobody could get properly drunk on American lager. A long night of the unit's finest hospitality would sort the men from the boys. Lubrication provided by Carlsberg and San Miguel.

Rounded off with Tequila and some sexy Wanchai pole dancers. Followed up with a couple of hours on the assault course first thing in the morning. With 90% humidity thrown in free of charge. The usual welcome.

It was his mission to make the visit of their Delta visitors memorable. Show them who was boss when it came to Special Forces world ranking. Nothing less would be expected. The last time Jameson had trained with them at Fort Bragg, he'd been shown no mercy. He had no intention of going easy on them on his home turf. They all knew the game.

"Jameson, SDU," he answered the phone as he checked his watch. They'd been expecting him in the mess twenty minutes ago.

He noticed his heart rate had increased a notch. Unexpected phone calls did that to him. He was still waiting for the big one, a major counter terrorist operation for which SDU trained continuously. Anything juicy would do. An aircraft hijacking. A massive armed hostage situation. Terrorists barricading themselves in a consulate with explosives. It had been a lean couple of years. They were overdue some serious action. The team were champing at the bit.

"Steve, It's Smithies here." The hairs on the back of his neck rose. The tone of Smithies's voice told him this might be the one. Jameson locked eyes with the unit 2ic who was standing in the corridor. He signalled for him to wait. His pen was already in hand, ready for the brief.

The assistant commissioner said: "I have a job for you. We have reliable information regarding a major robbery on Nathan Road at 9.30 tonight. A big gang, heavily armed. Automatic weapons, possible grenades. Get the unit to Marine headquarters by 8 p.m. Avoid the press, no convoys. Call me at HICOM Kowloon for a full briefing when you have got the wheels in motion. Any questions?"

"No, sir. Wilco," he responded.

The next three hours turned into a blizzard of activity. The Yanks were disappointed that their night out was postponed but they understood the rules of the game. When a call came through you dropped everything.

Shortly before 8 p.m. Jameson was in the Marine HQ car park leaning against the bonnet of the unmarked Land Cruiser. It was dark. The neon lights of Harbour City and Ocean Terminal illuminated the vehicles around him with an eery red glow. He could see the pier and Star Ferry, just a hop and a skip from the bottom of the hill. Ship horns sounded, somewhere distant in the harbour.

It must have been an obvious place to construct a police station, he decided. It would have had commanding views when it was first built. Now the urban clutter of ugly concrete surrounded it.

The location was perfect. As a jump off point it was ideal for blocking the route to the pier. The white paint and nineteenth century columns and arches were classically colonial. They could have been standing in India or Sri Lanka. The history of Empire had always fascinated him. He loved the feel of places like this, it was one of the best parts of the job. Nearly as good as leading the famous 'Flying Tigers' as the locals liked to call the unit.

He heard radio chatter as the observation posts checked in one by one. He glanced at his watch. It had been tight but everything was in place. They had been lucky. The team had still been at base after a late afternoon game of soccer on the drill square. The annual grudge match against the training staff was coming up. They were taking no chances. Pride was at stake.

The turnout had been flawless, one of their quickest yet. The team was looking sharp. Most of them were gathered nearby. A few were restless, the younger ones. All they could do now was wait. They were chatting and joking, killing time. Some checked kit. Others stood smoking. They looked relaxed. He guessed they were expecting it to be another over-hyped flop. Hurry up and wait, as the old saying went. They were due some luck. Recent operations had been duds. Poor intelligence rankled. He knew frustration was mounting.

"OPs one to eight in position." The voice came from the back of the large Mercedes van where the headquarters team had set up camp. An impromptu command post crammed with people, whiteboards and radios.

He looked at the familiar faces and felt a sense of pride. His boys. His team. When push came to shove, he knew he could trust every one of them to perform. His briefing had been short. They all knew the ground well. They knew what was needed. No recce required.

Eight OPs was more than usual. Eyes in the right places and effective communication would be critical. The info seemed too good to be true. Bring it on, he thought. When it kicks off, we will be ready.

He sub-consciously felt for the safety on the MP5 sub-machine gun strapped to his chest, then checked the rest of his kit. After ten years in the unit he did it automatically, like all the old hands.

"Inform HICOM we are in position. Ten minutes until show time. Fingers crossed. We are overdue some luck, eh boys?"

21

"ACP OPS," McClintock barked into the telephone. "Urgent." After a short delay Smithies picked up. McClintock put him on speaker. "Gerry, it's Brian. We've had some more thoughts."

Sam noticed McClintock had already stopped calling him 'sir'. Sam liked McClintock's use of 'we'. The DVC outlined their thinking on how the two raids might have been planned.

"Right," said Smithies, "I'll pass that on. By the way, we've decided to bring in New Territories. They will provide support on the crime side. I've already spoken with Big Ronny. We need to prepare for when it kicks off. Better safe than sorry, eh?"

"Good idea," McClintock said, nodding. "One more thing. If this does involve police officers, we think it unlikely they would use their own service weapons."

"Why?"

"Detective Specials are just too recognisable. They are in every cop movie. They would stand out like a dog's dick."

The distinctive snub nosed .38 calibre Detective Special revolvers were carried by all plain clothes officers in the Force.

"Good point," Smithies conceded. "What are you thinking. An imitation firearm? Maybe a pistol?"

"Or a grenade."

The line went silent.

A grenade would make a lot of sense, Sam realised. Far less chance of leaving a forensic trail if it detonated. It would be enough to pull in cops from miles around. Jenny had seen grenades in the bags. It was a distinct possibility. The perfect distraction. It would take hours to sort out the scene. Especially if there were casualties.

"In that case I'll turn out EOD to stand by at Kowloon Headquarters." Smithies hung up.

"This is all coming together nicely," said McClintock.

The telephone rang before Sam could respond.

"McClintock, DVC Tsim Sha Tsui."

"Baldwin here." Sam heard a deep patrician voice on the other end of the speaker. It was the Commissioner of Police himself.

"Good evening, sir."

"I've been thoroughly briefed by the ACP OPS. I'll be frank, I have some reservations, it's not exactly textbook, is it? However, I've given it my approval. I'll be monitoring the situation from PHQ."

Sam could see McClintock standing straighter. He was no longer looking at Sam. A serious look was etched on his face.

Baldwin went on: "Turning to other matters. This is a sensitive case. I've spoken with ICAC. We've agreed they will deploy their resources against the three police officers identified from midnight tonight. In the meantime, New Territories will take the lead."

"Understood, sir," McClintock said.

"I would like you to pass on my regards to your young lady for her actions yesterday," Baldwin said. "I cannot guarantee anything of course, though I am sympathetic to her situation. We will do our best for her. We can't tolerate corruption, but it sounds as if she had her head turned by our friend Silas Chu. Let's wait and see. A successful result in your operation would help the argument."

"Thank you, sir. That's appreciated."

"Good luck," Baldwin said.

McClintock waited until the CP was off the line before he cut the connection on his own phone. He raised his eyebrows at Sam.

"He's a canny fellow. He'll stay clear of this in case it goes wrong. If it goes right he'll be elbowing Bathgate out of the way in front of the cameras."

At 8.45 p.m. they were all assembled in McClintock's office. Sam was next to Ricky Ricardo. Liu, Cheung and A-Bo were standing by the door. Everyone was armed. Even McClintock had drawn a revolver. Rumour had it he was a terrible shot.

The DVC had just finished speaking. The briefing was short and to the point. McClintock had described what they were expecting to occur in the division that evening based on 'firm intelligence'. Jenny, Sham Shui Po and police involvement were not mentioned. He was taking no chances with leaks.

"Are you all clear on your responsibilities?" he asked.

They all answered in the affirmative. Sam was relieved that Cheung kept his mouth shut.

"Let's go over it one more time," the DVC said. "Ricky, Mr. Cheung, you will stand by in the station in the MP car. I'm relying on you both to manage any scene on Nathan Road. It's going to be fucking chaos down there, especially if there are casualties. You know the drill. Close the road, cordon the scene, and set up a command post. Deploy EU and PTU as necessary. Ambulances are standing by which will be released by HICOM as required. Let's hope they're not needed.

"Sam, Mr. Liu," he went on. "You will organise a beat conference on Ashley Road junction Peking Road at 9.15 p.m. I want no one anywhere near the operational area from that point on. The column of PTU officers on Operation Moorgate will be re-deployed before that. Once everything kicks off, I want you to lead your team towards Salisbury Road. Your job is to relieve SDU. You will take over any crime scenes pending the arrival of the PTU Reserve Platoon standing by in Yau Ma Tei."

"Lastly, and just to be on the safe side, the divisional radio console will be relaying an instruction to all beat duties to retire from the operational area at 9.20 p.m. I'll be Field Commander, accompanied by A-Bo, and float between the two scenes as required," he concluded firmly. "Capiche?"

"Yes sir," they replied as one, some more confidently than others.

"Good luck. Let's get to it." Sam hoped that McClintock was feeling as chipper as he came across. If the operation went horribly wrong, all of them would suffer, not just the dead and the injured.

By 9.00 p.m. Sam and Liu were walking slowly down the pavement on the western side of Nathan Road, next to the Kowloon Mosque. The dark of the night sky was obscured by a million lights from the shops, bars, restaurants, and billboards. The scene reminded Sam of a holiday resort or a fun fair.

McClintock had reminded them that success hinged on police activity appearing completely normal. This gave them justification to be walking towards the operational area. Provided that the suspects stuck to their timings, they had thirty minutes to complete their charade before the show commenced.

Sam and Liu were talking quietly, running through the finer details of what might happen, trying to look as if they didn't have a care in the world. He was listening for messages on his beat radio. It was quiet. The rest of the sub-unit were unaware of the impending storm about to break over them. Further down the road he could see a team of four PTU officers, alternating between stopping potential suspects and chatting up pretty shop assistants.

The PTU lads were distinctive in their boots and dark blue berets. Every young constable could expect to be rotated into PTU for a nine-month period after he'd learnt the ropes in a sub-unit. They were like the Force's fire brigade. Over a thousand officers who could be deployed anywhere in the territory at short notice to deal with riots, crowd control or special operations. It was an exciting posting. Sam was looking forward to his turn. He knew there was a queue of officers ahead of him in the district.

Sam glanced at his station sergeant. Liu looked cool, almost indifferent. Sam was finding it hard to concentrate on their conversation. In his mind he was picturing SDU setting up observation posts in windows and on rooftops around them. It was a strange feeling. He didn't know where they were but he felt they were being watched. Scrutinised. Measured.

The Special Duties Unit was on a whole different level from PTU. They were the Force's elite paramilitary tactical unit, trained by the SAS for counter terrorist operations. Selection for SDU involved passing 'Hell Week' which called for the highest level of physical and mental stamina. Passing selection was a major achievement. They were the hardest men in the police force. Occasionally applicants died in the process. No woman had ever applied.

Sam's mouth was dry and his hands were sweaty. He felt his left hand unconsciously checking the cover of his holster. He realised he kept doing it, he couldn't stop himself. If Liu noticed, he said nothing. Sam felt like a gunfighter entering a strange and hostile town for the first time. His eyes darted around the busy street, his senses overwhelmed by the hundreds of people and vehicles in his eyeline. He glanced at his watch again. The hands seemed to have barely moved since the last time.

"Relax," said Liu, "you'll be fine. Try to think about something else. Enjoy the atmosphere. Look at the girls. Just stop looking at your watch will you?"

Sam looked over at Liu and laughed nervously. Then checked his watch again.

At exactly 9.10 p.m., two men walked calmly out of a ground floor seafood restaurant on Ap Liu Street, Sham Shui Po. They turned left along the street for fifty yards. Turning left again they cut through an alleyway towards Cheung Sha Wan Road before turning left one final time. They paused in a dark and cluttered back alleyway running perpendicular to the main road. They looked unremarkable, dressed in dark clothing and light jackets. They carried small, cheap men's leather handbags. After casually glancing around to check that they were alone, they drew black balaclavas and leather gloves from their bags, covered their faces, and donned their gloves.

Their target was an illegal gambling den run by the Wo Shing Wo triad society, an organisation with whom Silas had never been able to reach a lucrative accommodation. That triad had always considered itself too powerful to pay protection money to corrupt cops. Silas had crossed swords with them on several occasions. It was time for payback.

The entrance was well disguised, concealed in a filthy courtyard behind a ramshackle four-story building dating back to the 1920s. The larger of the two men knocked on the door using a coded sequence of knocks. Seconds later the door creaked open several inches to reveal a tough looking male in his 20s. The bulging arms and black vest displayed vivid dragon tattoos adorning his arms and neck to best effect.

The doorman remained calm despite the pistol pointing at his forehead. As an experienced triad enforcer, he had been in many difficult situations before. He stared at the barrel six inches from his face and awaited an instruction.

No words were exchanged. A single shot rang out. The steel-tipped bullet punched into his skull before exiting in a spray of blood, bone, and brain matter.

The two figures pushed open the door, stepped over the body and advanced along the short corridor. The din of raised voices grew closer and louder. The sound of the gunshot had been unmistakeable. All eyes were on the doorway as a fragmentation grenade tumbled towards them. Panic and screaming ensued as the fifteen gamblers desperately tried to distance themselves from the metal orb sliding menacingly along the floor.

The violent blast ripped apart bodies, clothing and furniture as sharp shards of shrapnel travelled through the room at supersonic speeds. The two suspects withdrew and discarded the pistol next to the first body at the scene. They removed their gloves and balaclavas, replaced them in their hand bags, and walked briskly back down the alleyway.

They calmly re-traced their steps. They stopped only to toss their bags onto the flat roof of a neighbouring outhouse, before returning to the restaurant. Once inside they quietly resumed their seats. They had been away for a total of less than six minutes.

They nodded to their host. He was overweight and sweating heavily. He stood out due to large dark glasses and a blue baseball cap. He wore his white polo shirt collar up, like a teenager on a first date. He had bruised fingers and extensive cuts and bruises across his face.

He had remained seated quietly throughout, appearing to be engrossed in his newspaper. He reached into the jacket which hung on the back of his chair. A smile appeared on his lips as he surreptitiously passed each of them a small brown envelope containing crisp golden $1,000 notes. He stood up, pulled on his jacket and walked into the night. It had started.

McClintock was pacing the floor in his office, sipping tepid coffee. He knew the waiting was always the worst part and there was tension in the room. A-Bo was watching him out of the corner of his eye. McClintock felt like a caged tiger in a zoo. He wanted to rip someone's heart out but he had to maintain an outward appearance of calm.

They were both startled by the sound of the telephone. McClintock grabbed for the handset. He answered it before it had a chance to complete its first ring.

"McClintock, DVC," he said loudly.

The voice at the end of the line was the one he was expecting.

"Brian," Smithies said calmly, "Operation Condor is live. We have multiple injuries from a grenade attack at a triad establishment in Sham Shui Po. Proceed as planned."

The line went dead as McClintock looked at the Duty Sergeant.

"A-Bo we're on. Pass the messages," he commanded.

A-Bo nodded and turned his head so that he could speak easily into the beat radio clipped to his black leather cross strap.

"ADVC OPS, Sergeant 2715 over," he said evenly into the microphone.

"Send," came the immediate response.

"Condor, Condor, Condor," replied A-Bo.

"Roger," Ricky Ricardo replied.

"Sub-Unit Four Commander, Sergeant 2715 over."

"Roger, Condor," replied Sam.

"Let's go," McClintock said. He was filled with a huge sense of relief. If nothing had happened in Sham Shui Po he would have been the one left with egg all over his face. They knew now that the raid was still going ahead. He placed his cap on his head and adjusted it carefully. It was time for action. Days like this could make or break a man's career.

"Are you as good with a revolver as I am?" he asked A-Bo.

The Duty Sergeant gave him a polite shrug.

22

Senior Superintendent Miles Foxton was enjoying himself. He hadn't been out on the motorbike for weeks. It felt good to be back in the saddle. On the bike to his right he saw Station Sergeant Fung from his headquarters team. They were old traffic buddies. He was the obvious choice for a leisurely patrol around Kowloon. Foxton felt duty bound to fly the flag and occasionally leave his comfortable air-conditioned office. Patrols like this hardly felt like work, he thought smugly. Putting the fear of God into errant taxi drivers was fun. He took perverse satisfaction from their hatred for traffic cops. The books of traffic tickets in his tunic pocket were his weapon.

It was 9.32 p.m. and they were riding along Salisbury Road. The heavy 650cc Honda motorbike under him felt powerful, almost beastlike at times. Controlling the power could be challenging for novices, but not him. Approaching the red traffic light, they worked down through the gears, engines roaring in complaint as they gradually slowed. The junction with Nathan Road lay ahead.

The weather was warm, but not uncomfortable. The evening sky was clear and moonlit. The road was dry and the traffic seemed reasonable for the time of night. The radio was quiet. Foxton smiled to himself. Life was good.

As a long-time Traffic man, it was a point of personal pride that he still rode. He never let his subordinates forget it. He even took the bike home most nights. He liked to think of himself as a real cop. He had maintained firearms proficiency when others of similar rank had already quietly surrendered their holsters. The thought of patrolling naked, as he saw it, filled him with dread. His routine was one evening patrol every month, usually involving a damned good curry with the boys in the canteen. Sometimes they even managed a cheeky beer afterwards.

Retirement was looming and Foxton was becoming maudlin about the whole concept. He was thinking how he would miss all this when he got back to Sussex. He would have to get used to spending seven days a week at home with his wife and her parents. Gardening and the company of geriatrics did not appeal.

The spotter in OP2 was ecstatic. The intelligence was correct. For once. About time too, the spotter thought. There were just the two of them manning OP2. There were three other pairs in observation posts overlooking the same stretch of Nathan Road, two on each side. Between them, they could see anything that moved on that stretch of road. According to the briefing they had received an hour earlier, between them they had it stitched up tighter than a nun's knickers. It was 9.29 p.m. The gang was early. They were just eighty yards away and the spotter's view from their eyrie was perfect.

"HICOM, OP2 over."

"Send," replied the familiar voice.

"HICOM, robbery in progress, TP3 and TP4. We have eyes on eight suspects, so far."

"Roger so far."

"Two lookouts with long-barrelled weapons, so far."

"Roger so far."

"Two teams of three suspects robbing TP3 and TP4, so far."

"Roger, so far."

"Description. Eight males wearing dark clothing and face coverings. Two with suspected AK-47s, the others carrying pistols. Over."

"Roger out."

Through his earpiece the spotter heard the command post and the other three OPs nearby confirm the message. His eyes were locked on the scene below him on Nathan Road. He dare not blink for fear of missing a detail, a movement, a threat. These men were their targets now. The OPs were playing lead, conducting the orchestra for the first half of the performance. He heard his partner's shallow breathing beside him. He knew the rifle sight would be zeroed in on one of the two lookouts.

"Confirm two AK-47s," the sniper reported calmly.

No response was required. He nodded. It struck him that the scene looked strangely normal. Pedestrians ambled along the pavement seemingly unaware of the drama around them. The lookouts' AKs were concealed under long jackets. Only the most observant passer-by would have noticed them. Even if they did, they might simply ignore them. Nobody wanted to cause trouble. Best to look away. The doors to the two stores had been closed and locked. The alarm was yet to be raised.

His spirits soared. The plan was coming together beautifully, he realised. Ten minutes and the targets should be on their way. Then the real fun could begin. It would be a shame to miss the finale close to the pier but he knew theirs was an important job. They just needed to be patient.

He was startled by a sudden message.

"HICOM, OP3 over." The voice was strident, the alarm palpable.

"OP3, send."

What had the spotter missed? A momentary sense of panic set in. He had seen nothing.

"HICOM, we have a problem. A security guard has seen the robbery in TP3."

He shifted his gaze. To the right, further along the pavement, he saw a flash of blue behind a small white van unloading boxes on the road side. He relaxed as he realised OP3 had a clearer view. He had missed nothing. This was the reason they had set up four OPs, he reminded himself.

The security guard shifted position. The spotter could see him more clearly now. He was huge, a white turban atop broad shoulders. The blue safari suit and gold braid on the shoulders was unmistakeably a uniform. He looked like he was waiting for the gang to re-emerge, like a poacher hunting a family of rabbits. His gaze was fixed on the glass doors twenty yards to his left. He was peering through the van windscreen, through the raised open door at the rear. It provided cover whilst the guard stalked his prey. A shotgun appeared tiny in his massive hands. The spotter adjusted the scope and checked the gang's lookouts. Both were calm. They hadn't seen the guard.

It was 9.32. The gang had been inside for three minutes already. They would need to be quick if they were going to raid six targets before the cavalry arrived.

It was over in a flash. The shop door opened without warning. One of the suspects emerged carrying a black leather bag slung over one shoulder. It looked heavy. They were leaving with a good haul.

The guard made his move. He cocked his Remington shotgun and confidently moved out from behind the van. That was brave, the spotter thought. He worried it would not end well. There was not a cop in sight and he knew none were coming.

It took just seconds. The spotter saw the nearer of the two lookouts respond instantly. The guard was still oblivious. He never saw his killer raise the AK-47 to his shoulder and fire almost in the same movement. A single shot was enough. The Sikh security guard was hurled backwards by the force of the impact. He sprawled on his back, still clutching the shotgun tightly. A growing pool of blood surrounded his head.

Eight stories above they had heard the shot. Pedestrians scattered and started screaming in terror.

"HICOM, OP2, shots fired, shots fired," he reported urgently. The shit had well and truly hit the fan.

Traffic was light and Foxton could see further ahead than usual. He was relieved that for once the road was not completely clogged with taxis, buses, and mini buses. They were stationary at the traffic lights waiting to make a right turn onto Nathan Road. A battered red Toyota taxi sat in front of them, spewing unpleasant diesel fumes in their direction. The driver had jammed on his brakes zealously when the lights changed colour to amber. He wasn't taking any chances with two traffic cops behind him. Foxton felt conspicuous. Their large white motorbikes were festooned with lights and police markings. Bright white bibs and sleeves lay over their uniform tunics. High visibility was part and parcel of the traffic game. He felt God-like.

Something caught his attention, it sounded like a large bang. It was muffled by the sound of his idling engine and the helmet covering his ears. He raised himself up in his seat to see if he could identify the source. Fung seemed to have heard it too. He scanned the road ahead but could see nothing. Fung looked over and shrugged his shoulders. It must have been a vehicle backfire, he thought.

The lights changed to amber then green. He resumed his focus on the vehicles in front and released his clutch. Engines purring, they slowly turned into Nathan Road. They changed lanes and overtook the nervous taxi driver in the nearside of the two northbound lanes.

As they cruised up Nathan Road, Foxton became aware of movement. People were running, the pavement to his right was almost deserted. Unsure of what he was seeing, he slowed his bike to near walking pace. They gradually came closer. They were separated by the central divider, chest height metal railings atop a concrete base. A body lay on the pavement. The blood was visible even from a distance.

Amidst the chaos he saw a lone figure not running, leaning against a lamp post. He was staring in their direction and carrying something black. He pointed it at them. The source of the earlier 'bang' suddenly became viciously clear.

Foxton glanced around and realised the road in front was blocked by two overtaking buses. Weaving was his best chance for survival. He yanked the handle bars to the right as he shouted a warning. The sudden move had not been anticipated by Fung. The two front tyres touched. They came tumbling to the ground in a cloud of dust, sparks and metallic squeals.

Fung looked appalled. He was muttering oaths and curses whilst trying to retrieve his bike. Foxton slapped him on the back and pointed at the gunman. They both started running.

"Console, shots fired, shots fired," shouted Foxton into his radio as he dodged behind the taxi from earlier. "Armed robbery in progress."

The taxi driver stared at them and looked amused. Two traffic cops who'd fallen off their bikes would make a great story. A bullet crashing through the front windscreen sent him ducking for cover.

Foxton and Fung moved, finding better refuge behind the concrete walls of the Kowloon Hotel. They drew their revolvers and cursed their bad luck.

23

The moths were annoying him. He wished he had a net or bug spray to deal with them. Anything to stop them flying around in front of his face. He knew it was the lights on the billboard below the roof that were attracting them. There was nothing they could do. It was hopeless. There were thousands of them. Nobody had mentioned moths when he signed up for SDU selection.

It was the spotter's first operation. His nerves were starting to fray. Exercises could never replicate the real thing. He knew he was a great shot. He had excelled in training and his instructors had told him he would be a good sniper. He would have to prove them right in a live operation, but not yet. Tonight he was the sorcerer's apprentice. The monkey, not the organ grinder. The spotter, not the shooter. He was a patient man. He was prepared to wait his turn.

He glanced over at his partner to his right. The sniper had said nothing for minutes. He knew he was taciturn at the best of times. He was famously dour, a man of few words, and less warmth. He wished the sniper would say something, acknowledge his presence even. He was feeling ready to burst with excitement. It would be good to give it an outlet. He knew it wasn't the time. The sniper would not approve.

He saw the sniper blink as a moth brushed his eye. He was relieved it was not just himself getting irritated by the wildlife. Or the situation. He chided himself for letting his mind wander. He focused back on the street below.

They could see everything but do nothing. He had never felt frustration like it. His heart was pounding and he felt like screaming. He felt helpless. Useless. He decided to keep quiet. He could hear OP1 providing a running commentary for the command post. It gave him time to think.

"I've got a clear shot on all five," his partner advised.

He did not respond. He ground his teeth and took a deep breath. He could see them himself. Perfect targets, barely moving. Lined up like tenpins at a bowling alley, in the open and without any cover. The bright shop lights were the robbers' enemy. There was barely any shadow. No civilian stood within twenty yards. He felt like they were stuck in purgatory on the road to sniper heaven. So near and yet so far.

"Hold your fire," he said. He knew the statement was unnecessary, but it felt good to say something. It would be better if they got the order to fire.

The sniper grunted an acknowledgement.

In this unit time served was everything. Experience was counted in decades not years. He glanced over at the powerful Lee Enfield Enforcer rifle in the sniper's hands. The index finger was still straight. It was not time yet to caress the trigger or to take up the pressure on it. Discipline held.

The sound of automatic gun fire drew the spotter's eye back to the scope. He felt another twinge of panic. He tasted bile in his throat.

"What are they doing?" the sniper demanded in a low voice. The shots were being fired towards somewhere beneath them. At this height they couldn't see.

OP1 filled the void.

"HICOM, OP1. The gang have opened fire on two Traffic officers. Over."

He wondered how that could be possible. The area was supposed to be clear of uniforms. They had seen them all leaving. Surely Traffic must have known about the operation? All it took was one person who didn't follow orders. Either that or there must have been a breakdown in communication.

He scanned his field of vision through the scope. Thoughts of sniper heaven – that perfect killshot that came out of nowhere and took out the enemy – evaporated. They had lost their chance. All but one of the targets had now found cover. All he could see was the first lookout whose AK-47 regularly snapped off rounds over the road at a point somewhere beneath them.

The spotter heard the sound of shots fired in return. Quieter, more feeble. Probably a police revolver, he realised. A uniformed officer only carried six rounds. Whoever it was would have to conserve their ammunition.

"The original plan is fucked," the sniper said. It was the most he had said since they set up. "This lunatic is going to kill a lot of people. I need to take the shot. Get approval."

The spotter hesitated. This was a big call, even for the most experienced sniper team in the unit. He was reluctant. The ramifications could be huge.

"Do it or I will take the shot," the sniper warned. He was known as the coolest man in the unit. Now he was angry. The spotter could tell from the changed inflection in his partner's calm voice. This situation was irritating both of them.

"HICOM, OP2, urgent. Requesting permission to engage suspect one. Civilian lives at risk." He wondered if they would realise the urgency of his request. He knew everyone in the unit would have heard him. He felt the tension in his stomach.

"OP2, wait one."

The silence of the radio felt almost painful. Below, another revolver spoke, the sound echoing around them. The tall buildings acted like canyons, magnifying any sound. Traffic had stalled and the quiet was eerie and unnerving.

Their target fired a burst of shots over the road. This time on full automatic. Spraying rather than aiming. Like they did in the movies, he thought. Sooner or later he'd run out of ammunition. On full automatic the AK-47 delivered 600 rounds a minute. The banana-shaped magazine only held thirty rounds. How many magazines did the target have hidden under his jacket?

"What the fuck are they waiting for?" the sniper demanded. It felt like time was standing still. It was not an easy decision. It was one for the big chief. Probably the Regional Commander or even higher. He didn't envy him.

"OP2, HICOM."

He barely dared breathe. He could hear blood pounding in his ears. His palms were sweaty. For the first time he was glad he was spotting and not shooting.

"OP2, permission granted. Take out threats to life."

"HICOM, roger," he replied.

The sudden sound of the shot next to him caused him to jump. He had expected a delay. A conversation. Even a warning.

His training kicked in. He re-focused on the scene below. The target had been plucked off his feet, knocked backwards for several yards. The powerful 7.62 mm round had caught him plum in the chest. It had been the easiest of shots. The target never stood a chance.

The sniper had already worked the bolt action and there was a new round in the breech. They were ready for another target to appear.

Nobody moved. The hunters suddenly realised they were being hunted. There was an invisible killer. Then the spotter saw heads appear behind vehicles, looking this way and that, searching for the enemy. Night-time only added to the confusion.

"HICOM, suspect one down," he reported. He tried to keep his voice level, professional, matter of fact. He failed. He couldn't help but sound triumphal. He had no doubt that would be mentioned in the debrief.

"Nice one," the sniper said. There was sarcasm in his voice. Master was unimpressed with his new apprentice.

Movement caught the spotter's eye. One of the heads seemed to be readying for a move. The head was scanning left and right, then up and down. Evaluating threats. Assessing the odds. Building up courage.

"Watch the one behind the mini bus," the spotter suggested.

"On him."

He saw the head looking along the payment. Realisation dawned. The target wanted to retrieve the dead man's AK-47. They wanted to fight their way out. It had to be.

"He's going for the AK," he said to his partner.

Go for it. Make our day.

He heard a shout in Mandarin. Two of the targets moved at the same time. One ran across the road and found a gap in the barrier. He squeezed through and disappeared out of sight. The other ran in the opposite direction towards the AK-47, lying on the road. He kept low until he reached the gun. He snatched it up and was starting to turn. The bullet from the sniper's Lee Enfield struck him down before he could. Centre mass again. The man didn't move. One round, one kill. Just as they had always been taught.

"HICOM, OP2. Suspect two down," the spotter reported. He managed to keep all emotion out of his words. This time he felt nothing for the two men lying dead.

"Better," came the verdict from his partner as he worked the bolt action to be ready for the next shot. Praise indeed.

The spotter wiped his hands on his trousers. "Two down, six to go." There was no hiding the satisfaction in the voice. He allowed himself a brief smile and resumed his vigil.

Another head appeared in the doorway of a different goldsmiths. It was close by, next door but one. There were anxious shouts in Mandarin. Then three of the gang emerged and ran across the road, passing out of their sight. OP3 took over the commentary. They had better sightlines now.

"HICOM, OP3, the gang is heading north not south, over."

The spotter swore under his breath. His elation turned to disappointment. The gang were heading in the wrong direction, away from the ambush.

A minute passed. The silence was excruciating.

"HICOM, OP3, six suspects left Nathan Road turning onto Peking Road. We have lost them, over."

The spotter realised he was bathed in sweat. It was acrid. It felt sharp in his eyes. Now he allowed himself to relax. Their race was run. It was time for others to pick up the baton. He glanced to his right, at his partner. The safety on the rifle was back on. The sniper returned the look. He was shaking his head in dismay. The quiet rage was back.

"What a fucking mess," he declared. "HICOM has got two minutes to catch them otherwise they are gone."

24

Sam was nervous. They had arrived at their meeting point ten minutes earlier. The other six were already there, waiting and wondering what was going on.

The position had been selected carefully. As the crow flies, they were just 200 yards from the targets on Nathan Road, separated by tall buildings. Close enough to respond quickly. Far enough to be out of the way.

Ashley Road was busy. Groups of tourists and shoppers milled around bars and restaurants. Traffic crawled along the narrow crowded street, navigating past double parked vehicles. Piles of boxes unloaded from small vans cluttered the pavement carelessly, creating a neon-lit obstacle course. It felt claustrophobic.

They were standing close to the junction with Peking Road, poised to move when the word came. The group attracted curious glances from passing pedestrians and motorists.

Liu was briefing them on their role in the operation. Sam could see the surprise on their faces. Two of the PCs fresh out of Training School were looking jittery. The others were grinning. Playing supporting act to SDU sounded exciting.

Sam glanced at his watch. Five minutes to go. He decided to say something. He felt it was expected. Time to channel his inner Churchill.

"Listen up. As you've heard, SDU are leading the operation. We are in support." He waited whilst Liu translated. He knew simple English delivered in bitesize pieces was essential to get his message across.

"We move as a team. We are Bravo team. ADVC OPS leads Alpha team." He waited. He heard Liu adding detail. He knew he would.

"If we need to separate, stay in pairs." Liu directed the pairings. He mixed youth and experience. He left the Auxies together.

"Questions? No?" He concluded with a smile and an exuberant thumbs up. "Good luck then." He looked from face to face. Sam thought he could detect steel in their responses, a willingness to get the job done. Possibly a thirst for revenge.

He found the tension unbearable. His first instinct was to head towards the action. On any other day, they would have been making their way cautiously to the scene. Revolvers drawn, advancing to contact. Passing reports to console. Knowing that heavily armed EU officers would arrive within minutes.

Standing around seemed counterintuitive. Almost obscene. Restraining himself was hard. He tried to busy himself by examining cars parked nearby. Then shop windows. Even neon advertising signs. Anything that took his mind away from the waiting. From the lack of action.

"Did you hear that?" Liu asked

Sam had heard nothing. He shook his head.

"A shot. Distant. Nathan Road direction. Anyone else hear it?"

Sam saw blank faces. He was straining to hear anything over the music from the bar entrance opposite. He glanced at his watch. It read 9.32. His heart was beating faster.

"Again," Liu said. This time he heard it. The others heard it too.

"Draw revolvers," instructed Sam. He was not taking any chances.

"All round defence, find cover," ordered Liu. He stepped into a dark alleyway and motioned the others to follow.

Sam realised the radio was still silent. Not a single message had been broadcast since the earlier warning from console to clear the area. He had known it was coming. It had still made his heart beat faster.

He heard more bangs. This time a rapid succession of shots. Pedestrians had heard them too. Some of them paused and looked concerned.

"AK-47," Liu said quietly. Sam realised the information from Jenny had been correct. He guessed Liu was thinking the same. His thoughts turned to the escape phase of the plan. He felt disappointed to be left only with the aftermath. SDU would be having all the fun.

The radio sparked into life. It was a message to all regional duties. The operation was moving to the next stage.

"Armed robbery in progress. Repeat armed robbery in progress. Tsim Sha Tsui, Nathan Road, junction Middle Road. Operation underway. RC's instruction. All beat duties avoid the area until further notice. Out."

Sam felt butterflies in his stomach again. These messages were not helping to calm his nerves. His arms and legs felt weak. Like when he was a kid with Dad, anxiously waiting for kick-off as they stood on the side of the pitch.

"Okay, *daai-lo*?" Liu asked. He was staring at him with a mild look of concern.

Sam realised his nervousness must be showing. Liu appeared serious but relaxed. Like an experienced boxer about to enter the ring. Confident with his own game plan after years of training. Unconcerned about the opponent.

They heard more shots. This time fully automatic. Liu gave a low whistle. Sam saw the streets rapidly emptying. Groups scurried into shop doorways. People ducked down behind cars, talking anxiously. Wondering where the shooting was coming from. Gesticulating. Speculating. He realised they were giving the cops a wide berth now. Just in case.

Another loud bang caused Liu to smile. Sam didn't know why. He frowned.

"SDU sniper," Liu explained. The others were staring at their station sergeant with interest.

They heard it again. This time there was no doubt. It was a different sound. Deeper. Louder. More trenchant.

"That wasn't part of the plan," Liu reminded him.

"So?"

"That means there's a problem."

Across the street a group of noisy young diners emerged from a restaurant. One saw Sam's team and nudged the others. They glanced at the partially deserted street and retreated to safety.

"Tsim Sha Tsui Bravo Team, HICOM, over." Sam was surprised. He had been expecting to hear from McClintock, not headquarters.

Liu was the first to react and acknowledge.

HICOM instructed: "Team Bravo, urgent, stand by Ashley Road junction Peking Road. So far."

"So far." Liu was staring at Sam. For the first time the station sergeant's mask of calm had slipped. He was looking concerned. They were just yards away from where they needed to be. He wondered why the location mattered.

"Shots fired. Suspects heading your direction on Peking Road. So far."

"So far," Liu replied.

"RC KW orders to block their escape. Arrival imminent, repeat imminent. Over."

25

Sam and Liu looked at each other. He didn't need to say it. They all knew what the message meant. A heavily armed gang would be passing by in front of them within seconds. They were twenty yards away from the junction. Liu took over.

"Move," Liu ordered. "Quickly." Liu started walking rapidly towards the junction. He beckoned the others to follow and ordered two pairs across to the other side of the road. The pair of Auxies stayed with Sam and Liu.

The two groups moved slowly forward in unison. They hugged the walls, revolvers pointing forwards. Fearful civilians ducked out of their way.

Sam was feeling positive. They had the combined firepower of eight revolvers and the element of surprise. With luck, they could deter the gang from crossing the junction. If they were in time.

"Remember lads, aimed shots. Wait for my lead," Liu reminded them.

They continued to creep along the edge of the pavements.

When it happened, the collision was instantaneous. They saw the gang cross into the junction no more than ten yards away. The gang was walking briskly, marching brazenly down the centre of the road. Pedestrians gawped at the weapons, unsure if it was a movie or real life.

The gang looked only forwards and behind. They paid no attention to the cluttered street to their left. There was a dozen yards between the front and rear of the gang. They carried identical black leather holdalls over their shoulders. Traffic had stopped.

Liu chose that moment to engage.

"Police, stop or we shoot," he shouted loudly in Cantonese, then repeated the words in Mandarin.

Sam nervously jabbed the emergency button of the radio at his hip. He'd been holding his revolver with both hands. They felt slippery, unsafe. He needed to dry his hands. There was no time. He braced for action. He moved out from behind Liu to give himself a clear shot. He spotted a target. The distance was about fifteen yards.

The gang now noticed them, reacting to Liu's formal warning. The leader swivelled to bring his AK-47 to bear. He had the weapon at his hip. Sam feared the worst.

No instruction was necessary. A fusillade of .38 calibre rounds erupted. It was as devastating as a naval broadside. All the hours on the range were finally being put to the test.

The leader was caught in the head and chest before he could pull the trigger. Another fell to the floor. Perhaps they hadn't reckoned on the speed and aggression of the police response.

Sam blocked out the noise and concentrated. He fired a fraction of a second later than the others. His target had decided to stand and fight. Sam's round hit him just after he fired two shots from a shiny black pistol. He fell. Sam heard a scream to his right. He saw an Auxie lying on the pavement, bleeding heavily from a wound to the thigh.

"Help him," he shouted to the officer's partner. He turned his eyes back to the carnage in front. Three robbers were unhurt. It was every man for himself. He saw two run forwards through the junction, dumping their bags as they went. Another turned back. Shocked pedestrians were starting to come out of hiding and picking themselves up off the pavement.

"Shots fired, shots fired," Liu was yelling into the radio. He was edging forward, revolver at the ready. He approached the stricken suspects. Two seemed beyond help. One was moaning in pain. A kick in the head increased the wailing. Two of the constables grabbed the injured gangster. Rough hands yanked arms behind his back. Handcuffs added to the agony. Sam heard a voice calling for ambulances. He saw a wound dressing in the hand of one of the Auxies, tending to his partner.

Sam called to Liu: "Get them. You go left, I'll go right," he screamed.

Liu began running. Sam bolted after his quarry. The gangster knew he was being followed. He kept glancing over his shoulder as he ran. Sam was wary of him suddenly turning around and firing. The man still held a pistol in his hand.

Sam gave chase back down Peking Road then right down Hankow Road. He knew he was fit but how long would he be able to keep it up? He was forty yards behind. He felt safe at that distance. He tried to remember how many shots he'd fired. He thought he had just three rounds remaining.

The pace was manageable. He was unconcerned about losing him at this speed. He knew he should try to provide a commentary. He started paying attention to street names. Reporting was impossible. The channel was jammed with excited voices. He thought he heard Liu's voice sounding stressed. His words were unintelligible. Sam reasoned SDU would have the pier sewn up tight if any of the gangsters headed in that direction.

They passed the Peninsula Hotel. They reached Salisbury Road. A green Rolls Royce was just pulling into the hotel drive. Sam expected the gangster to jink right in the direction of Star Ferry. Where was the SDU ambush team? All he saw was traffic backed up in both directions.

The gangster seemed to have other plans. He ran straight over the road, weaving through the honking traffic, into a small park. Sweat dripped into Sam's eyes. He could feel himself tiring. Pace yourself, he thought. Pace yourself. This was easier than a PTS training run up Brick Hill. He needed to be able to function at the end of the chase. A sudden vision of an Olympic skier with a rifle came to mind. He felt less certain of his ability to shoot straight after a long pursuit. His knees were starting to ache. The black uniform dress shoes he wore were not designed for a long-distance chase.

They ran through the park, passing a group of startled Japanese tourists. He carried his revolver in his right hand and his cap in his left. His cap had wanted to fall off. He decided it was better to ditch it, to keep his hands free. He tossed it towards them. The visitors scattered like it was a bomb.

The suspect showed no sign of slowing down. He looked a small wiry type. He carried no weight other than the black bag over his shoulder and the pistol in his hand. Just my luck, thought Sam.

It can't be far now. They would reach the *daai fei* in less than a minute. SDU would have them in their sights. The radio went momentarily silent. He remembered he hadn't reported his location. He slowed slightly and grasped the opportunity. Through gasps he called for assistance.

"Console, Inspector Steadings, over," he wheezed.

Keep it brief, Sam thought. They know the score, they know you need support.

"One suspect, harbour side Space Museum. Heading Kowloon Pier, over."

He didn't wait for a response. He heard his message repeated by the sergeant manning their channel. He sounded anxious. Almost paternal in his concern.

In front, he saw the suspect glance over his shoulder. He appeared tired. His pace was slowing.

Sam exited the park and turned onto the promenade. The grass underfoot turned into concrete. The sea was on his left. It looked oily and dark. It smelled unpleasant, sulphurous. Like rotten eggs and other mysterious odours.

In the distance he heard powerful engines rumbling. A menacing-looking grey *daai fei* sat near the pier, less than 100 yards away. At the stern, three powerful motors billowed smoke ominously.

Sam's quarry had seen the speedboat as well. His confidence seemed to grow. He slowed to a fast walk. Sam matched his speed. He realised the moment of truth was coming. He took deep breaths, readying himself for the showdown. There was no sign of SDU. Something must have gone wrong. It was going to be up to Sam now.

He reminded himself distance was his friend. Handguns were notoriously inaccurate. After a long chase both of them would be lucky to hit anything. Thirty yards should be a safe distance. Unless he was dealing with a marksman. He cast the thought aside.

He could see three people on the *daai fei*. None looked like the gang members they had seen earlier. They looked fresh. Alert. Dangerous.

A crew member wearing a baseball cap pulled up an AK-47 and pointed it at Sam. His options were limited. He took cover beneath the parapet of the walkway. He would have to wait for assistance now. He dropped to one knee and drew deep gasps of humid air into his lungs.

He was soaked with sweat. He wiped it away from his eyes with his forearm. He dried his hands on his damp trousers. He glanced behind him. The tourists and lovers had fled. He was alone in the dark.

He raised his head and squinted at his opponents. He saw his target turn and advance towards him. He raised his pistol in Sam's direction. Sam felt trapped. Outgunned. He wondered why he wasn't panicking. He was surprised he could still think clearly. A cold fury gripped him. He readied himself to shoot.

Another glance above the parapet was met with a burst from the AK-47. The two shooters were working as a team. They had a plan. Pin him down and kill him.

He decided to act. He dried his right hand again. He needed to deter his foe. To put him off. Delay him. Show him he meant business. He steeled himself. After three, he told himself: one; Two…

A loud bang rent the night air. He was confused. It seemed a familiar sound but he couldn't place it. Three.

He jumped up and shouted a warning. It came out automatically. He had intended to say nothing.

The gangster was lying motionless ten yards away. The pistol still in his hand. Blood pumped from a deep wound in his back. The black bag was half open. He could see expensive watches inside. Rolex. Omega. Cartier.

Diamond encrusted watch faces glittered seductively under the amber light of the streetlamps.

Sam was standing in the isosceles shooting position drummed into them at Training School. He was aiming his revolver at his enemy, willing him to make a move. His mind blocked everything else out. Time had stopped. His concentration was total. Almost trancelike.

Another shot brought him back. It was close. The gunman was off the boat, advancing towards him. He looked short and overweight. The white baseball cap looked out of place. He was shouting. Cursing Sam in Cantonese. Too far away for Sam to shoot. Too close for comfort. Sam dived for cover. Knees and elbows scraped painfully on the concrete.

He risked a quick peep. He was met by a fusillade, the rounds skipped off the concrete near his head. He thought about using his radio, decided it was pointless. Running was hopeless. He crouched into a ball, trying to make himself as small a target as possible. Like he had seen in the movies. He was pinned down. Helpless.

He saw flashing blue lights in the harbour. Bright searchlights hunting for targets. More boat engines. Shouts and threats. The sound of a helicopter arriving overhead. The *daai fei* was leaving. The sound of gunfire. More shouts.

It was time, he decided. His breathing was slowing. He decided to try a shot. He cautiously moved his right arm and right eye from behind the protection of the concrete stanchion.

He shouted a warning. His attacker was still advancing slowly. He had a look of hatred on his face. He looked furious. Almost unhinged. Another barrage of shots sent Sam scuttling back into cover.

A warning rang out.

"Police, drop the weapon," came the command. It was not a voice he recognised. He took his chance. He jumped up, readied for a shot.

The gunman screamed in anger and frustration. He turned towards the source of the warning. Sam saw SDU-types wearing balaclavas in the distance. The sound of automatic fire echoed off the concrete walls of the Cultural Centre. The gangster with the AK-47 crumpled to the ground, hit several times.

The SDU men approached with their MP5s raised, sighting them on the target. They were wearing jeans and black tee-shirts with Browning pistols in holsters on their waists. The taller of the two slid the AK-47 away from the body with his boot. The other handcuffed the suspect. The baseball cap lay next to the body. Sam didn't recognise the face. The eyes were open. Unseeing.

They checked the guy that Sam had been chasing, rolling him over.

"Dead," one of them announced.

The taller one approached Sam. He removed his balaclava. His hair was wet from exertion.

"Jameson, SDU," he announced. "Are you alright?"

Sam nodded. He was struggling to think of anything to say. He wondered if he was in shock.

"You were very lucky, looks like we got here just in time. Let me give you some advice," he said with an easy smile. "Next time just take the shot."

Easy for you to say, thought Sam. Explaining seemed pointless. He nodded wearily and returned his revolver to its holster. He stared blankly at his rescuers then looked out over the harbour. In the distance he saw the *daai fei* circling aimlessly, the engines on fire. The sound of sirens, and the thump of a helicopter split the night.

He felt strangely disconnected from the scene. Lofty's old adage rang in his ears: 'If you can't take a joke you shouldn't have joined'.

Sam shook his head wearily and a smile formed. He started laughing. Wait till I see Jenny, he thought, doubled up with laughter. The SDU Commander stared at him for a moment then turned away to issue further orders.

26

"Who is he?" McClintock wheezed. He was out of breath. Sam guessed it must have been years since he had last sprinted in uniform.

The DVC was peering intently at the dead body at his feet. He had arrived just moments after the last shots were fired. A-Bo was standing behind him. Sam noticed that the older man had barely broken sweat. Looks could be deceiving.

The SDU station sergeant was rifling through the body's pockets. He wore black gloves. His MP5 was carried slung casually over his back. He handed over an expensive-looking leather wallet.

"Let's see what we've got," McClintock said as he opened it. Sam saw it was brimming with yellow thousand dollar notes.

"Holy fuck," McClintock said. He pulled out a faded police warrant card and examined it closely with a small torch.

"So, that's the detective sergeant we were looking for?" Sam said. "A-Siu presumably?"

"Yes indeed," said McClintock. He was scratching his chin. "I'm confused. I was half expecting Silas Chu to make a run for it, not this one," he said with a concerned look.

Sam glanced up. In the harbour the flames on the *daai fei* has been extinguished. It was surrounded by half a dozen sleek-looking Marine Police interceptors. Their flashing blue lights lit up the steps of the pier and the walls of nearby buildings. A large group of serious-looking detectives marched towards them from Star Ferry, clipboards at the ready.

"Right laddie, well done so far," McClintock declared. "PTU are on the way. They'll guard the scene. Stay here and brief the Crime boys. Once that's done, get yer arse back to the station and I'll see you there," he instructed.

Sam realised that cordoning so many crime scenes would require huge manpower. He wondered where they would find the vast quantities of blue and white police cordon tape. Processing all the witnesses and exhibits was going to be a mammoth task. It would likely take CID all night. The traffic would be screwed for hours.

"This is not over by any stretch of the imagination, mark my words," McClintock shouted over his shoulder as he jogged back towards the carnage on Nathan Road. A-Bo followed faithfully behind his boss.

"He's a strange one," Jameson noted. He'd been watching quietly from a few yards away. His MP5 was also slung over his shoulder while he was making notes in his pocket book. "Then again it's been a strange night."

Jameson walked off in the direction of the pier leaving Sam the task of explaining the two bodies at his feet. Sam realised he wasn't even sure who had shot the first one. He guessed it must have been an SDU sniper. He scanned the nearby rooftops but still saw nothing.

It was just after midnight and Sam was alone in the sub-unit office. The Regional Crime Unit Inspector had listened to Sam's version of the night's events and recorded the key facts. He had been advised they would be in touch again later and been curtly dismissed. The inspector seemed unconcerned by the absence of phantom-like SDU witnesses. It would all come out in the wash, Sam guessed.

He was making notes on a piece of A4 paper, determined to capture the details whilst they were still fresh in his mind. Ricky had told him not to worry about a detailed notebook entry and statement just yet. He planned to come in early the next day to complete the admin. Sam's head was spinning. He was relieved at the thought of being able to put off what would undoubtedly be many hours of work until later.

He was starting to come down from his adrenaline high. He felt strangely empty. His high-octane day was ending with a low. Individual incidents replayed themselves in his mind. He could not understand why his mood was bordering on depression. More than anything he craved to be able to talk to Jenny. He wanted to see her face when he explained how it had gone down. He knew that discussion must wait.

Sam tried to rationalise his feelings. He wasn't sure if his bullets had inflicted the fatal wound. He didn't care. You were just doing your job, he told himself. It was you or them. He felt devoid of emotion as he recalled events. He felt not a shred of remorse. It seemed odd.

The injury to the Auxie officer felt different. He couldn't shake the thought that he was responsible for the injury. He went over the lead up to the shooting again and again, dissecting their actions and reviewing the options. The impromptu ambush had never been part of the plan. It was an unscripted addition requiring rapid improvisation, he reminded himself. He felt they had done as well as could be expected in the circumstances. Lady luck had been smiling on them. Mostly.

He was disconcerted by his conflicting emotions. Pull yourself together, he told himself. Questioning yourself is inevitable. Other people can judge how successful you were.

The door of the office crashed open. McClintock stood there grinning maniacally. He was dishevelled. Sweat stained his olive green uniform and his hair was a sticky mess.

"Gift for you," he announced. He threw Sam's cap across the room forcefully, like it was a boomerang. Sam caught it and smiled. "We guessed this must have been yours. Did you lose anything else out there?" he asked.

"No sir," Sam responded cheerfully. The unexpected visit had succeeded in snapping him out of his funk.

"Mess. Now!" McClintock instructed, "I'll see you up there. Mine's a San Miguel. A large one. You owe me for getting us all into this mess, you wee shite." He disappeared out of the door as quickly as he entered. Sam heard him stomping loudly down the corridor to his office.

That's what I call leadership, Sam thought. As he tidied up his papers, he started visualising the cold beer that awaited him in the mess above.

The mess was brightly lit but silent as he entered. He glanced through the window and took in the night time vista of Kowloon. It looked alluring, even majestic. The sound of a siren was slowly retreating into the distance. Probably an ambulance.

He was not the first arrival. Ricky stood patiently behind the bar. He looked delighted to have company. Sam sat on a tall wooden stool opposite. Ricky pulled a frosted glass out of the freezer.

"What can I get you?" he asked.

"Carlberg and a San Mig please. The boss is on the way." Sam knew most old hands were loyal fans of San Miguel. He preferred Carlsberg. He knew both were locally brewed and were reputed to be full of chemicals. In his experience it was a toss-up as to which led to the worse hangover. Ricky produced another frosted glass and deftly emptied a can into each.

"Cheers Sam, well done today," Ricky said as they touched glasses. Sam thought he was looking far more upbeat than he had earlier in the afternoon. He seemed relieved at having dodged a career-defining bullet of any kind. This should look good on all their records.

"Thank you, sir, cheers," Sam replied. He emptied half the glass in one go. He immediately regretted the impact of the cold beer on the back of his throat. His brain felt numb.

Sam noticed Ricky staring at him intently. He seemed to have something on his mind.

Ricky asked, "How was it? I can't believe I've been in the Force for 25 years and never drawn my revolver in anger. And now you've opened fire within weeks of passing out. Unbelievable," he said, shaking his head. Sam wasn't sure if Ricky thought he was lucky or unlucky.

"More importantly," Ricky asked, "How are you feeling?"

Sam took his time to answer. The image of the injured Auxie writhing in pain kept flashing in his mind.

"I'm not sure," Sam answered honestly, "I feel a bit numb. Does that make sense?" he asked.

"Of course." Ricky nodded his head in agreement. "It's been a rough few days. Well done though, I'm proud of you all. Cheers." He drained his glass with a flourish and pulled two more tins from the glass-fronted refrigerator. They were beaded with condensation.

"Drinking without me, you mutinous bastards?" McClintock boomed as he strode through the door.

Ricky handed McClintock his drink. He sipped it eagerly and closed his eyes in ecstasy.

"Let me buy these," McClintock insisted. "After all, it's not every day you can say you're the best DVC in the best division in the best Force in the world. Eh laddie?"

"Cheers, sir," Sam said raising his glass again. "To the best sub-unit in the best division," he added cheekily.

McClintock drained his glass in one smooth motion then wiped his mouth.

"Now you're getting it," McClintock responded. "C'mon Ricky, don't just stand there for fucks sake. Fresh horses man. I'm dying of thirst over here," he cackled.

Ricky rolled his eyes comically in exaggerated exasperation. To Sam it seemed that Ricky had just been temporarily appointed as the most highly paid barman in Hong Kong.

Sam saw McClintock was full of nervous energy. He could barely sit still. Without waiting for his drink he launched into a blow-by-blow account of the day's activities. Sam glanced over at Ricky and they shared a knowing look. He knew there was no escape. It was going to be a long night.

27

"What next?" Sam asked. He was standing in McClintock's office in uniform after starting his shift at 3.00 p.m. They were alone. Unusually both doors were closed. That will get people talking, thought Sam.

"We wait," McClintock answered tartly. Sam could see that he was unhappy. He seemed on edge and testy. Sam guessed the lack of sleep and a San Miguel hangover were not helping. Sam was not feeling great himself. They had been up for half the night before common sense prevailed and he crawled away to find a bed in the barrack. Unlike McClintock he had not been required for morning prayers at 7.30 a.m. No wonder the man was grumpy, Sam thought. The daily morning ritual of reviewing the previous day's events was a chore at the best of times.

The events of the previous night hung over the station like a fog over a campsite. It was cloying and unpleasant. There was no escaping it. The division was agog with stories, rumours and suspicion. The normal routine was yet to fully resume.

The local press remained camped outside of the main gate. They had been joined by the international press. One London tabloid had described it as the 'Tsim Sha Tsui Shoot Out Shocker'. Sam had seen several carefully selected TV camera crews escorted into the compound to film segments.

"Any more news on Silas Chu?" Sam asked.

"Nope. That is the loose end which needs tidying up before we can put this whole thing behind us." McClintock had resumed his normal position. He had his back to the room, surveying his empire through the large office windows.

McClintock had only just returned from a meeting with the Regional Commander. It probably explained his mood, Sam realised. He didn't seem his normal self. Sam wondered if McClintock's chickens were coming home to roost after blatantly circumventing the chain of command.

The DVC was silent. Sam felt self-conscious. He decided to chance his arm with a risqué question.

"So how was the RC?" he asked cautiously.

"You really are a cheeky little fucker," McClintock responded sharply as he turned to face Sam. Sam reddened at the comment. McClintock was smiling. The gambit had worked.

"Let's put it this way," he continued, "as bollockings go, it was world class, richly deserved, and enjoyed by all concerned. However I, or should I say we, live to fight another day," he announced. He was laughing now. Sam joined in, relieved at the outcome.

McClintock described the meeting. It could have gone better was his summary. With Patrick called away to PHQ, he had been left denuded of top cover. Gordon Bathgate had taken the opportunity to joyfully eviscerate him in front of the Region's top team. They stood gawping like witnesses at a prison execution as Bathgate ripped him apart. Bathgate would neither forgive nor forget McClintock going above his head to Smithies, and he had told him as much.

Fortunately, punishment options were limited. With the Commissioner having openly supported the plan hatched by Smithies and McClintock, Bathgate's hands were tied. For the moment. It was an interesting lesson in top level Force politics, Sam realised. If he were to make a career of it, he'd have to learn the rules of the game.

The eyes of the world were upon them. Transferring McClintock to any other posting would quickly be picked up by the media and seen as criticism. The Force needed to circle their wagons.

The DVC said, "The breaking news is that *O-Gei* have taken over the case."

"*O-Gei?*" asked Sam. The list of acronyms, abbreviations and unit nicknames in the Force seemed endless.

McClintock rolled his eyes in disapproval.

"Organised Crime and Triad Bureau to you my dear boy," he replied patronisingly. Sam recalled the name now which he'd first heard during a familiarisation visit to PHQ close to the end of their training.

"*O-Gei* taking over is no bad thing," McClintock went on. "It's a big messy case. It needs PHQ resources. PHQ will want to keep a tight grip."

Sam played along and nodded. He knew nothing about *O-Gei* and PHQ politics.

"However ..." McClintock had paused for effect. He was looking at Sam intently. Sam got the feeling bad news was coming. "It's not over yet and here's why."

Sam said nothing. He didn't know where McClintock was going with this.

"The good news is that the gang is history and the CP is delighted." Sam nodded. He was still amazed by the result. Part of him couldn't believe that it had gone so well. Liu had played his part by chasing the last two suspects into the waiting arms of SDU. "The bad news is that Silas Chu and A-Ken are still at large."

Sam agreed. Everyone had been puzzled that the two men hadn't attempted to make a break for it on the *daai fei*. Surely they must have realised the game was up. Why only A-Siu?

"What happened doesn't make sense," Sam said. He was confused why A-Siu had given up his chance to escape to confront Sam.

McClintock hesitated before he answered. Sam felt his stomach start to somersault.

"This may come as a bit of a shock," said McClintock quietly. "The feeling at PHQ is that you were his target."

McClintock let the impact of his words sink in. Sam was confused.

"Say again," asked Sam incredulously. "Me? But why?"

"This is highly confidential," McClintock continued. "It will form part of the ongoing *O-Gei* and ICAC investigation. They suspect that Silas was tipped off."

"How can that make sense?" asked Sam. He wondered why the raid had gone ahead if there had been a leak.

"Think about it," McClintock said. "Silas knew the game was up for him as soon as Jenny escaped. Right?"

Sam nodded his understanding.

"But that wouldn't affect the raid because he didn't think Jenny knew their plan. With me so far?"

Sam nodded.

"It's the very fact that you became A-Siu's target that highlights the leak. Otherwise, how would they know about you?"

Sam wasn't convinced. It seemed like pure conjecture. Surely he had just been in the wrong place at the wrong time.

"We can prove it," McClintock insisted sombrely.

"How?" Sam asked. He had started to sweat now.

"It was on the pager recovered on the body. There was a message from Silas just before 9.30 p.m. blaming Jenny and you for betraying the raid. Someone close must have tipped him off."

It was Sam's turn to stare through the windows. The timing was crucial, he realised. Not long after McClintock's briefing. There had been only six people in the room. McClintock was suggesting it must have been one of them. Someone who was briefed about the raid and also somehow knew about him and Jenny. He rejected the thought.

"With New Territories, Marine and SDU all involved, it could have been any one of hundreds of officers," Sam suggested.

"You'll never make a detective," declared McClintock savagely. "No one outside this station knows anything about you. We have a leak, and it's on this fucking corridor. Now think." His finger was jabbing angrily in Sam's direction.

McClintock was staring at him. He was feeling dim and depressed.

"Is there a way to identify the source?" he asked.

"Silas and his *mah-jais* all had pagers. It's just a matter of *O-Gei* getting hold of the records. We know the approximate timings."

"How long will it take?" Sam asked. He was concerned about Silas's associates. They might pose risks to Jenny. Or himself.

"*O-Gei* are applying for search warrants. We need to be patient."

Sam was still seeing only some pieces of the jigsaw.

"What about A-Siu?" Sam asked. He was still confused by the guy's behaviour on the pier.

"This is where it gets murky," McClintock replied. "A-Siu was divorced and had a young girlfriend on the Mainland. He was also recently diagnosed with liver cancer. It looks like he was trying to get back to her with a share of the proceeds. Once on the *daai fei* he must have had a change of heart. Maybe when he saw the Marine boats. Then when he saw you he probably decided he had nothing to lose."

"So you think he knew who I was and deliberately targeted me?" Sam asked. He was keen for confirmation.

"We know it for a fact. The last instruction received on A-Siu's pager was clear. 'Kill the *gweilo*', it said."

Sam was speechless. He should have applied for a quiet posting at the arse end of nowhere after all.

"Now for the good news," McClintock declared. He turned over a piece of paper and pushed it across the desk towards Sam.

It was a memo signed by the Regional Commander.

"The RC thinks that it's best that we don't take any chances. He has temporarily authorised a personal issue firearm for you. Of course, it wasn't his suggestion," he declared smugly, "but he understood my argument. Eventually." McClintock ended with a wink and a smile.

"It's just a precaution. Try not lose it. Please?" he said caustically.

Sam felt a shiver go down his spine. The thought of inadvertently leaving a weapon in a restaurant toilet or on the back seat of a taxi was not one to contemplate. It seemed to happen to others all too regularly.

"Liu will help you with a plainclothes holster. Apart from him, only Ricky, Alan and the armoury staff know about this. The revolver is in my safe. Sign this register. You are to keep it on your person at all times. When you come on duty, draw arms as normal. Lock the personal issue away for the duration of the shift. It's not exactly kosher but it should be safe enough. Happy?" he asked.

McClintock opened his safe and Sam secreted the weapon in his trousers pocket, concealed by the flap of his tunic. He felt unnerved by the additional responsibility.

"Now bugger off and let me phone the wife," McClintock ordered. "If I don't get home tonight, it will be knickers-on for the rest of the year. Then you will really see me angry."

Back in his office, Sam kept turning over the meeting with McClintock in his mind. After all the recent excitement, he was finding routine work dull. Concentration remained elusive.

He decided to focus on admin. With Jenny absent, he knew he needed to step up. Keeping things moving was critical if he was to avoid an unpleasant logjam of files. He quickly triaged the ones in his In tray. Files requiring further thought were dumped into the Pending tray. That included his first Death Report for the Coroner. It looked intimidating. Definitely one to save for another day when his mind was fresh and clear.

It was Sarah's turn in the office. She had been surprisingly pleasant so far. The usual tension had evaporated. They had worked harmoniously without Sam feeling the need to remove himself.

"Are you okay, A-Sir" she asked. She was looking at him curiously. He realised he must have been staring into space for a while. He had become lost in his thoughts. Jenny, the raid, and the unwelcome news from McClintock was a heady mix.

"Is everything alright," she asked again. "Can I get you anything?"

He noted the concern in her voice. He forced himself to smile.

"I'm fine, thank you." His denial sounded lame, even to him. "I just need something to eat," he lied. "Would you mind fetching noodles and coffee from the canteen. Please."

She smiled sweetly. "I'll be right back, A-sir," she promised.

His thoughts returned to the threat described by McClintock. He felt out of his depth. He was afraid that he was losing control of events. Further contemplation was curtailed by the telephone. In the absence of Sarah he elected to answer it.

"Inspector Steadings, Sub-Unit Four," he said loudly. He spoke in Cantonese. He felt self-conscious and awkward. In all probability the caller would want to speak to Sarah, not him.

"Your Cantonese is still crap," came a familiar voice. "Is that the best you can do? You should be fluent by now. Now that you're famous. What is the Cantonese for Golden Balls anyway?" asked his mate Ralph ironically.

"Cheeky sod," Sam responded cheerfully. "What's the Golden Balls thing?" he asked.

"Haven't you heard?" Ralph joked. "That's your new Hermitage nickname. Golden Balls Steadings has a nice ring to it, don't you think?" Sam could hear the mirth in his friend's voice waiting for a reaction.

"Hilarious," Sam responded sarcastically. He wondered which joker had come up with that gem so quickly. "Fancy a cuppa after B shift?" he asked.

He was thinking that banter and tea might well morph into something stronger. It would not be a bad thing in the circumstances.

"Sounds great," said Ralph. "Say just after midnight at your place?"

Sam was still laughing to himself when Sarah returned with a heavily loaded plastic tray. She gave him a strange look. She appeared disconcerted by his rapid change of demeanour.

Sam smiled at her and winked. He knew the locals thought all *gweilos* were mad. Foreigners were all *chi-sin*. One day she might understand the magical restorative properties of *gweilo* humour and alcohol.

28

The shift had ended without incident. Sam was in the office with Station Sergeant Liu. They both wore plainclothes. A loaded Smith and Wesson revolver lay on the desk. Liu was taking his mentoring role seriously. Sam reminded himself that Liu had probably spent years carrying firearms covertly.

He looked on intently as Sam threaded the dark leather holster onto the belt of his chinos. Sam could already feel how uncomfortable the arrangement was going to be.

"Now holster the revolver and see how it sits," he directed. Sam could feel the heavy steel of the revolver start to pull his trousers down on one side.

"It will have to do for now. You need to wear it with a heavier belt next time," he advised.

I bet they don't have problems like this in Miami Vice, Sam thought to himself. Although uncomfortable, the weapon was a reassuring presence.

"One last thing," Liu said. "Pull your shirt out or wear a jacket from now on."

Sam complied.

"All done. Shall we go?" Liu asked.

"Go where?" asked Sam. He was bemused by the question.

"Didn't the DVC tell you? I'm taking you home from now on," Liu said cheerfully.

Sam could only smile. Maybe McClintock's not so bad after all, he thought ruefully.

Twenty minutes later, Sam got out of Liu's Toyota in front of the Hermitage. Traffic through the tunnel had been light. They had not been delayed by police roadblocks, road works, accidents, or any of the other usual causes of late-night traffic frustration.

Liu wanted to escort him to his apartment door. Sam declined. He insisted he would be safe once inside. Despite his protestations he felt surprisingly nervous. He climbed the steps to the entrance and found the entrance lobby empty. He turned around and waved to Liu who returned the gesture and drove off.

Sam found himself scanning up and down the road. It was not something he would usually have done, he realised. He was still getting used to the weight of the revolver. The heavy steel was cold against the skin of his stomach. He was having to resist the temptation to constantly touch it.

The Hermitage was unusually quiet. No one else was visible apart from a sleeping security guard who was slumped in a decrepit rattan chair in the large basement garage beyond. It was half full of an assortment of jeeps, motorbikes, and small saloon cars. Several seemed abandoned. They were covered in deep layers of dust and festooned by enormous cobwebs that hung like sails from the ceiling. Sam could sense decay and decadence. He knew the empty parking spaces would be worth a fortune on the open market. Here they were taken for granted as free storage space by the young men of the building.

He shivered involuntarily. This is ridiculous, thought Sam. He was becoming scared of his own shadow. It had dawned on him earlier that he had reason to be cautious. The Regional Commander would not have been willing to authorise a personal issue revolver otherwise.

Lift or stairs, he wondered? He was remembering movies where elevator doors opening had produced nasty surprises for the occupants. He elected to take the stairs instead. He walked as quietly as he could. He stopped at the top of each flight and listened for unusual sounds. His right hand remained on his revolver.

Two minutes later he had climbed to the third floor. He gingerly opened the fire door onto the corridor and cautiously made his way to his apartment. He was amused to find that some wag had beaten him to it. A pair of large golden Christmas baubles hung off his door. A tribute to his new title.

He turned to check the corridor behind him and pulled out his keys. He was relieved to be able to bolt the door behind him. Home sweet home, he thought. For the first time his apartment felt like a sanctuary from the madness outside rather just somewhere to eat and sleep.

It seemed like Sam had only just stepped through the door when there was a firm knock. It made him physically jump with fright. He quickly unholstered the revolver and pointed it towards the door. There was no other sound.

"Who is it?" he asked.

"Who do you think it is? Chairman Mao?" came the irritated response. Sam's elevated heart beat returned to normal. He cautiously approached the door and peeped through the door viewer. He saw only the shape of his squad mate.

"Come in," he instructed. As Ralph entered, Sam quickly checked up and down the corridor. He secured the door and faced his visitor.

"Are you alright?" Ralph was wearing a look of concern. He was staring down at the revolver in Sam's hand. "And what the hell are you doing with that?" he asked pointedly.

"It's a long story. I'll tell you over a drink. Tea or whiskey?" asked Sam. "I'm out of beer." He holstered his revolver. His hand was shaking slightly.

Ralph held up a white 7-11 plastic bag. Sam could see damp cans of Carlsberg clinging to the thin plastic sides.

"In that case, it's just as well I brought some supplies," Ralph replied.

Sam was relieved. He wanted to save the whiskey for the next time he saw Jenny. The cans were refreshingly cold. He swiftly opened one and toasted Ralph.

"Take a seat," said Sam. He gave Ralph the smug look he deployed whenever he had inside information. Sam undid his belt and slid the holstered revolver off. It looked oddly out of place on the table between them.

"I smell a rat," Ralph announced as he wiped his mouth. He was eyeing Sam quizzically. Folded arms emphasised his complaint. "It's got be more than a coincidence that I find you at home with a revolver the day after a major shoot-out. Right?" he asked.

Sam said nothing. He was wondering how much it would be wise to disclose. Friendship sometimes meant entrusting people with confidences. Some stories were just so good that they needed to be told. He remembered they had a nasty habit of leaking out. Loose lips sink ships, he realised.

"I see you're not denying it," said Ralph. He was taking Sam's silence as an admission.

"It's complicated," Sam replied. An image of a bruised and filthy Jenny pleading for his help came to mind. He realised it had been less than 48 hours earlier. He unconsciously glanced at the door and checked the bolt. The beer had yet to work its magic and relax him.

"There is more to this than a simple armed robbery. I can't say more at this stage. McClintock will have my guts for garters," he explained.

"Fair enough," said Ralph amenably. He put his hands in the air in mock surrender. "At least tell me the bits you can," he pleaded.

Sam rubbed his hands together and made a start. It took him nearly thirty minutes to describe the robbery. He left out all mention of the lead up. Some aspects were judiciously amended so that the facts fitted his narrative.

"Jesus," said Ralph in admiration when he had finished. He had been silent until then. Sam had kept his eyes on the harbour throughout. He worried about emotion creeping in. He thought avoiding eye contact was his best defence.

"Talk about being in the right place at the right time." Ralph whistled his appreciation.

"We were bloody lucky. There's no doubt about that," Sam said seriously. He shivered slightly. Things could have turned out very differently."

"More tea vicar?" Ralph asked. He helped himself to another can from the batch he'd transferred into the refrigerator on arrival.

"Thanks, but I need the toilet first," Sam announced. As he walked through the bedroom he placed the revolver on his bedside table. He carried on to the en-suite bathroom beyond.

Thirty seconds later he was washing his hands. The toilet was flushing loudly behind him. He vaguely heard Ralph's voice. He was saying that there was someone at the door. Sam was surprised. It was unusual to have even one visitor after midnight.

He suddenly heard shouts and bangs. The sounds of a scuffle were punctuated by a loud scream. His mind was racing. His mind made the leap and he raced out. He grabbed the holster and drew the revolver.

"Sam, help," screamed Ralph as Sam entered the main room. He could see Ralph backed up against the far wall of the apartment. Traces of blood were smeared on the paint behind him. A deep wound on his shoulder was oozing blood.

He had a chair in his hands. Razor-sharp twelve-inch steel butchers' knives were slashing at him. Small towels tied to handles acted as grips. He was fending off two attackers. The men were short, stocky, and rough looking. Sam could see triad tattoos on their tanned muscly arms. They were shouting obscenities and taunting their cornered victim in Cantonese. Cruel grins marked their lust for blood.

The two assailants were manoeuvring around the table to attack from both sides. They were oblivious to Sam. He saw a third man standing in the doorway. The lookout, Sam guessed. As he emerged, the sentry shouted a warning.

The distance from Sam to Ralph's assailants was a matter of feet. It was almost touching distance. He was concerned about lack of reaction time if they turned on him. Shoot now or warn first was his dilemma. He decided to err on the side of caution. He loudly shouted "Police, stop or I shoot" in Cantonese.

The warning caused the nearest to turn. He lunged at Sam with a bloodied beef knife. The knife slashed down from shoulder height. A murderous scream filled the room. It died in his throat. Sam was ready for him. He deftly stepped backwards into the bedroom to give himself space. A single shot pierced the attacker's chest. It was deafening in the confined space of the apartment.

Sam's attacker slumped to the floor. The soiled beef knife bounced and slithered towards his feet.

"Police, stop or I shoot," Sam repeated loudly. He carefully advanced out of the bedroom to see the remaining suspects fleeing. He glanced at Ralph and saw him clutching his arm.

"Call 999, watch him," he shouted to Ralph who was crouched down besides the table. A bloodied hand covered the deep wound on his shoulder. Bright red blood seeped through his fingers. He could see the blood dripping on to the polished wooden floor. Sam felt sick with concern. Anger coursed through his veins.

A shot echoed along the corridor. He slowly edged out of the apartment to give chase. Sam was confused. He had seen no firearms. He advanced cautiously, revolver held high. He wondered who was shooting at whom.

He was confronted by the sight of an attacker lying motionless. A lake of blood was rapidly spreading from his head and shoulders. A short and tubby *gweilo* stood over him. He was naked except for a pair of white Y-front underpants and a string vest. His red face, extravagant moustache, and a mass of dark hair on his chest made the scene more ridiculous. He took a long drag from an unfiltered cigarette held by nicotine-stained fingers. In the other hand he held the type of snub-nosed revolver beloved of detectives.

"Are you alright fella?" he asked. The voice was strangely calming. It came wrapped in a deep Northern Irish accent. It made the incident sound trivial. As if it was a regular occurrence. Just a minor neighbourhood irritation. Like an over-enthusiastic fox caught ransacking a bin.

"Fine thanks," replied Sam. He could hear his heartbeat pounding in his ears. "My mate Ralph's injured. We'll need an ambulance."

"Friends of yours?" the *gweilo* asked, waving his revolver casually at the dead suspect at his feet.

"It's complicated," said Sam. He preferred to deflect the question. The Irishman took another puff on his cigarette and poked the dead triad with his bare foot.

"How did you get involved?" Sam asked. He was curious as to the origin of his unlikely saviour. More heads were emerging from doors along the corridor. Several approached warily, some with revolvers in hand.

"I'm Mike," the Irishman said evenly. "Moved in here last month. I'd just come off duty. I was in bed listening to the World Service. Someone was shouting something awful and I thought I should take a look."

The accent was strong. Sam was struggling to understand some words. He pitied the locals who worked with him.

"I heard a shot," Mike went on. "Then this one and his pal ran towards me with knives. Silly boys. I just fired at the nearest one, so I did. Job done I reckon," he said smugly. He sucked greedily on his cigarette. Smoke billowed along the corridor.

Job done indeed, Sam thought to himself. He wondered if anyone else had ever had a similar baptism of fire straight after leaving Training School.

"Can anyone can lend me a pair of handcuffs?" Sam asked hopefully as more coppers emerged from their apartments.

29

He had definitely felt better, he decided. Once again Sam was in front of his boss. He was still wearing the same outfit he had left the station in seven hours earlier. He needed sleep and a shower. Preferably in that order.

It had taken hours before he was released from the crime scene formerly known as his apartment. It was after 6.30 a.m. by the time he arrived at the station. A 45-minute nap on a sofa in the Officer's Mess had been interrupted by the Duty Officer roughly shaking his shoulder. It was accompanied by an urgent summons back into the lion's den.

"Look what the cat dragged in. You've been busy again," McClintock said. Sam felt exhausted and he guessed it showed. He knew he was dishevelled and unshaven.

"Tell me everything," the DVC instructed.

Sam explained his version of events for the sixth time in six hours. It was becoming tiresome. It had started with the first EU car to arrive. It was followed by their Platoon Commander, a CID Reserve Team inspector, and then the Duty Controller. It ended with an aggressive character from a Regional crime unit. He seemed to resent being woken in the middle of the night to take over the case. It had taken all of Sam's self-restraint to deal with the endless questions semi-courteously.

McClintock waited patiently. He allowed Sam to finish before probing.

"A bloody good job you were armed," he said. Sam had guessed McClintock might launch into a bout of self-congratulation. Though not so quickly.

"It's lucky you weren't by yourself," McClintock continued. "The end result might have been very different if they had got the drop on just you," he said seriously.

The same thought had crossed Sam's mind. He reminded himself not to tell his mother about it.

"The good news is that you kindly left one alive," he declared sarcastically. "I have no doubt that he will sing like a bird once *O-Gei* get their hands on him. Though it might be a while before he is released from hospital." He sounded disappointed.

"The other good news," he went on, "is that the EU Platoon Commander was smart enough to get rid of your empty beer cans. That means there will no steward's enquiry about drinking whilst in charge of a firearm. You owe him a beer I reckon," McClintock suggested with a smirk. His attitude did not surprise Sam. He guessed it was but a minor infraction of the rules in McClintock's strange world.

"As for that lunatic Irish neighbour of yours', he's probably in line for a Commissioner's Commendation. You might owe him a beer too. And Ralph whilst you are at it. Thankfully his wound should heal fine."

McClintock sat back in his chair and crossed his arms. He laughed. "Bloody hell Sam, you really are a one-man disaster zone."

Sam was not seeing the funny side. He said nothing. He just wanted to get the grilling over with. He was feeling lightheaded and woefully under-prepared for an early morning jousting session.

"Next steps," McClintock announced enthusiastically. "I've been talking to the powers that be and they feel that you need to keep a low profile for a while. That means moving you to more secure accommodation."

Sam had only been in his new apartment for a matter of weeks. Already it was feeling homely in comparison with his basic mosquito-ridden Training School room. He wondered where they might put him.

"The arrangements are still being confirmed," McClintock said. "It looks like you are going back to Training School. Into the visitor accommodation, you will be glad to hear."

That's a relief, thought Sam. He had heard good things about those rooms. They were like a hotel suite rather than the series of cell-like spaces he had occupied during the preceding nine months. The lack of air-conditioning had been a real struggle in the heat. The fans were noisy and dehydrating.

"Once it's all confirmed, I'll get you escorted back to the Hermitage. You can pack up some things before heading over to PTS."

Sam nodded his understanding. He started thinking through the list of things he would need.

McClintock said, "From now on you will not go anywhere alone. On duty or off. A vehicle will take you to and from Training School. When off duty, you will remain inside the grounds. When on duty you will have an orderly with you at all times. That means wherever. In the office. In the barrack. On patrol. In the shithouse. Am I quite clear?" he asked, tapping his desk with a finger to make his point.

"Yes, sir," Sam responded quietly. Perhaps his choice of career had not been the wisest after all? So far as he could recollect, the advert in the Daily Telegraph had not hinted at anything like this. Accountancy, as his father had suggested, might have been a better option. Dull but safe.

"You look buggered," said McClintock. He had come to the end of his lecture. His voice had lost its edge. "Get some sleep upstairs. I'll let you know when everything is sorted out. And by the way, well done last night."

"Thank you, sir," Sam said.

McClintock laughed once more. "Fuck me," he said. "You need a *baai kwan daai* more than anyone I've met. Now cheer up and get some kip."

Sam had heard about *baai kwan daai* ceremonies. They sounded like a classic Force excuse for a piss-up. A mixture of Chinese religious incantations, roast pigs, and an afternoon of beer. All for the sake of celebrating a success or commiserating bad luck.

He glanced over at the 18-inch statue of the Chinese god of war, triads and cops staring at him malevolently from the window ledge. He wondered what his father would have said about all that. They were a good Catholic family and pagan gods had not been part of his upbringing. Needs must, Dad, he thought with a smile, as he trudged out.

30

After three hours sleep, Sam was feeling better. A long hot shower had brought him back to life. The facilities in the inspectors' changing rooms were basic. The iron-framed beds were angular and awkward. The mattresses thin, lumpy, and suspiciously stained in places. Nonetheless, he was grateful. He always kept a clean set of clothes in his locker. After a shave he felt ready for the day. He had surrendered his revolver to the CID team as an exhibit. Without it he felt distinctly naked, though not unsafe in a station containing dozens of armed officers.

With no instructions in hand, he decided to check for news. Ricky Ricardo was on the phone. As Sam popped his head around his office door frame, the ADVC Ops smiled. He signalled Sam to head further along to McClintock's office.

"Ah, sleeping beauty awakes," McClintock commented drily. He waved him in. "Feeling better?"

"100% thank you, sir. I needed that." He wondered what he had looked like several hours earlier.

"Good stuff," McClintock replied. "Everything is arranged. Alan will sort out transport and an escort as soon as you are ready. Your revolver is still with Hong Kong Island. Draw another from the armoury and off you go. CID might be in touch about last night but any enquiries like that will come through me. Your whereabouts are not to become public knowledge. Take the rest of today to get your shite together. I'll see you back here for B shift tomorrow. Happy?" he asked.

"Yes sir," Sam replied. "Thank you."

"So, what are you waiting for, you plonker? Get going," McClintock chided. Sam smiled. He was starting to warm to his DVC's unorthodox man management techniques. "And try not to shoot anyone this time," McClintock shouted behind him. He laughed uproariously at his own joke.

Sam's first stop was the sub-unit office. He scribbled a note that he was going to be absent for that day's shift and would return the following day. That will confuse them, Sam thought. No doubt Station Sergeant Cheung would have something to say.

Sam grabbed his belongings from the barracks and headed to Alan's office. As he entered, Alan simultaneously raised his eyebrows, shook his head, and laughed.

"Ready?" he asked.

Sam smiled and nodded.

"David here will escort you." He pointed towards a uniformed constable sitting patiently in the corner. Sam noted that the numbers on his shoulder were backed with red, a sign of a confident English speaker. The constable was engrossed in a book on conversational English.

"When you get to Training School, report to the Admin office," Alan explained and shook Sam's hand. It felt ominous, as though he was in need of the good luck that the gesture implied.

"Your wish is my command, A-Sir," David announced extravagantly as he stood up. Sam laughed. He was constantly amused by the oddities the bilingual Force regularly threw up. Together they headed into the compound to find their driver.

Forty five minutes later they were approaching the Hermitage. Sam noted that David had started taking his bodyguard duties most seriously. At a glance he appeared bookish and weak. His old-fashioned reading glasses and small frame hinted at a past as a clerk. But he was sharper than he looked.

As the battered Sherpa police van approached the single inspectors' quarters, David scanned the road cautiously and directed the driver to do a drive past. Satisfied that the coast was clear, he ordered a U-turn before they finally parked up outside. To Sam it felt excessive but he was reassured nonetheless.

Sam suggested that the driver wait with the vehicle, but he shook his head. Sam guessed he had received explicit instructions from Alan. He locked up the van and accompanied them up the steps, all the while scanning for any threats. The two constables seemed to be enjoying themselves. Playing nursemaid to a *gweilo* would be a refreshing change from normal beat duties.

The only person visible was a slumbering security guard in the garage. Sam was pleased to be able to slip home unobserved. As the small party cautiously exited the lift, David led. The driver brought up the rear. Sam indicated where they needed to go.

All physical traces of the previous night's incident had been removed from the corridor. Only the lingering smell of bleach remained. The Hermitage cleaners were known to have to put up with challenging behaviour from their rowdy clients. Sam imagined cleaning up bloodstains was a new low.

He unlocked the apartment door. David drew his revolver and edged past, holding his weapon at 45 degrees, ready for any threat. He disappeared inside the bedroom and ensuite. A shout declared them safe.

The apartment had the same cloying smell of the corridor. Signs of a struggle were more apparent. Small flecks of blood pockmarked the wall. Deep cut marks on a chair evidenced Ralph's desperate attempts to defend himself.

Sam was in no mood to hang around. He quickly packed essential clothes, toiletries, and sport kit into a battered suitcase. A pile of police manuals caught his eye. He briefly considered taking them to start preparing for the next round of professional examinations. He decided that his state of mind would not be helped by hundreds of pages of mind-numbing police procedures. He abandoned the idea.

"Next stop, Training School, please," Sam requested cheerfully as he locked the apartment door. He walked along the corridor wondering how long it might be before he could safely return.

The drive to Training School was unremarkable. The driver took the route over the hills, past the Second World War bunkers at Wong Nei Chung Gap. It was a longer but more pleasant journey than through the Aberdeen tunnel. They were in no hurry and he enjoyed the drive.

It felt strange to be driving through the metal gates of Training School again so soon after leaving. The familiar sounds and smells were comforting. The office team were a model of efficiency. He was given a numbered key to his new room within 60 seconds of arrival.

"It's the usual arrangements, A-Sir", the pleasant bespectacled Chinese lady told him. "Sign for any food and drinks on a mess chit. Your laundry box will be emptied daily. Any problems just let me know. Mr McClintock is an old friend. I remember when he was here as a trainee. Always happy to help if we can." She was beaming with pride as she guided Sam to his swish new temporary quarters. She obviously knew some of the background causing Sam's return to Training School.

Sam thanked then dismissed his escort and set about making himself at home. He was pleased by his new surroundings. The plush rooms were normally reserved for visiting or retired officers. They were large and comfortably furnished. Sam thought they compared favourably with hotels he had stayed in. A small kitchenette tipped the balance. The sensation was like moving from one star to four-star accommodation. This will do me for a while, he thought contentedly.

Through the trees he could see the main gate. It was less than a hundred yards away. The flow of traffic was constant. The porous perimeter seemed less than ideal. He was not wholly reassured by the elderly guards manning the gate house. It was too close for comfort.

The building was the grandest part of a mess complex that housed nearly 200 trainees. It was a place where daily life centred around the restaurant and bar. Sam wondered if they would welcome a visitor. He would have to find out.

He was removing the last items from his suitcase when he heard a series of loud knocks on the door. He froze. The sound reminded him of recent unwelcome visitors. He placed his hand on the revolver on his hip. As he approached the door, he could feel his anxiety building.

"Who is it?" he shouted. He deliberately stood to one side of the door, in case it burst open unexpectedly.

"Who do you think it is?" came the familiar voice.

Sam instantly relaxed. He opened the door. A diminutive figure stood in the doorway.

"Well, well, well," Lofty said with crossed arms. "What have we got here then. Were you missing us already?" he smirked.

"Of course, sir. You and the mess."

Lofty gave a knowing smile. "Cover up that bloody revolver. I'll see you in the mess in ten minutes. Your round," he instructed.

The invitation cheered Sam up. He felt upbeat for the first time all day.

It was a strange sensation walking into the Officers' Mess. A dozen training staff were standing by the bar. He nodded at the familiar barman. A-Tong was cheerfully wiping glasses with a white cloth as he waited for his next customer. He looked smart in his white jacket. The bar was spotless. It was like coming home to a familiar haunt.

Lofty had worked quickly. A posse had been rounded up with supreme efficiency. Sam suspected many of them had not taken much prompting to down tools and head to the mess.

It had only been weeks since he had last leant against this bar. Already the dynamic with the instructors felt different. He felt welcomed as a peer rather than a trainee. He had earned his spurs. The disparity with the nearby trainees seemed stark.

"Whahey," shouted an excitable voice from the crowd. "Here he is, Golden Balls Steadings. Or is it Shoot Out Sam?" he jeered. The crowd of mainly expat instructors cheered his entrance. He felt like a new Emperor at the Coliseum. He was momentarily embarrassed by the scene.

Contrary to Lofty's instruction, Sam found it impossible to buy a round. The crowd was possessed of unusual generosity. The mob swelled as the afternoon went on. Yet more instructors arrived after finishing the day's duties. "Just one quick one," was the mantra. No one believed it. Especially their wives.

Sam faced a barrage of questions. Eventually he gave up attempting to tell his story. The constant interruptions made it impossible.

News of his arrival had percolated into the darkest recesses of Training School. Even some of the big beasts came out to play. The most senior staff were not accustomed to roughing it with the vulgar crew camped in the bar. These creatures preferred to drink in the refined surroundings of the Gazetted Officers' Mess at PHQ. Associating with plebs was undesirable.

A hush came over the congregation. Sam turned to find the Commandant looking at him wistfully. Sam was unable to read his attitude to the impromptu party.

The Commandant was accompanied by his faithful Deputy. He was respectfully standing two paces behind the Commandant's right shoulder. With their doleful appearance, they looked like a pair of undertakers about to go to work on their latest cadaver.

At just over five feet tall, Chief Superintendent Gerald Chan was the shortest man in the room. Sam knew he suffered badly from Little Man Syndrome. He was known to compensate for his lack of height with aggression. Feared by trainees and instructors alike, he was an ice-cold operator. He possessed the uncanny ability to instantly suck the life out of any room.

"Good afternoon, Mr. Steadings," he said seriously. "Welcome back to Training School. I understand you've had an interesting few days," he observed.

"Yes, sir," Sam replied formally. He reverted to trainee mode. He had automatically straightened his back and stood to attention.

"Well done the other night," Chan said. "Enjoy your stay. Try not to drink too much." It was unprecedented banter from a man with no known sense of humour.

"A-Tong. Buy all the gentlemen a round on my tab," he ordered to everyone's astonishment. He turned on his heel and left the room.

"Jesus Christ almighty," an impressed Lofty declared. "You really are Golden Balls if you can get a round out of that one."

The party resumed. A-Tong was distributing ice-cold beer cans by the armful. Sam saw Lofty staring at him. His old instructor was shaking his head in astonishment. Or admiration.

By 7 p.m., ranks were thinning. They had earlier been reinforced by a group of trainees who had decided to join the action whilst passing through. Sam was feeling both the pace and the lack of sleep. He decided that discretion was the better part of valour. He was suddenly aware of the heavy metal revolver pressing into his side.

Sam had the opportunity to exit stage left when Lofty indicated that he had to go home. With Lofty on a third and final warning from his wife, he knew that even the highly trained and ever loyal A-Tong would be unable to convince her that he was no longer in the mess. Lofty had reluctantly taken her call on the bar phone. Sam overheard him promise that he was leaving immediately. He emptied his glass and departed to hoots of derision from his compatriots.

"Sorry gents, but I'm also going to call it a day," Sam announced. After a round of handshakes and backslapping, he shook off determined efforts to persuade him to stay and walked out. It was a short stagger to his new accommodation. He was not sure whether he was feeling more tired or hungry. The key thing was to get out of the mess intact and then re-group.

He was keenly aware that it was all too easy to get dragged into a late night session if he wasn't careful. That was the last thing he needed.

The Training School was quiet. Off duty trainees walked past in small groups, identifiable by their PE kit attire. It was already dark. The white walls of the guest house were lit up by spotlights. With a heavily forested hillside for a backdrop, it looked exotic and welcoming, like a country club. The atmosphere felt almost romantic.

The secluded path took him behind the admin block. It was silent other than cicadas announcing themselves loudly in the trees. He passed a smartly attired local officer dressed in a suit. The man greeted him jovially before continuing on his way.

As Sam climbed the stairs, he felt relaxed. Worries about his safety were momentarily forgotten as he enjoyed the warm night. He had never stepped inside the building previously though he was familiar with the block from his rounds as Duty Officer before he passed out.

The annex was quiet, he had seen few lights in the windows. His room was on the first floor. The staircase and corridor were open to the elements. As he approached his room, a small lizard scuttled across the floor in pursuit of an injured moth.

He was disconcerted to see a shape at the end of the passageway. Someone was leaning on the balustrade, seemingly staring into the dark shadows between the trees. The figure looked strangely familiar. The subdued lighting made identification difficult. He started to feel tense.

As he walked closer the figure turned and spoke. "Hello stranger," she said. After several days of incessant surprises, Sam felt too tired to be astonished.

He was delighted to see Jenny. As she approached they embraced. They kissed warmly.

"Am I pleased to see you," he said. They walked towards Sam's room, His arm was wrapped tightly around her waist. As soon as they were inside, they kissed passionately.

"Who would have thought we would be neighbours one day?" Jenny said.

"Please explain." Sam was frowning. The combination of fatigue and alcohol was slowing his thought processes.

"Isn't it obvious?" she asked. "They've put me here. I'm in the room next door," she said with a giggle.

"But what about protection?" He worried about the risk to her life. Jenny would be a key witness in any future corruption trial.

"Don't worry," she said. "After the attack on you, they reckoned both of us would be safer here. There's a CIB witness protection team at the end of the corridor. They've promised they'll be keeping a low profile."

Sam thought of McClintock. This must be his doing, he decided. He was grateful for the companionship. That explained the officer he had seen outside.

"Hungry?" she asked.

He nodded enthusiastically.

"Any preference?"

"I'm starving. Anything will do," he told her.

Jenny picked up the telephone and called her minder. She listed the dishes she wanted delivering.

"All done," she told him. "Now tell me what's been going on," she demanded. She pulled him on to the sofa. "I've heard you've been busy," she said admiringly.

31

Sam woke with a thick head and an uncomfortably cold back. He was directly in the path of a powerful air conditioner mounted in the wall opposite. For a moment he wondered where he was. He glanced around the room as he recalled the previous night's events. He was relieved to see his revolver still sitting on the glass-topped rattan side table.

The colourful floral curtains were closed and he was alone in the king-size bed. He could hear the sound of Cantonese songs wafting through the open door. He had lost track of time. From the sounds of activity, the training day was already in full swing. He heard a loud and ragged volley of firing in the distance and remembered they were just yards away from the firing range.

He stretched his limbs lazily. The combination of a long talk with Jenny, energetic sex, and a good night's sleep had been cathartic.

He had done most of the talking. Jenny had little to tell. She had been put on ice. After taking over her protection, the CIB team had quietly brought her into Training School earlier that evening. Her presence was a secret. Her meals were to be hand delivered and she was not permitted to enter the mess.

The team had told her of Sam's presence. They had tactfully withdrawn and guarded from a safe distance. Very thoughtful, thought Sam. They had been well briefed.

"Good morning," she said. Jenny was silhouetted in the doorway, bare footed on the cool parquet floor. Her favourite silk kimono reflected brightly in the shimmering sun and created an aura around her.

"What time is it?" he asked groggily. He was concerned that he might be late for duty.

"Relax," she said, "it's only 9.30. You've got plenty of time. Jump in the shower," she suggested. "Breakfast is on the way. Then we've got visitors," she added tantalizingly.

The visitors arrived at 11.30 a.m. Three were unknown to Sam. They were senior police, Legal Department and ICAC representatives. Tall and middle aged, they were dressed in matching dark suits.

They filed into the living room of the apartment solemnly, like guests paying their respects after a death. A smartly dressed guard discretely closed the door behind them.

"Morning, Sam, morning, Jenny," McClintock said. "Are you making yourselves comfortable?" His tone was friendly, but the wording seemed ambiguous. Sam was unclear if McClintock was driving at the quality of the accommodation or implying carnal relations. The thought instantly brought colour to his face. He must be able to read me like a book, Sam thought dismally.

"It's perfect. Thank you, sir," he replied respectfully. He was deliberately taking the lead and hoping that Jenny might be spared.

"Let me make the introductions," McClintock said. "This is Deputy Commissioner of Police Milner. Phillip

Tan from Legal Department. Derek Carlton from ICAC."

Sam eyeballed each of them in turn. They stared at him impassively.

"Morning, sir," he replied to them collectively after McClintock had finished. Jenny kept silent. Her eyes were fixed on McClintock. Sam knew she was wary of him.

"I'll try and keep this brief," Milner said. "I know that you've had a difficult few days. However, we have a knotty problem on our hands and we need your help to resolve it." He paused momentarily for effect. "If you are willing to assist us," he added.

Sam said nothing. He was trying to imagine what type of situation could need their involvement when the Force had over 25,000 officers available. He had not seen a newspaper or television report for 24 hours. He felt out of touch.

The silence seemed deafening. It appeared no one was willing to speak. It was as though they were all hoping someone else would pick up the thread.

"It might help I set the scene for all of us," McClintock said. "There have been developments. The police and ICAC are still looking for Silas Chu and A-Ken," he said with venom. "Unfortunately we have had no strong leads on their whereabouts, though we believe they are still in the Territory.

"The problem is that the situation has escalated. Silas Chu is now viewed as a security threat and not simply a fugitive," he said gravely. "The suspect you shot at the Hermitage has been interviewed. At some length," he added with emphasis. "He told us that Silas put out a contract out on you both, hence the attack on you and young Ralph. That contract has now been cancelled."

"I'm confused," said Sam. "If it's been cancelled, where is the problem?" He tried hard to ask the question in his most reasonable voice.

Milner stood up and went to look out of the window. He was staring at a group of trainees practising taekwondo self-defence moves on the field opposite. Without turning he continued the explanation:

"As you might expect, we have certain, erm, contacts shall we say on the Mainland. Both official and unofficial," he said. "Since the raid, we have been putting out feelers. Last night we had word that Silas had cancelled the contract because another heavily armed team are on the way from the Mainland. Intelligence indicates that they are led by Silas's brother-in-law, Dragon Wong. They are here for you two." As he said it, he turned theatrically and pointed in their direction. "So now do you follow?" he asked.

"One more thing," he continued. "We have it on good authority that Silas is now persona non grata on the Mainland. If he is found in Guangdong he will be handed back to us. His family are under surveillance. He has nowhere to go. He is effectively trapped. Cornered animals can be dangerous," he warned.

Sam nodded his head in confirmation. Jenny had gone pale. Sam reached for her hand and noticed her eyes were moist.

"The Governor is extremely troubled, as are our masters in London," explained Milner. "He has ordered that we take all necessary measures to protect the public from further injury. Despite civilian fatalities, the initial public response to recent events has been positive. Police came out of it without undue criticism." He paced up and down the room as he spoke.

"But events in Beijing are escalating. The Governor is worried that public confidence is on a knife edge. If this level of violence continues it could have a negative impact on the public's trust in the authorities. The bottom line is that we need this situation resolving, quickly and decisively. Before it gets out of hand," he said sternly.

McClintock took up the narrative again. Sam formed the impression that the discussion had been pre-prepared, even rehearsed.

"And that, ladies and gentlemen, is where you two come in," McClintock said with a smile. Before McClintock had even said a word about the plan Sam knew they were not going to like it. He shrugged his acceptance.

"We need some bait and the good news is that you are it," he declared gleefully."

It was official, thought Sam, they were dealing with a sadist. He could feel Jenny squeezing his hand tightly.

"Let's get down to business," McClintock announced. He was relishing his role too much for Sam's taste. "We need to move you out of town to avoid the risk of collateral damage and prying eyes. A number of locations are under consideration. One will be confirmed in due course."

Sam was starting to feel that he and Jenny were simply sacrificial pawns in an important game of chess.

"In the meantime," McClintock said. "You will stay here. Security will be beefed up. A detailed plan is being worked up at PHQ. It will primarily be a police operation."

McClintock glanced over in Carlton's direction. He nodded.

"This is where ICAC come in," McClintock revealed.

"I can't say too much, but ICAC investigations have uncovered certain connections to Silas within the Force. The plan is simple. We will drop a trail of breadcrumbs under the noses of those connections and then let nature take its course." Sam thought it was an odd way of describing it. It reminded him of a David Attenborough documentary that ended with crocodiles ripping apart a hapless wildebeest.

"Once we are certain the bait has been taken, the trap will be sprung." McClintock ended by dramatically smashing his fist into his palm. It was accompanied by a loud slapping sound.

"So why are Legal Department here?" asked Jenny. She spoke for the first time. Sam knew she would be nervous. She would need to understand any legal implications for her.

"Good question, Inspector," Phillip Tan responded coolly. "I'm here because the Governor wants this operation to run absolutely smoothly." He gave as warm a smile as a lawyer is capable of delivering. "I'm also here to give you reassurance. From our review of the facts, unless new evidence emerges, we will probably not be laying charges in respect of your involvement with Silas Chu. Am I right, gentlemen?" he asked looking from Carlton to Milner in turn.

"What does 'probably' mean?" Jenny asked sharply.

"We are looking for certain assurances from you before we make any firm commitments," Tan went on. "We are broadly comfortable with your version of events. We are looking for your cooperation to maximise the likelihood of a successful outcome."

"And?" Jenny demanded in response to Tan's deliberate pause.

"If Silas is fit to stand trial, we want an assurance that you will give evidence in court against him and his associates."

"And if I do that, then what about my career in the Force?" she asked plaintively.

"I'll see what I can do, my dear. That is my best offer," Milner now said stiffly. "Subject to a full, fair and impartial disciplinary investigation."

There was silence. Sam realised Jenny had few choices available to her. Her best and only option was to place her trust in the people in front of her. Sam saw her head nod in acceptance.

"What next?" asked Sam. He realised there had been precious little detail given.

"Never you mind," said McClintock patronisingly. "Let's just say that I think you will approve when you hear the details." Sam saw the four men share knowing glances. Jesus, a conspiracy within a conspiracy, he thought. He saw McClintock staring at him with an evil grin.

32

The house had been carefully chosen. Sam understood their reasoning. The building sat alone in a small bay on the coast of Sai Kung. No other buildings were visible in any direction. It seemed amazing to find something so remote in a city so densely populated. He still found it difficult to believe that over 80% of the colony's land mass was designated as Country Park.

It was a village-style house, two stories plus a flat roof, whitewashed to help cope with the heat. The New Territories had thousands of similar buildings. Archaic planning laws and inherited rights preceding the arrival of the British had created a paradise for a lucky few. They avoided life in a multi-storey box in one of the many new towns that had sprung up as the population boomed.

The house was probably thirty years old. It was in reasonable condition structurally, but it felt unloved. It needed a good clean, a lick of paint inside and out and air-conditioning. The only cooling was provided by squeaking ceiling fans in each of the rooms. They were covered in ancient spiders' webs decorated with the desiccated husks of long deceased insects.

The kitchen was basic. A large canister stored beneath the brick-built counter fed two gas stoves. A barely functioning refrigerator rattled noisily as it battled the fierce daytime heat. The ground floor bathroom was equally spartan. To Sam the squat-style toilet looked awkward and uncomfortable. He reminded himself to take extra care with his keys and revolver around its gaping mouth.

Bare bulbs clinging to rusted ceiling sockets provided a basic level of illumination. The pitiful lighting only helped to accentuate the mould and dirt. An old wooden table dominated the main ground floor room. It was surrounded by an unruly crowd of rickety rattan and wooden folding chairs.

Sam felt underwhelmed by the safe house. He reminded himself of their reason for being there. He made a note to keep his negative thoughts to himself.

He took Jenny by the hand and led her upstairs to view their sleeping arrangements. Each of the three large bedrooms contained an iron-framed double bed. The mattresses were stained and mouldy. They flipped them over to check both sides. Amidst clouds of dust, they selected the least unpleasant option.

Satisfied with their decision, they followed another dusty staircase up to the rooftop. The heavy wooden door leading onto the roof terrace protested loudly as Sam levered it open with his shoulder.

The view was stunning. It was an idyllic green and blue vista of open sea and islands. Below they saw a narrow path down to a small beach. To their right lay the overgrown track along which they had walked earlier.

The house lay within a small bowl, surrounded on three sides by low hills. He knew the thick vegetation contained all manner of animal life. Though tigers were a distant memory, other terrors remained. The bushes concealed huge centipedes and a multitude of venomous snakes. Aggressive wild boar the size of small cows were common. They were the reason the police had its own pig hunting team.

Mess lore had it that many a British squaddie on exercise in the hills had come to grief on local fauna. The story described a vicious bite from some creature sharing their trench, often to their most sensitive body part during the middle of the night. After observing some of Hong Kong's vibrant insect life for himself, Sam was a true believer. Following an unpleasant incident with a cockroach, he had started checking his shoes every time he put them on.

"Let's get stuck in," said Jenny cheerfully. "If we are going to be here for a few days we might as well make ourselves at home." She smiled and raised her eyebrows. Sam liked the insinuation.

The telephone rang just as they reached the ground floor. Its harsh tones gave them both a start. Sam was the closest to the cradle on the wall. He allowed the telephone to ring five times as agreed.

"Rupert Smith. How can I help you?" he asked, using the name he had been given earlier.

"Are you all settled in?" McClintock asked.

"We've just arrived, sir," Sam replied. "Everything looks fine. It's grim but we are aiming to be shipshape in a couple of hours." Sam was surveying the filthy floor as he said it. He decided his estimate was on the generous side.

"It's not meant to be a bloody palace. Man up," McClintock replied viciously.

Sam pulled a face. He had given McClintock an opening and he regretted it.

"Yes, sir. We've got everything we need. We've tested the radios and got a weak signal on the Sai Kung channel. We will be fine, so long as the rest of it goes to plan," he said gloomily.

"Don't you worry about that, laddie," McClintock continued, less harshly this time. "The crumbs are only just being laid. You will be safe enough for the time being and you have this line to the Ops Room if you need anything. Remember, the radios are for emergencies only so stay off air unless the shite hits the fan. Save the batteries. Capiche?"

McClintock's use of his favourite term brought a smile to Sam's face. He consoled himself with the thought that the gruff Scotsman had looked after them well enough so far. He had probably earned a degree of trust.

"How's the wee lassie?" McClintock asked. Sam looked over at Jenny. She was standing by the window and watching him closely. Her arms were crossed defensively.

"She's fine, thank you, sir." The smile they shared belied their nerves.

"Look after that one," McClintock said unexpectedly. "She's a good girl and probably a keeper. Good luck." He abruptly ended the call.

"Yes sir!" Sam responded loudly, mimicking a parade ground response as he heard the line go dead.

"You know that old bugger might have a real heart in there after all."

"Really?" Jenny didn't sound convinced by Sam's theorem. "Let's get to it. Time to unpack. How about I start down here and you do upstairs?" she suggested.

"Yes, madam." Sam threw a salute and she responded with a sour expression.

They started by emptying the contents of their two large khaki rucksacks on to the table. The plan had called for them to bring everything they needed for a five day stay. The pile of tinned food and pans reminded him of a camping expedition in Wales when he was in the Scouts.

They had expected the house to be dirty and came prepared with an array of household necessities and cleaning materials. Spare clothes and bedding were the bulkiest items. A mosquito net was thrown in as an afterthought. For entertainment they had a book each, and a small battery-powered tape recorder.

Sam insisted on bringing two powerful twelve-inch Maglite torches. They could double as clubs if required. A pair of small binoculars and a map of the local area completed their equipment.

They were both sweating heavily following the forty-minute walk from the drop off point. The weather had not helped. It was a hot and sunny day. The humidity did the damage. Their clothes had clung to them relentlessly from the moment they started hiking along the airless track.

"Time for something cooler," Jenny declared as she changed. Sam followed her lead by stripping down to shorts, tee-shirt and flip flops.

They started by opening the windows to let fresh air in, and dust out. After checking the water and gas, they set to work with two old mops. Progress was more rapid than he had expected. Within an hour everything had been tidied away. The house was looking habitable. The revolver, radios, torches, and binoculars were left on the table, ready for immediate use.

"Time for dinner?" Jenny asked as the last rays of that day's sun dipped behind the ridge to the west.

"Noodles, noodles or noodles?" he enquired as she made a start on their first dinner on the run.

An hour later they had finished their meal of spam, eggs and noodles and had retired to the roof with a folding chair each. They had time to kill and they were chatting in the warm night air. To Sam it felt strangely romantic. With the operation yet to swing into action, they knew the risks were minimal. They could relax and enjoy their new surroundings.

They were taking no chances with the insects. Two dark green mosquito coils burned slowly at their feet. Sam was getting used to the pungent smoke. It seemed easier to take when not in the confines of a room.

The dangers of their current situation were never far from his mind. Their conversation kept coming back to it, however hard either of them tried to focus on other topics. Sam was using a third chair as a side table. He kept glancing at the revolver sat on it. Its presence was reassuring. In his heart he knew that a single weapon would not be enough to save them if the worst were to happen.

The night was dark. Thick cloud cover prevented a view of the stars. From their vantage point they could see miles out to sea. The lights of passing ships and outlying Chinese islands were almost indistinguishable at distance. The tranquillity of the spot was striking. As they sat in silence, Sam thought how wonderful it would be to live in a house like this with a secluded beach and amazing views.

"We've got to enjoy it while we can," Jenny said, as though reading his thoughts. "Fancy a dip?" she asked. She turned to face him. She cocked her head whilst pouting ever so slightly, like a pet begging for a treat.

"At this time of night?" he asked, feigning outrage. He was trying to mask his desire to take up the indecent offer. Images from the romantic beach scene in From Here To Eternity entered his mind unbidden.

"You're not chicken are you? Or a shy little boy?" she taunted. She grabbed both of his hands and stared intently into his brown eyes.

"Just you wait. Let me get my torch and my mosquito repellent." Failing to plan was planning to fail he recalled.

The walk to the beach was no more than two hundred yards. The old path was well made and easy to navigate, even in the dark. Stone steps marked the steeper sections.

They walked hand in hand. Sam carried his small rucksack containing their towels and his revolver. Jenny used a torch to light the way. They left the house unlocked, confident that their belongings would be safe in such a remote location.

Sam found a large rock protruding from the sand and used it as a shelf. Jenny stripped off all her clothes and encouraged Sam to do the same. She led him naked into the warm waters lapping gently against the shore.

"Comfortable yet little boy?" Jenny asked. The dark water was up to their waists. She held him tightly.

"Yes, thank you, madam," Sam whispered. He laughed and suddenly grabbed her. They toppled and crashed under the waves. Salt water and sand filled his mouth. What a life, he thought as he came up for air, then Jenny, giggling with pleasure, tried to push him under the waves again.

33

Roger Milner was sitting uncomfortably in his office. The sweat gathering under his armpits was staining his khaki uniform. He knew it wasn't just the heat. He was staring at the television in the corner of the room. The volume was turned down. The words were unimportant.

"Bloody parasites," he muttered to himself. The press were excited. They had found something newsworthy to chase in time for the evening news. It didn't happen every day.

Commissioner of Police Peter Baldwin raised a patrician eyebrow. He said nothing.

The sensational story had broken earlier that afternoon. It was at around the same time Sam and Jenny had been dropped off for the walk to their temporary abode. It was the type of piece that journalists love. Corruption and abuse of power were the headlines. Lust, greed and violence the ingredients. Mayhem, fear and death the outcomes.

It had the legs to run for days. Best of all it correlated with recent developments. Newsworthy stories that the public were already tracking. It was a story rooted in fact, backed by police statements, and supported by ample photographic and videotape evidence.

It was the ATV news department that got the scoop. They had edged out their bitter rivals at TVB and beaten their newspaper colleagues for the first time in living memory. Though the source had been anonymous, that did not detract from its value. The news hounds quickly established its veracity. Sources both official and unofficial corroborated it. The evening news editor excitedly despatched investigative reporters and camera crews to the key locations.

An unremarkable block of apartments in Mei Foo Sun Chuen was first. It was followed by the main gate at the Police Training School. Then Police Headquarters and Tsim Sha Tsui police station. The report was accompanied by footage from several days earlier. It showed graphic scenes from the grenade attack in Sham Shui Po. Images of a body covered with a sheet after the armed raid in Tsim Sha Tsui. They were interspersed with images of a *daai fei* burning in the harbour. Photographs of a pretty young lady dressed in police uniform flashed onto the screen.

"Surely Roger, I do not have to remind you of the importance of a free press?" Baldwin asked.

"They have their uses. Sometimes," Milner conceded grumpily. He was privately enjoying the pastiche of clips that had been put together in haste. He was less comfortable at the thought of having to drive past the phalanx of reporters and cameramen when he returned home. He was certain that his photograph would appear in at least one or two Chinese newspapers in the morning. It would not be the first time.

"Let's just hope all this doesn't come back to bite us on the arse," Baldwin warned.

Milner's irritation with his leader was growing. His habit of stating the bleeding obvious was wearing thin. It was blindingly clear neither of them would be able to distance themselves if the shit hit the fan. They both knew complex operations had a nasty habit of blowing up. This one was particularly risky.

He was starting to regret his earlier enthusiasm for the project. Letting Smithies talk him into it might have been a mistake. He worried he was getting soft. He would never have agreed to something like this when he was still working in Africa. Week-long horseback patrols in the bush were a distant memory. It was a simpler life back then, before people worried about human rights and all that rubbish, he thought bitterly.

"All we can do now is wish them luck," said Milner. He could feel the weight of responsibility bearing down on him.

"Yes", agreed Baldwin. "Them and us."

"Strike one," Smithies declared happily. He was watching the same television programme in the comfort of his own home. He had changed the channel after putting down the phone. The message had been gratifying. The first piece of bait had been successfully taken. He was watching the evidence in front of him on the evening news. A wave of relief was washing over him. He smiled at the thought of what was to come.

It had taken some time to develop Operation Breadcrumb, as he liked to think of it. It had started with an anonymous tip. It had developed into a highly choreographed series of actions and scripts. The trap had to be set carefully, otherwise the various clues and hints could be missed. Lay it on too thick and they might get suspicious.

Identifying Silas's associates within the Force had been surprisingly straightforward. ICAC intelligence files helped. Investigations of Silas's activities and analysis of pager messages and landline records did the rest. The activity had garnered dozens of names. Cross-referencing sources had whittled the list down to seven. Those closest to Silas and likely still to be in contact. Some senior, most junior.

Activity on Silas's pager account had declined since he disappeared. They suspected he might have another account under a false name. Identifying the account was a priority. ICAC seemed confident it would be revealed quickly.

Smithies was feeling smug. The operation was the most creative he had ever put together. The key decision was putting which crumbs in front of what nose. There was no clear science to it. It was all too easy to get it wrong. The whole operation could yet fall apart.

Their approach was logical and sequential. Each crumb should elicit a clear response. If the morsel was not taken, they would move on to their next target. Each time they would use a different crumb. The source of activity could be easily tracked.

Their first target had been self-selecting. Pager analysis revealed he had maintained contact with Silas after his disappearance. His actions appeared naïve rather than criminal. Most likely it was blind loyalty. Indiscrete and sycophantic, he seemed a perfect choice.

He was an experienced detective sergeant based in Mong Kok. He had been associated with Silas for over 20 years, ever since their stint together as CID newbies. They were known to have kept in touch through regular dinners and trips to night clubs. Checks of travel records disclosed excursions to Macau and Guangdong together.

Smithies's weapon of choice was gossip. Juicy stories were highly prized within the Force. Every station and team had individuals proficient in the art. They were especially prized at promotion time. The speed and reach of the grapevine was legendary. The ability to use gossip as a conduit was a not-so-secret weapon.

A known purveyor of high quality tittle-tattle was found. He was well known to the intended recipient. He could be trusted not to ask too many questions. Smithies was amused by reports of the conversation. He had enjoyed developing the script.

"Have you heard that bitch Jenny has done a runner?" The question seemed to have been posed innocently during a supposedly chance encounter in the station canteen.

"Never? Where was she?" asked the sergeant.

The informant had moved his face closer. He looked around the station canteen furtively. He ensured no one could hear their words. Exactly as they planned.

"I've heard from a good source in Crime Wing. She was under CIB protection but did a bunk. The CIB boys and the big bosses are furious."

"*Diu lei lo mo*, fuck your mother, no fucking way!" the sergeant growled. Astonishment had been etched on his face.

"It gets better," the informant went on. He had deliberately built up the level of expectation with a pregnant pause. "I've heard that her *gweilo* boyfriend got her out after smacking one of the CIB lads. They are both fucked now. Can you believe that?" he asked. "What a fucking carry on. Just imagine if the newspapers got hold of that."

What a story. What a performance. What a start to Operation Breadcrumb. Smithies smiled. Sometimes it was just too easy.

"You are really odd sometimes you know," Mrs Smithies said angrily. Despite twenty years living in Hong Kong, her proficiency in Cantonese had never progressed beyond taxi-level. She had been contentedly watching one of the two English language channels. Smithies had rudely changed the channel without so much as a word of explanation.

Smithies rarely talked shop with his wife. He was not about to start now. The operation was highly confidential.

"What was that about anyway?" she asked.

"Nothing to worry about, my dear" he replied. "Unfortunately, it will mean I need to get back to the office. I'll see you in the morning," he promised. He walked briskly out of the lounge before she could protest.

"But you've only just come home!" she screeched. The high pitched sound frightened the overweight poodle at her feet. It jumped to its feet nervously.

Smithies grabbed his jacket and made for the door. The complaint was repeated, louder this time. He didn't respond. For once he sympathised with her complaint about his regular absences and irregular hours.

He knew himself too well. It was not in his nature to sit at home twiddling his thumbs with an operation underway. Far better, he thought, to return to PHQ and monitor developments from PolMil. He would feel happier sleeping on the office couch. Home was too far away from the action.

If it came to the worst, he could always pop into the mess for a quick one. The Force was full of *gweilo* drunks. They came in useful at times.

His mind returned to the operation, there were so many imponderables. The plan seemed workable. The cover story about the CIB witness protection team would likely hold. He had been surprised at the willingness of one of the team to volunteer for a punch in the face. He had been parading his black eye around PHQ all day. It was a superb performance.

Faking an injury, hamming up incompetence and simulating operational failure were not typically included in the CIB job description. They were handpicked. They knew the stakes they were playing for. If anyone could be trusted to maintain operational security, it was them. If they pulled it off, the deception could easily be unwound. He would be nominating them for Oscars at this rate.

Leaving SDU out had been a tough call. More pressing operational needs took priority. Another Mainland gang was on the loose. SDU would be required if their safe house could be located. They could not afford to be tied up on a stakeout for days on end. That's why he'd been forced to call in a favour elsewhere.

Smithies unlocked his Mercedes. He looked at his face in the rear view mirror and reflected on his journey. On nights like this, part of him envied the *gweilo yat laps* on the frontline. He wished he was 21 all over again. He started the car and commenced the familiar trek to PHQ through the evening traffic.

34

The briefing was short and to the point. Military etiquette required it. Everyone in the room already knew their role. If nothing else, it was an opportunity to eyeball the other units.

The briefing room was large and well-equipped. It was packed with rows of wooden folding chairs. The room sat at the heart of HMS Tamar which was the Royal Navy's base on the Admiralty waterfront The dockyard had held that position for over 140 years, interrupted only by the savage Japanese wartime occupation.

The 22-storey building was distinctive. Local wags likened it to an upturned gin bottle. A narrow stem-like base widened as the building climbed. It was painted white. Reflections from the polluted water in the dock basin bounced off the windows in waves. It glittered in the June sun like a mirror ball in a Mong Kok dance hall.

The walls of the room were festooned with charts and instructions. The maps were of Hong Kong, southern China, the wider region, and the world. Photographs of ships, aircraft, tanks, and vehicles were prominent. They were mainly Chinese, with some Russian.

These days, the room was rarely used. It most often saw briefings for crews of visiting US Navy vessels. The

Royal Navy was but a token force, their best days were behind them.

The operation was to be a naval affair supported by the Royal Air Force. The Army's sole representative was the Governor's Aide de Camp. Unlike the others, he had dressed in plainclothes for convenience.

With one exception, attendees were male. The bulk were Royal Marines. They were joined by a sprinkling of naval officers and an RAF liaison officer. The lone female was an attractive Navy legal officer. If she resented the constant sideways looks she was receiving, she did not show it.

The Royal Marines looked suntanned, fit, and serious. They sat in two rows at the front, directly facing the briefing officer. He was describing the ground they were to operate on using a large map. He waved his rapier-like wooden pointer energetically.

The Marines were taking notes. It was more out of politeness than need. It was important to pay the briefing officer due respect. Even when you had already heard it several times and knew it all backwards.

The officer was wrapping up the briefing. He was a brute of a man, 6' 5" tall, with shoulders more usually seen on a rugby pitch. His face was craggy and weathered. The colours of his Tom Selleck-style moustache matched his unruly straw-coloured hair. His blue eyes danced around the room. Hawk-like, his attention focused on the faces in front of him. He checked for compliance or confusion.

Like the other Marines, he wore standard military DPM camouflaged battle dress. A black fabric belt and heavy leather boots completed the outfit. No weapons were on display, they would come later. The group gave off menace nonetheless. The atmosphere was tense, like a changing room before a cup final.

The briefing had followed the standard template. The appropriate headings had been covered. It had been delivered clearly and precisely, and in the correct sequence. His orders could not be misinterpreted.

"Special instructions," he announced. He glanced over at the legal officer. Their eyes met briefly. The tension in the room had risen.

"In view of the unique circumstances, the Governor has granted authority to use lethal force to apprehend the targets. No warnings are required if suspects with firearms are identified."

He was moving his eyes along the two rows and looking at each man in turn

"Let me repeat that," he said seriously. "No warnings are required if firearms are seen. Any questions?" he concluded loudly.

Protocol meant that questions were always to be invited. It was less common for questions to be asked. Asking questions was not good form.

A few of the Marines shared wistful glances. They seemed excited by the coming operation. They were already putting away their pens. They were ready to be dismissed.

"A question over here if you don't mind, old boy," came the plummy voice. Heads turned to look at the cause of the interruption. It was the RAF representative. He was an overweight Flight Lieutenant in his forties with a huge handlebar moustache. He wore a faded green flying suit. It was tight-fitting and streaked with sweat marks and food stains.

"Go ahead," said the briefing officer.

"Can we return to the weather forecast, please?" he asked politely. "I'm not sure I agree with the picture that's been painted. That might cause us some problems."

The other heads had turned towards him. His face had turned puce. The effort of raising his head over the parapet was showing.

"I'm not sure that I'm following you," the briefing officer replied.

"My concern is if we overrun," said the airman. "This operation is based on a 72-hour window. What if the opposition don't play ball? What happens if it needs to be extended?" he asked.

"If you recall," the Marine replied patiently, "the operation includes a contingency for replacement or re-supply of the team on the ground." He had said it calmly. His irritation was visible.

"Super," came the sarcastic response. "Good luck with that. Just be aware that neither your fast boats nor my helicopters will be any good in a bloody typhoon." He was standing now and pointing an accusatory finger. He had crossed a line. His victim's face was showing anger. The briefing officer looked ready to explode.

"What typhoon?" he asked aggressively.

"The typhoon that just changed course over the Philippines and is barrelling towards us at a rate of knots. That typhoon."

The officer shook his head in dismay. He stared back angrily at his accuser. There was no meteorologist present to rebut the accusation. It was time to move on.

"Dismissed," he ordered.

Their kit checked and double-checked, the team boarded the ship. They were silhouetted against the bright dock side lights. Their faces were blackened with camouflage cream, ready for the journey. Ready for action.

Heavy packs were slung over shoulders. Long 7.62mm SLR automatic rifles were held tightly. A fearsome weapon with a vicious bite, it was rumoured to penetrate brick walls even at distance.

The first leg of the deployment would be on one of the Royal Navy's patrol ships. At least one of the three Peacock class patrol vessels was usually at sea. Patrolling the maritime boundary and flying the flag was vital. They were as regular as a train timetable.

Operational security was paramount. Prying eyes was a concern. Even at night, the congested waters of the inner harbour were busy with vessels of all sizes. They were taking no chances.

The sea was calm. The winds were light. The journey to the east would take just ninety minutes. The voyage was unhurried. A casual observer would have seen nothing unusual.

Their route took them past Star Ferry, beyond the bright neon lights and advertising boards of Wan Chai and Causeway Bay. On the port side lay Kai Tak Airport. Its notoriously difficult runway jutted into the bay outrageously. The approach was famously demanding. Every landing was a recipe for disaster. The spectacle of planes diving down over the rooftops of Kowloon City every few minutes was a tourist attraction in its own right.

Beyond lay whale-like oil tankers and freighters. They rested quietly, dozing under a carpet of work lights. They dwarfed HMS Plover. At just 700 tons, she was a minnow. The behemoths were one hundred times her size.

The vessel was well-lit, hiding in plain sight was the intention. They cruised slowly, their 76mm gun pointed menacingly to the fore. Beyond the inner harbour, they passed under the ghostly shadow of Sai Wan Hill battery. It was a faded echo of more turbulent times.

Safely beyond the harbour confines, they picked up speed. The deck throbbed. The two screws at the rear generated a mesmerising white wake. A refreshing breeze blew over the ship's decks.

Their course took them to the south-west, towards the cleaner, deeper open sea. Ahead lay Tung Lung Chau Island, they skirted the south side. Their destination was a secluded bay. They were clear of other maritime traffic.

As they rounded the southernmost tip of the island, navigation lights dimmed. They were almost invisible in the dark summer night. The two fast patrol craft of the Marines Raiding Squadron were waiting. The Marines heard them before they saw them. They approached slowly, one each side. They deftly rafted up against rough scrambling nets. The stench of outboard engines filled the night air.

One by one, the Marines lowered their heavy packs into the boats waiting below. Weapons slung securely over their shoulders, they clambered down the heavy netting.

The dark narrow bay appeared as a gash in the sombre coast. Reconnaissance had revealed that the white sandy beach sloped gently. Occasional rocks dotted the shoreline. Dense vegetation beyond concealed steep slopes.

Confident of the terrain, the two craft approached the empty beach at high speed. It was the Marine way. They leapt into knee deep water. It was a short sprint to the trees.

Within seconds of grounding, the boats reversed engines. They disappeared back into the dark night as quickly as they arrived. The roar of powerful engines receded into the distance. Only feint luminescent lines marked their passing. The first phase was complete.

The leader knelt in the damp sand. He was on one knee, map in hand. He carefully scanned the features around him. He was satisfied they were on target. A twisting trail led to the ridge. A small gap in the trees marked its path.

The beach was peaceful. Cicadas noisily serenaded their neighbours in the trees above. The relentless racket drowned out the waves gently lapping on the shore.

The leader signalled the party to move off. Pair by pair, as they had been briefed. It was a good start. He wondered what the next few days might bring. He hoped they would finally get the opportunity to do the things they had trained so comprehensively to do. Live operations were few and far between. He intended to grasp this opportunity with both hands.

The Marines deployed into their positions. They knew what was required. No words of command were necessary. They moved without risk of ambush. This was not a Lympstone training scenario. There were no enemy hiding in the bushes. It would save hours creeping into position. Speed was more important than stealth.

It was 2 a.m. when they passed the house. It was dark and creepily quiet. The knowledge that it was occupied gave them a strange sensation of being watched.

Establishing observation posts in the dark was an uncertain business. The commander knew dawn might require some adjustment. It was a trade-off. Daylight brought unacceptable risks of discovery.

The plan was simple. The deployment catered for the scenarios they had discussed. There were only two routes in and out, to the beach or to the road. Access through the thick bush was unlikely.

The forest was both friend and foe. Dense foliage provided concealment. Impenetrable undergrowth trapped heat and humidity. Insect life was voracious. Mosquitoes homed in on any piece of exposed skin. Repellent seemed useless. Poisonous snakes were a concern. The Marines cleared away leaf litter to minimise unpleasant surprises.

The commander checked the glowing hands of his watch. It was 3 a.m. The radio operator checked in with the six observation teams. They were in position. The operator updated the Ops Room at Tamar through his bulky Clansman radio set.

It was a matter of watching and waiting. The team leader swiped an irritating mosquito away from his face. Making himself comfortable was proving difficult. He knew it was going to be unpleasant. Three days of lousy food and crapping in a plastic bag. They were living the dream. *Per mare, per terram.*

35

Sub-Unit Four's routine had been largely unaffected, even with the strange events of recent days. As an organisational model it was robust. The whole was greater than the sum of its parts. It verged on indestructible.

Briefings and debriefs took place with clockwork regularity. Officers went about their daily business quietly and efficiently. In operational terms, Jenny and Sam were not missed.

To lose one Sub-Unit Commander in unusual circumstances was unexpected. To lose both was unprecedented. With only media reports to rely on, wild rumours circulated. As time passed, stories became ever more lurid and exaggerated. Only one man knew the truth. He was saying nothing.

Station Sergeant Cheung had stepped into the breach. He was making the most of his moment in the sun. He was in his element. He was the older, more experienced, more senior man. Without consultation, he took on all the trappings of the Sub-Unit Commander role.

Power was centralised. He unilaterally decided that all decisions about leave, duties and administration should go through him alone. Liu was left to act as his unloved assistant. He was shut out of meaningful decisions.

Cheung became ever present in the station. He rotated between office, canteen and the NCOs mess. Liu stayed out of his way. He spent his time on patrol. The other NCOs were nonplussed. They were uncomfortable with the swift and unseemly power grab. The acquiescence of the usually confident Liu came as a surprise.

They wondered if he was just biding his time. Taking on Cheung head-to-head was not for the fainthearted. They understood it would only be temporary. If Jenny or Sam did not return, another inspector would be appointed. Tsim Sha Tsui was a key location. A station sergeant as commander would just not do in the long term.

Ricky Ricardo was aware of the situation. He seemed content to let things ride. He had bigger fish to fry than an NCO power struggle. He was under strict orders.

"Any questions?" McClintock asked when Liu came to his office for instructions.

Liu shook his head. "No, thank you, sir. I've got it."

He was wearing plainclothes. The sub-unit had just finished A shift. The pace of activity on the corridor was slowing as the nine to five crowd steeled themselves for the commute home.

"Good lad," the DVC said. "Keep me in the loop."

McClintock opened a desk drawer. He passed Liu a small envelope. Liu placed it inside the large manilla folder that he had brought with him as cover. It was empty.

After Liu had left, McClintock made the call.

"It's done," he reported. Nothing else was said. He placed the telephone back in its cradle.

McClintock sat back contentedly. He stared blankly at a spot on the wall above the doorway. All they could do now was wait. Fishing required patience. Smithies had been reluctant to involve Liu. It had needed all of

McClintock's charm to convince him. It was the only way. If they had a snake in the grass, it needed to be smoked out. Liu was ideal.

Smithies was being true to his word. He had kept McClintock informed throughout. By right, there was no need for him to do so. It was a favour to an old friend. It made perfect sense when the two inspectors were under his command. McClintock had insisted on remaining involved as their primary contact. He owed them that at least.

He was pleased the relationship with Smithies was still strong. He had wondered if he might have gone too far with him on the night of the robbery. He was fortunate Smithies knew him well. They had come a long way in the decade and a half since they first met. McClintock knew he was lucky that Smithies was his first DVC. Just as lucky as Sam was to have him. The thought made him chuckle.

His mind went back to Liu. He wouldn't be with them for long. A smart boy, they were fortunate to have him. He was running rings around Cheung. Such a loudmouth. If Cheung thought he was winning at chequers, Liu was playing chess. He was in a different league. Cheung's arrogance and stubbornness would cause his downfall. He was like an overweight Icarus flying too close to the sun. It was only a matter of time before he fell to earth. They both knew it. Cheung was oblivious.

The idea for the second round of breadcrumbs came during one of their regular discussions. Smithies had explained the problem and McClintock's native cunning came up with the solution. The challenge was to get information about Jenny's location to Silas in a credible and timely fashion. It involved much head scratching before they agreed a plan.

They had been lucky first time around. Role play was risky. Anything could go wrong. They needed a silver bullet. A simple method that could pass muster without flagging up suspicion.

Designing the solution required creative thinking. It had come as a surprise when Smithies suggested using his contacts from the Masonic Lodge. McClintock knew he was a regular at Zetland Hall. Many senior officers were. Not all of their reasons for joining met McClintock's approval but Smithies justifications had always been clear. He used it to expand his social circle. It was an excuse to get out of the house and away from his wife. It allowed him to rub shoulders with interesting people. It also provided useful contacts and access to the upper echelons of Hong Kong's expat society.

It had taken a single phone call from Smithies to a senior contact at HSBC. He immediately agreed to the unusual request. It was a favour. Any bank could have fabricated something similar. Jenny banking with HSBC made it all the easier. It took a programmer less than half an hour to draft the documents and make changes to her account. The account had been locked as a precaution.

McClintock had done the rest. A retired friend worked as a Post Office security manager. He had arranged for the envelope to be franked. McClintock had borrowed a blue pencil from the General Registry. He struck through the address typed on the envelope before roughly scribbling 'PSU 4 TSTDIV' across the front in bold letters. The scene was set. All that remained was for McClintock to brief his willing accomplice and hand over the bait. Delivery had to be precise, like a fly fisherman dropping a feathered lure on the nose of a hungry salmon.

The daily flow of correspondence around the station involved a heavily loaded wooden trolley. Its custodian was an overweight and bored-looking member of the Registry staff. He was a dishevelled simpleton in his mid-40s whom the Civil Service had taken pity on twenty years earlier. His role was solely collection and distribution of files. It was a stress-free nine to five existence.

McClintock worried what would happen to the letter once it arrived in the sub-unit office. Leaving it to chance was not a strategy. An Admin WPC might stash the document for Jenny's return. It needed someone to deposit it under Cheung's nose at the right moment. It needed Liu.

The return call from Smithies came late that afternoon. It was a relief.

"Game on," he announced. "ICAC monitored a call to Cheung earlier this morning. Cheung provided Silas with the Sai Kung address. We're moving to the next phase. Call your people first thing tomorrow. Good luck."

The call ended abruptly. He allowed himself a self-congratulatory smirk.

"That's my boy," he said.

36

The letter sat on the desk in front of him. Cheung read it over and over. He was sitting back in the wooden chair, fingers interlaced behind his head. It was the most exciting document he had ever seen. It had created an impact like a jolt from an electric shock. He immediately grasped the opportunities it presented.

Eileen had just walked out of the office. He was alone at last. He had read the newspaper from cover to cover three times whilst waiting for her to go. He had been intrigued by the official-looking envelope in front of him. Once alone it had taken him mere seconds to open it. He had unsealed it carefully. He used a letter knife opener to gently prise open the flap in case it needed to be made good.

He pulled out the contents gingerly. There were three documents within. He discovered a covering letter and two offer letters. He skim read the contents. Clever bitch, he thought to himself.

The covering letter was written on HSBC headed paper. It was dated three days earlier. It was addressed to Jenny. The address was c/o of Commissioner of Police, Police Headquarters, Arsenal Street, Hong Kong. He asked himself why. Why not address it to her home address at Mei Foo Sun Chuen?

He knew PHQ often received correspondence addressed to individual officers. Routing correspondence through PHQ was a common ruse for lenders chasing indebted cops.

He could think of no valid reason. The conclusion was obvious. She had planned this for some time. She must have known her time in the Mei Foo property was limited. Why else provide PHQ as a forwarding address?

Why not use the address given on the second document instead, Cheung wondered? The covering letter had carefully explained that the bank would be delighted to re-mortgage both of Jenny's properties. Separate mortgage quotations for the two properties were duly enclosed. Acceptance was required within thirty days. Legal documentation would follow.

The first quotation was for her Mei Foo property. It was described as a three-bedroom apartment of 1,400 square feet. Based on a valuation of HK$1.2m, the bank would be delighted to offer a 75% mortgage for a 25-year period at an interest rate of 6.25% per annum.

Reading it made him furious. The conniving bitch had refused to return the property to Chu-sir. Now she was seeking to profit by mortgaging the property to pocket HK$900,000 in cash. Chu-sir will be livid, he thought. That bitch will be toast.

Reading the second quotation assuaged his anger. He realised it offered a pathway to resolving Chu-sir's problem. The quotation was for a property with a Sai Kung address. It involved a two-storey village-style house of 2,200 square feet. Assuming a valuation of HK$800,000 the bank would be pleased to offer a 75% mortgage for a 25-year period at the same interest rate.

Something perplexed him. If she already owned both properties, why not provide the second address as her correspondence address? He knew Sai Kung, he had worked there previously. The address meant nothing to him. Was it a new development, he wondered? He re-read the quotation. It described the building as being brick built and 33 years old.

With a sudden movement, he snatched up the telephone. He aggressively punched in the number of an old colleague who lived in the area. Within sixty seconds he had his answer. Too remote, off the beaten track, no postal service. Jackpot.

He decided to find another telephone. The NCO's mess would do. He needed to be able to pass on the news without being overheard. He skipped up the flight of stairs to his destination. He was whistling tunelessly to himself. The letter was secreted in his tunic pocket for future reference. It was worth its weight in gold.

37

Silas Chu's safe house in Mong Kok was like so much of the Territory's older housing stock. It was crumbling, uncomfortable, and overdue demolition. The pre-war building sat on one of Mong Kok's quieter back streets. Despite its physical imperfections, it was ideal for Silas's purposes.

He had obtained the apartment years earlier for a peppercorn rent. He had several secure boltholes. They were intended for a time of need. This was the most secure of them all. It was known to only his closest confidantes. He was thankful for his foresight. He always kept his options open.

He had used it infrequently. He found it reassuring nonetheless. In hectic and stressful times, he enjoyed visiting alone. It was an oasis of calm within the city's most densely populated area. He felt safe, cocooned from the pressures and dangers of the outside world.

He ensured he kept up appearances. Anonymity was vital when he visited. He eschewed expensive clothing. Each visit he became a regular working-class man in a typical working-class area.

This time he was not alone. He was delighted to have company. He had Dragon at his side with reinforcements, three equally tough associates.

Silas had known Dragon and Luen Ko for years. They were like brothers. They had shared adventures and risks. They met during a regular visit to family in Guangdong. Dragon was a local triad leader operating under the front of a successful business. Luen Ko was his enforcer. The three of them were kindred spirits. Silas admired Dragon's strength. His name came from his unpitying attitude to those foolish enough to cross him. Luen Ko was hard as nails. Whilst Dragon ran the business, Luen Ko managed their underworld affairs.

During one visit, Dragon introduced Silas to his younger sister. Strengthening familial and business ties was as important as the love match. Like a French Princess betrothed to an English King, the arrangement was viewed through clear eyes. His reputation as a womaniser was overlooked. It was typical Chinese practicality. Marriage followed. Though they met infrequently, a generous allowance maintained domestic harmony. Silas's relationship with Dragon was unbreakable.

The shock resulting from the deaths of Luen Ko and so many of their associates was felt across Guangdong. The news caused dismay amongst the wider clan. They were appalled at Silas's betrayal by one of his coterie of female conquests. His name had been besmirched through treachery. If his position could not be recovered, revenge could be had. Honour must be restored.

The call to Dragon had been his first after the debacle of Tsim Sha Tsui. His previous life was over. All that was left was to salvage scraps from the ashes. It was time to settle old scores before moving on to a new life, wherever that might be.

It would be expensive. He needed cash. Quickly. Dragon was the solution. That part could wait. Those juicy targets were not going anywhere. The priority was sending a message to traitors everywhere. The priority was finding that bitch Jenny. Then she must die.

"Wow *daai-lo*," Dragon enthused. He slapped Silas firmly on the back. It was mid-morning. Dragon and his team had just returned from a night of whoring. The nearby fleshpots of Portland Steet were notorious.

Silas had been unhappy. Their plans to leave the apartment the previous night seemed an unnecessary risk. It took time before he was reconciled with the proposal.

Logic had won. He realised that the risks were manageable. He insisted they not carry firearms. If they were arrested as illegal immigrants, they would be first-time offenders. The worst they would face was a one-way trip back to the Mainland. They would be free to return to Hong Kong as soon they resolved any difficulties with the Public Security Bureau. All they would need was another boat.

They were taking big risks on his behalf. Restricting their pleasures was not a good way to launch the partnership. A happy team was a priority. It was an old lesson. It had served him well over the years.

He gave his blessing and the group had left after dark. He had stayed in the apartment alone. Thinking. Plotting. Hating.

Every message he received after his disappearance had given him succour. Most were from the criminal fraternity. A number were from old friends in the police.

With A-Siu gone, A-Ken stepped up as number two. He was busy elsewhere, tidying up their business affairs, collecting monies owed, and acquiring the fake documents they would need for their journey. Without a wife and family to worry about, A-Ken had willingly hitched his wagon to Silas. They were committed, like man and wife, for better or for worse.

The pager message from Cheung had come earlier, before the gang returned. It was the first time the station sergeant had been in touch since the night of the raid. Silas was grateful for Cheung's warning even if it had come too late for the others. He had heard from other sources that Cheung remained loyal. He arranged for his new contact details to be passed to him by an intermediary.

Silas recognised the number he was being asked to call. It was within Tsim Sha Tsui police station. It gave him pause for thought. Calling Cheung could be a trap. He doubted Cheung would be getting in touch without good reason. It was a calculated risk.

He took a pistol from the cupboard and concealed it in his waistband under a light jacket. He put an ear to the door. The corridor was silent. He cautiously padded down the steep staircase to ground level.

Silas glanced up and down the street. It was as busy as ever. He saw no olive-green uniforms and started to relax. He felt safe hiding behind dark sunglasses and a baseball cap. He walked the short distance to a Hong Kong Telephone Company pay phone. The booth offered clear views in either direction. He disliked surprises.

The call was answered after the first ring.

"Mess, Cheung," he said.

"Nice to hear a friendly voice," said Silas. "Do you have something for me?"

"I've got something you need." He spat the last word out.

The news from Cheung was sensational. Silas could barely concentrate on the rest of the conversation. He ended the call quickly. The walk to the apartment passed in a daze.

They were sitting alone. He had just told Dragon the story. The others were sleeping off the excesses of the night before. Dragon seemed impressed by the speed and efficiency of Silas's network. His previous investment in recruiting informers and men on the inside was paying off. He marvelled at the loyalty generated by lavishing attention and free dinners on the right people.

It was mid-afternoon when A-Ken arrived. He came laden with the items Silas had asked him to purchase. It was the first time they had seen each other since the Tsim Sha Tsui disaster. They embraced warmly, brothers-in-arms joined in an uneven fight. Silas made the introductions. The team settled down to make their plans.

Silas explained the background to his predicament. He held nothing back from the Mainlanders. The time for caution had passed. They had heard some of it before from Dragon. Other parts they had gleaned from newspapers. The Tsim Sha Tsui raid was big news, even on the Mainland.

He explained Jenny's role. The vitriol in his voice was raw. He was disappointed at his own lack of self-control. He removed his cap as the finale. He revealed the scars she had left him with. It elicited the desired response. He had shared the hatred. They embraced it as their own.

He reminded them of the terms of their business arrangement. The raids would be a 50/50 split. He was being generous. He was asking for little in return. Just their assistance in taking care of the girl.

He would provide high quality target intelligence, plus logistics support. Target details were a closely guarded secret, even from Dragon. The reason was completely practical, Silas told them. The suitability of targets changed day by day. Shipments of cash and valuables came and went. Police operations ebbed and flowed. The targets he had in mind went well beyond the usual fare of goldsmiths and jewellers. Information was still being received and assessed.

On Silas's instruction, A-Ken unrolled the 1:25,000 map of Hong Kong. He had purchased it earlier. He folded it carefully then taped it to the wall. It showed only the area encompassing eastern Kowloon and Sai Kung.

The men listened to him with serious expressions as Silas brought them up to date with recent developments. He described the escape of the girl and her *gweilo* boyfriend from protective custody, presumably to prevent her being arrested by ICAC. He had heard it from multiple sources. It must be true. He described Jenny's suspected hiding place. Their smiles reappeared. His 'highly reliable' source was unnamed. He marked the location with a pen. They studied the map eagerly. He highlighted key local features. The villages, paths, and roads. The nearest police station.

"How do we know she's there?" one of the gang asked. "All we have is an address." It was a reasonable question, Silas acknowledged.

"You are right. On paper it looks thin," he conceded. "I have a gut feeling she will be there. You have to trust me on this. I know that bitch. She is fucking smart. This feels right," he said emphatically.

"What if she isn't there?" another asked. "What then?"

"In that case, we wait for something else to turn up. If it doesn't, we carry on with the robberies. We can deal with her later. Right?" he asked. He looked from man to man.

"We're behind you, *daai-lo*," said Dragon. They nodded in unison. Silas started laying out their next steps.

"*Daai-lo*, should we do a recce first?" A-Ken asked. Silas had not expected A-Ken to speak up. He realised why he asked. It was not a question at all. He was staking a claim, establishing his authority as Silas's right-hand man in front of their new partners.

Silas went quiet. He calculated the pros and cons of the suggestion. A thorough recce was always good practice, he conceded. Understanding all the risks was important but the potential for delay concerned him.

According to Cheung, it was an easy target. There were no neighbours to complicate matters. The only difficulty was its remote location. But that was a bonus.

He knew the old Silas would have made an instant decision. Everything had changed since they had become wanted men.

"Thoughts anyone?" he asked. He was scanning the faces around him. No one spoke. Dragon took his opportunity.

"For me, the information is not detailed enough. We need to confirm that bitch is present and what the target looks like. Sorry if that's not what you wanted to hear. That's how I see it." Dragon was staring intently at Silas.

He was keen to placate their concerns. Dragon was right. They both were.

"A recce it is. Let's get over there tomorrow during the day. If it's suitable, we hit them at night."

The heads around the table nodded in acceptance. Silas looked at A-Ken and smiled.

"I have a cousin in Sai Kung who could put us up. Shall I sound him out?" A-Ken asked.

"Perfect. Assuming he will, that's the plan. Get yourselves ready, we leave at ten in the morning," he announced.

Silas slapped Dragon on the back and placed his right hand on his forearm. He squeezed gently.

"Thank you," he told him. He was feeling emotional. This was his family now. It was the start of a new life.

"But no more whores until this is over," he requested with a smile.

A-Ken had parked the vehicle carefully so they could approach it discreetly. Their transport was basic. It was one of dozens of commercial vehicles parked at the nearby Yau Ma Tei Fruit market. They elected to use two taxis for the short journey. They could not risk running into one of the ever-present police patrols. A-Ken directed one taxi, Silas the other. It took a few short minutes for them to reunite at the entrance. A fleet of lorries sat poised for that night's frenetic distribution activity. The smell of exotic produce filled the air.

The battered Datsun lorry had originally been white. After a decade of use it was discoloured and pockmarked with dents and scratches. Though it wore no signage, shadows of markings lingered in places. The small cab was strewn with delivery dockets. Documents of all types littered the foot well and dashboard. A filthy roller shutter at the rear provided access to the cargo compartment. Worn tyres completed the impression of an unloved beast that had seen better days.

A-Ken scanned the carpark. It was clear of security guards. He waved the group over. They each carried a small holdall. Two carried bigger bags. They looked around nervously. Taking the taxi was a good move. They stood out like turds on a dinner table.

He unlocked the corroded steel padlock securing the rear compartment. The scarred roller shutter clattered loudly as it sprang upwards. He helped them climb in. They settled themselves for the journey.

The interior smelled ripe. The floor was matted with dried and decaying fruit. They cleared away fragments of damaged boxes and packing materials with their feet. A blizzard of tiny black fruit flies took flight. They landed indiscriminately. On faces and hands. In eyes and mouths.

A-Ken closed and padlocked the shutter. He was unshaven and scruffy. His outfit was deliberate. His yellow vest, cut off denim shorts and white gym pumps was typical of the local army of commercial drivers. The cab was stifling. He wound down the window and lit a cigarette. The engine started first time. A cloud of oily black diesel smoke erupted to its rear. The lorry slowly moved off through the crowded carpark, gears grinding loudly as it went.

The Kowloon traffic was heavy, it was slow going. Once across Nathan Road, he headed north, to the highway. It cut west to east across the top of the Kowloon peninsula, a hectic procession of congestion and pollution. Jagged peaks neighbouring Lion Rock towered above. Over the city, jumbo jets turned ready for their dramatic descent into Kai Tak Airport. The eastern harbour lay beyond, a stretch of filthy water crammed with flat-bottomed lighters fussing around rust-marked freighters.

The highway was bustling with commercial vehicles and taxis. The traffic was relentless. The journey was taking him away from the densely populated public housing estates of Kowloon East. He saw green hills beyond.

They reached Clear Water Bay Road. Countryside replaced concrete. They passed a patchwork of thousands of cookie cutter village houses wedged into small villages.

The traffic thinned, they made good progress. He always enjoyed the drive to Sai Kung. His mind replayed some of the joyous weekends spent drinking in the seafood restaurants dotted around the small town centre. He lit another cigarette. The radio was playing an Anita Mui ballad. He turned it up and sang along. Anything to take his mind off the job in hand.

His efforts were in vain. He suddenly noticed his hands shaking. He wondered why he was on edge. A-Ken tried to force himself to relax. His mind kept returning to the things that Chu-sir had told them earlier. He shuddered at the thought of Silas's plans for retribution. He was starting to question the risks they were taking purely to slake Silas's thirst for revenge. For the first time he pitied Jenny.

A-Ken had not seen his cousin Billy for several years. He parked up outside the fisherman's house on the outskirts of Sai Kung town centre. It was just as he remembered it. The house was near to the sea front. It sat close to the bars and restaurants popular with expats and locals alike. It was almost within sight of the small whitewashed two storey police station. The station looked out of place. Barred windows and defensive cupolas gave it a menacing look unbefitting an easy-going fishing village.

Billy was fifteen years older than A-Ken. His wife had died several years earlier. A-Ken knew Billy was appreciative of visitors. He filled his days with fishing and drinking Tsing Tao beer with fisherman at the nearby *kai fong* association.

Billy's welcome was warm and effusive. He had heard about A-Ken's difficulties. He launched into a barrage of questions. A-Ken politely diverted him. He worried how hot it must be in the unventilated cargo compartment. They had a whispered discussion. Billy suggested that he reverse the vehicle into his yard. He could unload his cargo discretely.

A while later they were sitting in Billy's lounge. His passengers were wiping themselves down with damp towels. They were grateful for the cool breeze of electric fans which rattled loudly. Billy produced ice cold bottles of water. They drank greedily. It would take time for their body temperatures to return to normal. It had been a hellish journey.

"What next?" Billy asked after he had been introduced.

Silas left it to A-Ken to explain their problem. Billy's local knowledge was critical. Using his house as a staging post was ideal.

"It seems to me that you have two choices. If you want to see the house we can drive up there this afternoon and you can walk down for a look."

There was a pause. The group shared puzzled looks.

"And the second?" Silas asked.

"Why walk when we can take my boat?" Billy asked.

38

The boat was a modest affair, twelve feet of fibre glass and a small outboard motor. It was enough. It had helped feed and clothe Billy and his wife for over twenty years. He had imagined taking out his sons in it. Teaching them the tricks of the fishing trade, how to fish, and his secret spots. That was before he realised parenthood was not to be their destiny. Now he was alone. He wondered what the rest of his life would look like with no wife at his side. He would have no children to dote on him in his old age, like he had doted on his mother.

There were three of them. The others had stayed at the house. A-Ken was keeping an eye on things. The boat was bobbing gently on the waves. They were several hundred yards off the beach. Close enough to get the lay of the land. Far enough to be discreet.

They had passed several vessels on the journey out from Sai Kung's small harbour. Each time, Billy had given the sole occupant a friendly wave of recognition. Further out, bigger boats plied the once fertile waters. They were relentless. They ploughed backwards and forwards parallel to the shore, day and night. It was ever harder to eke a living out of such heavily fished seas.

The small cove appeared inviting. It was the perfect spot for a private picnic. There were steps up from the beach. A path led to the house. The building was clearly visible, even without their binoculars. The house seemed run down. It sat by itself in an open area, clear of the treeline. Billy had seen it a thousand times. He had never given it a second thought.

Silas and Dragon looked excited. He took Silas's binoculars to check for himself. They could see no people, yet it looked occupied. One of the first-floor windows was open. Items of clothing were drying on a line strung across the roof. There was little doubt.

Reconnaissance complete, Billy re-started the engine. He pointed the small boat west in the direction of its home port. He loved the feel of the warm breeze on his face. The sensation of the boat ploughing into the small waves was exhilarating. He lived for it. He glanced at the sky. He sensed a change in the weather.

Silas and Dragon said little. Only their facial expressions betrayed their satisfaction. They were holding on tightly. The boat was bumping and bouncing. Billy was enjoying their discomfort. City slickers out of their depth. They were making him feel uncomfortable.

Billy had been involved in run-ins with the law himself. It had never been a barrier between him and A-Ken. Neither was he dismayed by A-Ken's change of situation. He would willingly support his own flesh and blood, as his father would have wanted him to.

Billy thought of himself as a simple fisherman. He had spent forty years working with the most down to earth people he could imagine. He reckoned he was a decent judge of character. He made up his mind about people quickly. Too quickly, as his wife regularly used to tell him.

Straightforward was the way he liked his people, and his life. Fishing was a leveller. Each man was only as good as their boat, their kit and their knowledge. He embraced the self-reliance, the living off your wits. It sorted the men from the boys. No taking orders. No kowtowing. No BS.

He was ambivalent about the law. On occasion he had helped friends out to earn beer money. Nothing serious. Just landing a boatload of Mainlanders along the coast from time to time. This felt different. He wondered if he was in over his head.

After several hours with his cousin and his associates, Billy's in-built BS meter was giving off high readings. Billy had grown up with many of the local triad gang members. These were a different breed. He was struggling to warm to them.

A-Ken's attitude to Silas puzzled him. Subservience was at the heart of their relationship. It came through clear as day, though they tried to disguise it.

Billy felt sorry for the kid. In his mind he was still an awkward teenager. He had read newspaper articles about recent events with interest. He had imagined A-Ken's involvement as being peripheral at worst. Having seen their power dynamic at close quarters, he was beginning to wonder. Silas had got him into deep water. He was starting to reconsider his own involvement.

A-Ken had told Billy they needed help with resolving an awkward problem at a secluded house. It was triad business. The story didn't add up. He wondered what the real purpose was. He didn't need glimpses of pistols to know he was dealing with an unpleasant bunch of people. They had something serious planned. They looked like killers.

Did he still want to be part of it, he asked himself. Was it too late to bail out?

39

"Any updates?" Smithies asked. He was in the operations room. The cold from the building's air-conditioning was numbing. It gave the place the aura of a deep subterranean bunker.

The Assistant Commissioner was making conversation. He knew he would have already heard if there was news. The room was windowless. Strip lights reflected mercilessly off the shiny white boards adorning the walls. A bank of bulky television screens dominated one side of the room. Jumpy black and white images displayed key traffic junctions. One wall was covered with a large colour map of the colony and surrounding territorial waters.

It was 5.30 p.m. He was just finishing up for the day. His initial enthusiasm was wearing thin, he had crumbled. He had called his wife to tell her he would be home for dinner as usual. He might return to PHQ afterwards. The game was afoot, as his grandfather used to say. It paid to be vigilant.

The inspector looked up with puppy dog eyes and stood up as Smithies approached. He wore a thick military-style blue sweater with patches on the shoulders and elbows. It made the long hours under the frigid air-conditioning bearable.

The man looked eager for instructions. So far it had been a very dull special duty. That would teach him to volunteer. A vacant-looking communications officer in her fifties sat in the corner of the room. She was thumbing through a Chinese comic book. Half a dozen incumbents had rotated through Smithies's office in her time in post. Her body language told him she was unimpressed by the latest incumbent. She glanced at her monitor briefly and returned to her reading. Smithies decided not to make a fuss.

"All quiet, sir," the inspector reported. "The military are continuing hourly sitreps. They have nothing out of the ordinary to report. Our two subjects have been observed inside the house. No one else has been seen in the vicinity.

"According to the Observatory," he added, "Typhoon Dot is strengthening and changing direction. Hong Kong will likely be affected by the outer wind bands overnight."

That's a nuisance, thought Smithies. He started calculating the time before the territory felt the full impact of the storm. It would have consequences for their plan. They were already well into typhoon season. The timing was unhelpful.

"Roger," he replied. "Let's see what the situation is in the morning. Depending on what signal the Observatory raises, we can take it from there. I'm going home for a couple of hours. I'll be at my quarters if you need me."

He walked down the corridor to the lift lobby. It felt like a ghost town. The building had emptied out like a mass evacuation at 5.00 p.m. sharp.

The typhoon was unexpected. The consequences needed thinking through. Thousands had been killed by typhoons in the past. The danger was not only of high winds and rough seas. It was the sheer unpredictability of its path. A mile in either direction could be the margin between safety and disaster. It was a lottery ruled by location and wind direction.

The Observatory's decision to raise higher typhoon signals would depend on the typhoon's speed and track. The timing was critical if they wanted to close down the operation safely.

"Bugger," he said out loud in frustration as he stepped into the lift.

"We need to develop some contingencies," Smithies suggested the following morning. "This typhoon potentially changes everything."

He was in a conference room close to the Ops Room in PHQ. Half a dozen of them were gathered around the highly polished wooden table. He was accompanied by several other senior PHQ wallahs. A Royal Naval Lieutenant Commander sat resplendent in all-white naval rig at the far end.

The meeting had been hastily convened. The advisory number one signal had been raised by the Hong Kong Observatory at 0230 hours. That meant the entire territory was on standby. The number three signal was expected later. For reasons lost in the mists of time, the signals jumped from one to three to eight. A number eight signal shut the city down. You didn't want to think about signals nine or ten, because they meant storm force winds in excess of seventy miles per hour.

"Yes indeed," replied the naval officer. "This typhoon has caught us short. I'm afraid I bear bad news." He looked embarrassed.

"How so?" asked Smithies.

"Commander British Forces has personally directed routine operations to cease once the number eight signal is raised." He paused momentarily. "That means we will be withdrawing the Marines as soon as it looks likely."

"Bloody hell." Smithies was taken aback by the decision. At this early stage of the game, it was uncharacteristic defeatism. The rank of the decisionmaker made it non-negotiable. Arguing with a Major-General was unthinkable. Only the Commissioner himself might be able to get away with it.

"Look at it from our point of view," the naval officer said apologetically. "We have troops in exposed positions. If something goes wrong, there will be no way to support them. It's just not practical to continue."

"Right." Smithies sighed in surrender. "There is no point trying to argue the toss. In which case, when and how do we get our people out?" he asked the rest of the room.

"We need to monitor the predicted track of the typhoon," said his deputy. "Once it looks certain the number eight is going up, we can get them to walk out."

"Agreed," said another voice.

Smithies could feel the others looking at him. The situation didn't feel right. They were missing something. A bad night's sleep on his office couch after beers in the mess was not helping his analysis. He didn't like to be seen to prevaricate. Not with the military in the room. It needed a firm decision.

"Agreed. Thank you, gentlemen." He pushed his chair back irritably and turned away. The niceties of farewelling their military visitor were the last thing on his mind. He sensed him retreating quietly. He had got the message.

Smithies peered through the windows. He could see thick grey clouds gathering over the harbour. He could not conceal his disappointment. What a bloody shame, after all this effort. He consoled himself with the thought that at least typhoons kept criminals safely off the streets.

It was nearly lunchtime when the telephone rang. It was a pleasant break from the monotony of the day. Sam was already close to finishing his thick Tom Clancy book. The Yanks had pasted the Russkies again thanks to expensive toys and massive investment in modern weaponry. It all seemed too easy. Not like the real world where the radios never worked properly.

The thought of days spent playing patience did not fill him with joy. There were other things he could do to amuse himself that did not involve their bed. He had been meaning to update his diary for weeks. It was a job he kept putting off. Discovering the local bird life was another option. He had yet to see or hear the gwork-bird that had irritated them daily at Training School. He made a mental note that he still needed to check out its real name.

"How are things?" McClintock asked brusquely at the other end of the phone line. "Not too bored yet?"

The man could read minds.

"All good here, thank you, sir. It is getting a bit breezy though. Jenny tells me a typhoon is on the way. Is that going to be a problem?" Sam asked.

"Typhoons are unpredictable beasties, laddie. They can quickly change direction. The latest info we have is that the number three is likely to be raised later today. Possibly number eight overnight. If eight is raised, we'll get you to walk out. A car will pick you up at the road."

Sam was silent for a moment. It all seemed slack. Unprofessional. Something felt wrong.

"What about the military?" They had yet to hear or see any sign of the Marines. He could only assume their presence. "Will they be coming out with us?" he asked.

"The military are the reason you're leaving. They are withdrawing as soon as the number eight signal looks likely." The exasperation was evident in McClintock's voice.

"What do you mean?" Sam said sharply. "Surely it's being coordinated so we're not left without cover?"

He glanced towards Jenny. She was standing in the corner of the room. Her arms were crossed. She was chewing her lip.

"Leave it with me," said McClintock stiffly. "We'll sort something out." He put the phone down before Sam could argue.

"Bloody hell," said Sam. "I'm not sure that I like the sound of that." Jenny was staring out of the window. Her body language was unmistakeable. She was unimpressed. Sam could not blame her.

40

The gang had left moments earlier. Billy watched them drive off. He could not describe his sense of relief. He had heard what they were planning.

Silas had wanted to use the boat to approach the house. The weather had other ideas. Billy's refusal to countenance the idea was the clincher. With the weather turning, he warned that taking a small boat at night was a recipe for disaster. The number eight signal was expected overnight. It was simply impractical. Fishermen everywhere stayed in bed when the number eight went up. Billy refused to break the habit of a lifetime for anyone.

That left only one option, the lorry. The map indicated the hike from the road was no more than a mile and half. Silas figured maybe thirty minutes in each direction. Another fifteen minutes in the truck. It wasn't the end of the world.

Waiting for night to fall made sense. They could use the dark to cloak their approach. The roads would become quieter as the typhoon neared. After that they would be conspicuous. Only cops were dim enough to be out and about in a typhoon. Driving a flimsy high-sided vehicle in 70 mile per hour winds was dangerous. They could not leave it too late.

A-Ken would drive them to the drop off point. He would wait for them at Billy's house. He could collect them once they were finished.

Billy had listened as Silas briefed the team. Silas seemed nervous and excited. It was a strange combination. He saw them preparing weapons and equipment. Billy had helped by collecting dinner from a local restaurant.

His conscience had been pricking him. He had a sinking feeling. He knew exactly what his long dead wife would have thought. He could hear her criticism ringing in his ears. Calling him an accomplice to murder. Telling him to act like a man. She had intensely disliked his occasional illicit activities. It was her disapproval that convinced him to stick to fishing. After that he avoided night-time assignations with snakeheads and smugglers. Anything for a quiet life at home.

It was just before 6.30 p.m. when the gang set off in the lorry. Another thirty minutes and it would be dark. A-Ken was alone in the cab. Silas and the others sat uncomfortably in the rear. They gripped bottles of water tightly. Damp towels cooled their necks. The storm had ushered in lower temperatures. Relief was palpable.

Billy waved A-Ken off. It was a six mile round trip. He expected him back in half an hour once he had dropped his human cargo.

Their departure had been delayed by one of Billy's elderly neighbours. Mrs Lin was seeking his opinion on the impending typhoon. She had experienced several direct hits in her time. She knew the risks. The delay suited Billy perfectly.

Billy's chat with the diminutive and ever talkative Mrs Lin was unhurried. The conversation was conducted in Hakka, a dialect common among the fishing community. After several minutes he felt that he had done his duty.

He politely brought the discussion to a close and wished her well.

The small lorry turned the corner at the end of the street. Billy gave A-Ken a final wave. He stood motionless outside his house for sixty seconds. The wind had suddenly picked up. Gusts blew leaves and papers around his feet. The street was deserted. The dark was arriving early.

He glanced around nervously. He was looking for signs the house was under surveillance. He saw none. Billy walked slowly into his house and picked up the telephone. He called the number he had been given earlier.

"Cheuk-sir, six birds have just flown the nest," he reported. He returned the telephone to its receiver. He crossed his arms and stared at the picture on the wall. It was his favourite photograph of his late wife.

"As you always said, my dear, better later than never," he told her. He blew her a kiss for good measure. Let's hope the cops hold up their end of the bargain, he thought to himself. He lit a joss stick and placed it on the small wooden, red-painted altar inside the kitchen. He hoped it would bring him good fortune.

Billy's trip to the restaurant earlier had been routine. His diversion to the police station, less so. A glass door marked the entrance. The room was small. It felt like a dentist's waiting room. An adjoining door led through to the Report Room. Half a dozen heavily scratched blue plastic chairs with rusty black legs lined the walls.

The young constable behind the counter looked bookish in his black plastic-rimmed glasses. His olive-green summer uniform appeared brand new. Billy decided he needed someone more senior, someone who looked less like an apprentice librarian. He asked if an inspector was available. It was a matter of great importance, and most urgent, he told him.

The officer looked perplexed. He said nothing. He motioned Billy to take a seat. He used the wait to peruse bilingual notices posted on the wall. He read about Report Room procedures, reward notices, and the right to access a lawyer.

Billy was in luck. The only inspector remaining in the station was the Divisional Commander. Terence Cheuk had arranged an evening shift because of the typhoon. He walked through and introduced himself. The constable disappeared to make a coffee. They were alone.

"How can I help you?" Cheuk asked. Billy recognised him. He remembered his face from a licence check at his favourite bar. His cherubic face made him look like a teenager.

"I'm here to claim a reward," Billy said. He saw a change in Cheuk. He looked more attentive. He was probably expecting another complaint against his officers, Billy realised.

"For anyone in particular?" Cheuk asked. At any one time the Force was hunting hundreds of fugitives. Some had a price on their heads for decades. Only recent notices were on the board.

"The big one," Billy replied coyly. He was teasing Cheuk and enjoying his moment. Despite the butterflies dancing in his stomach.

"Give me a clue," Cheuk demanded.

"The dirty cops from Tsim Sha Tsui. The ones connected to the shootout. These two," he said. He was pointing at photos of Silas and A-Ken on a black and white A4 sheet on the noticeboard. Wanted for murder.

Reward of HK$50,000 offered by the Commissioner of Police.

Cheuk was silent for a moment.

"You had better come through." Cheuk took out a pen.

"I can't. I need to get back. Let me tell you what I know," he said quietly.

41

In police stations all over the Territory, command posts were being established. Typhoon Dot was rapidly bearing down on the coast. Assistant Commissioner Smithies was in his Ops Room. It was his usual position during a major incident.

The update from the military had come minutes earlier. It had been delivered by the same liaison officer. The news was not good. Smithies was blaming himself for not foreseeing the cock up.

"Evening Gerry," he had started. His oily suaveness annoyed Smithies. His voice seemed artificially cultivated. He struggled to get past his public schoolboy demeanour. To him, it was condescension personified.

"Bad news, I'm afraid. CBF has directed our boys to stand down. A helicopter is on its way to collect them off the beach at seven. Before the winds get too high. The RAF are having a few maintenance issues with their Wessexes. The old man wants them put safely to bed. That won't cause you any problems, will it?"

He asked the question with classic military understatement. Does a bear shit in the woods, thought Smithies angrily. He decided to keep his disquiet to himself. Venting would do no good. This is what happens when you involve the military.

"We'll just have to deal with it, won't we?" he replied. "Thanks for letting us know." His voice was dripping with sarcasm. He put the phone down.

"Endex," declared Smithies to the team around him. "Can we urgently arrange an escort out for our people, please?"

"Who did you have in mind, sir?" asked the inspector.

It was a fair question. There was no provision in the detailed operational order marked "confidential" for this scenario. Smithies started thinking about his options. He might need to pull in some favours. The risks still felt manageable. But the dangers would only multiply if they were not addressed.

"Who are the CP's Reserve Platoon tonight?" he asked.

"Alpha Three were standing by at North Point, sir. They've been searching for a missing child in Aberdeen for the last two hours. The incident is ongoing." The reply was delivered with military precision. The lad had been trained well.

"In that case it's going to need to be EU. Let's not take any chances. Get on to Kowloon East. Start with the Duty Controller. Let's see where that gets us."

"In that case, why don't I have a copy of the operational order?" Superintendent Malcolm Wiggam demanded.

Smithies knew Wiggam well. He was a belligerent Australian. Obstinacy and bloody mindedness were the trademarks of his long and unremarkable career. With eight more months until retirement, Smithies knew Wiggam had no intention of bending over backwards to save a situation rapidly going South. He had a reputation for speaking his mind whenever he had an opinion to share. That was often.

"It sounds like a proper fuck up if you ask me, mate," he declared loudly. His loud voice was nasal and irritating.

"Malcolm, I'm asking you nicely," Smithies replied. He was loath to pull rank. He had banged heads with this fossil previously. Wiggam was reputed to manage his control centre team with the tact and diplomacy of an overseer on a Malaysian tea plantation. The response was not a surprise. It was Smithies's bad luck Wiggam was on duty.

"I don't give a flying fuck. If you think I'm sending two EU cars off on a wild goose chase when it's meal break time and the number eight signal is about to be raised, you must be off your tiny rocker, mate."

He slammed the phone down before Smithies had a chance to reason with him. He was unsure whether to laugh or cry at the petulance. They were all supposed to be on the same team but it didn't feel like it at times like these.

"Bloody typical. I'll deal with him later," said Smithies through gritted teeth. The inspector was looking nonplussed. He had heard every word.

The clock was ticking. Smithies was no closer to solving his problem. A sense of dread was starting to envelope him.

"Get me the OC SDU," he said finally. "At least I can rely on them."

He knew it was overkill. At least they wouldn't argue the toss, they worked for him directly.

42

The knock on the door came just before 7 p.m. It was accompanied by a posh English voice.

"Royal Marines here. May we come in?"

Sam could see green-clad figures through the ground floor windows. He unbolted the door.

"Evening, Sam," said the lieutenant. "I'm sorry to have to tell you this but we've been ordered to pull out." He shrugged apologetically. "It sounds like a balls-up if you ask me. Something to do with the typhoon."

Sam was stunned. "When are you leaving?"

It seemed imminent. The troops behind the officer were wearing their packs. Despite the wind, several were smoking. Gusts stripped away ash cones as soon as they formed. They looked relaxed, relieved to be pulling out. They were peering at him with interest. He guessed there would be choice comments about Jenny afterwards. It was the nature of the beast.

"The Wessex arrives in ten minutes," said the officer. "They want us out before the winds become unsafe. From what we've seen, you look to be secure. The only activity we detected the entire time was one fishing boat."

"What boat was that?" Sam was puzzled. The Ops Room had not mentioned it during their regular calls.

"It was a small blue fishing boat, a couple of hundred yards offshore. It only stayed for fifteen minutes. They looked a bit odd, more like day-trippers than fishermen. Three local chaps. One with a pair of binoculars," the lieutenant replied.

"Any descriptions?" asked Jenny sharply.

He called over one of the Marines.

"Wilson, what were those descriptions again?"

The corporal took a small notebook from his top pocket. His uniform was grimy. Dirt was lodged under his fingernails. He read out the descriptions one by one. It was the third that caught Jenny's attention.

"Chinese male, fat build, 5'6" to 5'8", blue jeans, white polo-type short-sleeved shirt, dark sunglasses, collar worn up. A white baseball cap. Carrying a small pair of binoculars. The boat registration was 67156," he ended.

"That's him," she whispered to Sam. "He always wears his shirts like that."

A look of concern bordering on panic possessed her face.

"Damn it," said Sam angrily. "Is there any way we can come with you?" asked Sam.

"I'd love to take you. It's not been authorised. We are already overloaded. No can do, I'm afraid."

"Right, thanks for nothing," said Sam. "I need to make a call."

He slammed the door before the lieutenant could say anything more. Jenny was standing motionless behind him. He picked up the telephone receiver and dialled.

"Ops Room."

It was the familiar local voice he had become used to.

"I need to speak to Mr Smithies or Mr McClintock or someone who can give me some fucking answers," Sam raged.

He was shocked at his own outburst. He knew it was unfair. He knew the other inspector was not calling the shots. The line went quiet. After a short delay, Smithies picked up.

"Evening, Sam," he said quietly. "We've had a change of plan and a few problems. Things are going to be alright. You need to trust me on this."

Sam said nothing. He didn't think he could trust himself to respond civilly. Blood was pumping loudly in his ears. He wasn't sure if it was fear or anger driving him. This was not supposed to be happening. It was either rank incompetence or a blatant disregard for their safety. He wondered if McClintock knew about it.

"Are you still there? Sam?" Smithies asked.

"When were you going tell us about the boat?" Sam demanded.

"What boat?" asked Smithies. He seemed confused by the question.

Sam had heard enough. He ended the call by slamming the receiver back into position.

"We need to go, right now," he said firmly.

He was staring at Jenny. She hadn't moved. She had a strange look of calm on her face. He tried again. His frustration was mounting.

"They've fucked up and we are on our own. Don't you understand?"

He heard the sound of an approaching helicopter in the distance. It was barely audible over the wind.

"I'm not running any more, Sam," she said quietly. "I'm sorry, but I caused this. It has to end here. It's not your fight."

She had steel in her voice. She was staring at him intently.

"Let's just go now, before it's too late." He knew he was repeating himself.

She shook her head firmly. "You go. I'll be safe here. Leave me the gun. Go and get help. Come back and get me."

The argument was interrupted by the phone ringing. He snatched it up. He had forgotten to use the correct protocol. He was past caring.

"Who is it?" he shouted.

He was losing his cool. He was embarrassed. He could not help himself.

"Evening, Sam," said the familiar voice. "Is everything all right there?" McClintock asked.

The DVC had picked up on the vibe. Sam could tell it from his voice. It was McClintock's therapy voice. The one he saved for special occasions.

"What do you know about the boat?" Sam asked roughly.

"I'm not aware of any boat." McClintock said quietly. "Neither is our friend Smithies. He asked me to call. You had better explain what you mean."

McClintock sounded genuine in his concern, Sam thought. He resolved to explain their predicament more calmly.

"We've been talking to the Marines about a boat they saw observing the house." Sam explained. "Jenny thinks one of the descriptions matches Silas."

McClintock was silent for a moment. Sam realised McClintock understood their predicament. He knew instinctively he could trust his boss to come up with the answers. Already he was feeling calmer.

"Listen carefully," said McClintock firmly. His business voice had returned. "I understand your situation. I'm going to get this shite sorted out and send someone down there to get you out ASAP. Jenny's right. Sit tight, stay in the house, and wait for the cavalry. Capiche?"

"Yes sir," said Sam.

He regretted his earlier outburst. McClintock was right. There was no logic in blundering out into the wind-torn countryside on foot.

"Good lad, now get off the phone. Barricade the doors and wait for support. SDU are on the way." The phone went dead.

McClintock's words rang in his ears. They had to make urgent preparations. They had little time.

"Help me with the table," he said to Jenny.

A sweep of his arm sent plates and cups clattering to the floor. She took hold of one end. He grabbed the other. Between them they toppled the table on to its side. It squealed as they coaxed it into position behind the front door.

"That won't delay them for long," she said.

It was a dismissal of his efforts. He felt a sudden flash of anger. It subsided as quickly as it arrived. She was only trying to help. The fear he was feeling must be nothing compared to her terror.

He forced a smile. It was enough. He glanced at the windows. The bars would provide some protection from intruders. Not for long if they brought tools.

"We need to slow them down. What else can we do?" He looked around the room desperately.

"This house needs to become a fortress," Jenny said.

"How?" He was not understanding what she meant.

"Think of it like a castle, with different layers. The roof is the safest place. We need to buy time. We need to make it difficult for them to reach us."

He liked the idea. Anything was better than doing nothing.

"Let's get the rest of the furniture up the stairs. We can use it as a barricade. Before we do, help me with something in the kitchen," he added mysteriously.

43

Steve Jameson, the SDU boss, was on edge. He had been, ever since the Tsim Sha Tsui operation. It was unusual. A nagging sense of foreboding was hanging over him. The intelligence about another armed gang had only exacerbated the feeling. He was struggling to relax. Another turn out felt imminent. He expected the pager on his belt to sound at any moment. He kept patting it to check it was still there, then testing the battery. It was his lucky charm.

The officers' mess at the Police Tactical Unit was rocking. By late afternoon, strong gusts of wind were whipping across the drill square. The Commandant had wasted no time declaring an early end to training. It was the signal to launch an impromptu typhoon party. The Commandant had ordered a round of pina coladas for the trainees. Local inspectors were eyeing the tall glasses on the glass-covered bar suspiciously.

Most of the single *gweilos* had decided to make a night of it. The mess bedrooms were fully booked. Only the Reserve Duty Officer was still in uniform. He was clutching a San Miguel in one hand, swagger stick in the other. Evening rounds of the camp and armoury checks were on hold. It was only a matter of time before the

Commandant and his entourage withdrew for the night and the party could properly get started.

Over fifty officers were present. The windows, covered as a precaution with large crosses of brown packing tape, were steamed up with condensation. The ancient walls of the old Army Nissen hut were crammed with military and police unit shields. It was an Aladdin's cave of photos, deactivated weapons, and other paraphernalia.

SDU were there in force. Longstanding rivalry with the training staff had erupted into fierce banter. Jameson was keeping out of the fray. He was content to be a spectator. He was still nursing his first beer. The others had enthusiastically chugged several. The ability to pick battles was a key leadership quality.

"OC SDU, call for you," shouted a voice from near the bar.

Jameson did not hesitate. Two of the SDU inspectors followed him over to the telephone. They were standing nearby, eager to hear the reason for the out of hours call.

"Jameson, SDU."

"Evening Steve." It was Smithies. His heart rate ticked up a notch.

"The wheel has fallen off. I need to ask a favour."

He listened intently. Smithies explained his requirements. Jameson reminded himself never to drink when his psychic radar was functioning so perfectly. He gave a hand signal to the two inspectors. It could mean only one thing. One ran out to their offices. The other started pulling the rest of the team out of the bar. Turn out.

"Jimmy, with me," he instructed. "We'll take three guys each in a couple of Land Cruisers. The rest can catch up. John, get the rest of the unit down there as soon as you can. I have a feeling we are going to need everyone for this. Any questions? No? Good. Let's roll."

Ten minutes later, Jameson was sitting in the front passenger seat of the Land Cruiser. Another Toyota waited patiently behind them. It was the best they could do until the rest of the unit responded to their pagers. They were scattered all around the city. The unit regularly practised turnout procedures. Their kit was always packed ready to go. It still took time. They could not afford to wait for the full unit. It could be a life-or-death situation. Every second counted. Getting feet on the ground quickly might make all the difference.

The Land Cruisers barrelled through the main gate of the base. The constable on the gate gave them a jaunty wave as he lowered the barrier behind them. Within moments, they had reached the slip road to the highway. The two drivers accelerated hard and darted into the traffic. The powerful engines screamed in protest. Startled road users hooted their horns in protest. Blinking blue lights offered no apology.

"What's the plan?"

The question came from the rear. Jameson was still tying his boot laces. Others were adjusting their kit. The Browning pistol at his waist was digging into his ribs uncomfortably.

"The only route to the house is the path from road. We need to leg it. Fast," he said.

His mind made up, Jameson radioed the team in the other Land Cruiser.

"Jimmy, ditch the vests and helmets," he ordered. "Speed is the key."

They made good time. The citizenry had voted with their feet. The weather forecast was unequivocal. The roads were quiet.

"OC SDU, call ACP OPS, urgent." The anonymous voice was distorted and echoey over the radio. It had been twenty minutes since their previous discussion. It must be important. He hoped it wasn't the order to stand down. He was feeling in the mood. One of the team responded on his behalf.

"Roger, wilco."

Jameson was thankful for the bulky mobile telephone. It was newly installed, a useful tool for communicating confidential messages. He knew they ran risks every time they used the radio. Too many journalists were using scanners. None were in sight as they departed. They were operating under press radar. He preferred to keep it that way. His call was answered instantly.

"ACP OPS, Smithies."

"It's Steve, sir." Jameson said. "You were looking for me?"

"Thanks for calling, there have been developments. Good news and bad I'm afraid," Smithies said. "We have received reliable information from an informer. Silas and A-Ken have been using a village house close to the centre of Sai Kung. They are with four Mainlanders, all armed, at least one with an AK." The line crackled and broke up for a moment then settled down.

Smithies continued: "Intelligence confirms an attack on our two friends is imminent. The gang are *en route* in a commercial vehicle. It is a white 1981 Datsun, registration TB 6341. With me so far?" he checked.

"Yes sir." Jameson was making rapid notes in a small notebook. The pieces were dropping into place. The stars were aligning for them.

"A few more things," Smithies went on. "Our informer is the owner of the safe house. A-Ken's cousin. He's come forward to claim the reward money. He says it's because he's unhappy with their plans. The informer owns a boat that is moored up next to his house. It was used for a recce. The typhoon prevented it being used for the attack. This is where it gets complicated," said Smithies. "From what the informer has overheard, the attack will not be an in and out job. Silas has revenge in mind. He's planning to take his time. I'm sure you can imagine what that involves?"

"We'll make sure it doesn't get to that stage," Jameson said grimly into his handset.

"We are told the vehicle will drop them off at the path, then return to the safe house in Sai Kung, and then collect them later. Now these are my instructions," Smithies explained.

Jameson scribbled furiously in the notebook that he was balancing on his right thigh. This was the important part. Especially if it all went wrong.

"Are we clear?" Smithies asked after he had finished.

"Crystal, sir."

Smithies ended the call. Jameson took a deep breath. He

started reviewing his options. He had limited resources. Time was against them. It was going to be tight.

44

The journey to the house in the bay was short. It was less unpleasant than their first trip in the lorry, but the weather had worsened. Once out of the town, the unpredictable winds backed and veered. The small vehicle shook like a washing machine on spin cycle. Sheets of rain were falling intermittently. The heavy drops were drumming loudly on the roof of the truck, like a swarm of angry bees.

Over the radio, A-Ken heard the news they had been expecting. The number eight signal had been raised. It seemed overdue. The headlights of the vehicle picked out swaying bushes and trees. He was thankful for the extra ballast provided by the bodies in the rear.

They arrived without incident. The unlit rural road was quiet. They'd passed hardly any other vehicles. Now he could see no lights in either direction. As he jumped down from the cab, the wind tugged at the door before he managed to slam it closed. Opening the roller shutter door created a maelstrom of paper and cardboard. The five passengers shielded their eyes to avoid the debris. There was no escape from the insidious wind. It came harshly from all directions.

Silas jumped out first. He was unsmiling. He looked serious. A-Ken patted him on the shoulder.

"See you later, *daai-lo*. Good luck."

He received a nod of appreciation. The others followed him out. He pulled the shutter down with a clang. Silas smiled and walked off. The others trooped past behind him. One by one they disappeared down the slippery path into the gloom.

A-Ken watched them go. He was not envious. The path looked treacherous. Their mission seemed unnecessary. It was a self-indulgent act of retribution from a spiteful man. He had not wanted to argue the point. It was a dangerous line to take.

He had done what was required of him. He had kitted the party out in matching dark blue waterproof jackets, from the supplies he had purchased. He had borrowed the vehicle from an old triad contact for a few days. A-Ken's supporting role as quartermaster was critical to the plan's success. He knew Silas was grateful.

He did not share Chu-sir's enmity for Jenny. He seemed to have become obsessed with her. Silas was a sadist. His retribution would be savage. It was his woman, so be it. Jenny was only getting what she deserved. A-Ken was not sad to miss the show.

The last in line gave a parting wave as they disappeared into the shadows. A-Ken looked up and down the road. He was alone. He started the engine and set out on the return journey with a cautious three point turn. Getting bogged down in a typhoon would be a disaster.

The light was disappearing quickly. They had timed it perfectly. He started to relax. He was relieved to be alone again. His mind turned to better times. He turned the radio up to sing along to one of his favourites. He had Jacky Cheung to take his mind off other things. What a dirty night. Poor Jenny.

Silas was pleased with their progress. He had equipped them well. It gave them a professional feel. His team. His target. His terms.

He knew the worst of the typhoon was yet to come. The return journey would not be as straightforward. The rain had suddenly become constant. Vegetation was wildly dancing all about them. The wind tugged angrily at his nylon hood. Only his hand kept it securely in place.

The gravel path was solid underfoot. It was easy to follow, even in the dark although rivulets erupting from adjoining hillsides made it muddy in places.

They made good time. Other than the odd stumble and trip, they were not obstructed. Within half an hour, their target loomed into view. They turned a corner to find the house sitting alone in the middle of the clearing. The white-painted building seemed to glow in the dark. The scene had an unnatural feel. It was eery and forbidding. He could see no lights or signs of life.

They halted under cover of the trees. For a moment, he let his doubts overtake him. He briefly wondered if they were on a wild goose chase. There was only one way to find out.

He split them into two groups. He planned to approach from two directions, attacking the front and rear simultaneously. Dragon would take the back door.

They approached cautiously. The windows were protected with ornate, rusted metal grilles. The wooden door at the front was large and weather-beaten. It looked promising.

Wind howling around the eaves concealed the sound of their approach. Silas peered through a window. The house inside appeared empty and unloved. Signs of occupation lay scattered around the floor. His hopes soared. His heart rate rose in unison.

He had seen enough. He signalled his two assistants. They drew equipment from their bags. They looked up at him eagerly, like Boy Scouts lighting their first camp fire. Silas ordered them to commence.

Long black-painted crowbars attacked the narrow gap between the old door and the frame, searching for weak spots. They applied pressure gradually. Silas heard wood splintering and the door bulging and flexing.

Without warning, the door lock gave way with a pop. The door itself opened backwards several inches. It obstinately refused to move further.

"Use your shoulders," Silas urged.

He stood away from the doorway, pistol raised. He was eager to use it. Shoulders applied weight to the door. The gap slowly widened. It seemed obstructed. Something heavy.

The gap grew to six inches. Silas ordered a halt. He shone his flashlight through the opening. Sturdy table legs extended out from behind the door.

"Again," he urged. Within seconds it was wide enough to squeeze through.

"You first," instructed Silas to the smaller of the two. "We'll cover you."

The man threw his crowbar into the grass and grabbed his pistol. He squeezed through stealthily, weapon in one hand, torch at the ready in the other. A moment later he was inside and the rest of them followed.

A white tee-shirt lay crumpled on the floor. Silas recognised the police logo. His excitement surged.

"They're here," he said. He heard a sound. It was hard to hear anything over the howling made by the typhoon outside. Shadows emerged from the rear. It was Dragon.

"Check upstairs," Silas ordered. He found a light switch and flicked it but there was no response. He felt broken glass underfoot. The bulbs had been smashed. Light reflected off the shards at his feet.

Dragon led the way to the staircase. He pointed his heavy AK-47 into the dark space. It was pitch black.

"Torch," Dragon demanded. Three beams illuminated the steep narrow staircase. The chipped concrete stairs were navy blue. Battered wooden handrails clung precariously to the sides. A tangle of furniture lay at the top. It was formed into a crude barricade. Chairs and folding chairs interwoven, tied together with twine.

It was obvious they had been expecting him. Silas laughed at the amateurism. The barricade would delay them by mere moments. He ordered its removal. Two of his men cautiously crept up the stairs, searching for a place to commence demolition.

Suddenly a flash lit the stairway. The explosive sound of a gunshot echoed around them. A body fell down the stairs and landed at Silas's feet. Blood was pumping out from a head wound.

Dragon unleashed a deafening fusillade of covering fire from his AK-47 while they all retreated from the staircase. His muzzle flashes revealed no enemy. A shower of plaster chips and dust fell around them then Dragon cursed long and loudly as his weapon fell silent. The magazine was empty.

The injured man was dragged away to safety in the main room. Most of his skull was a bloody crater of brain and bone tissue. His eyes were barely open. His breathing was shallow. There was no way that he would live. They all knew it. Dragon knelt at the dying man's side whispering quietly into his ear. A minute later, with a rattle from his throat, life passed from him. Sightless eyes stared upwards, as if in a final plaintive plea. Dragon released the man's hand.

Silas placed his hand on Dragon's shoulder. He acknowledged his pain. He knew what losing a brother in arms felt like. A-Siu came to mind. Silas hauled Dragon to his feet.

Dragon glared at him. "We need a plan to get up that staircase. We need some kind of shield."

The heavy table by the front door provided Silas with inspiration. It would not guard against an AK-47 round but the round had sounded like a .38 from a police issue revolver.

"What about that?" Silas asked, pointing at the table.

"The wood looks thick," said Dragon, nodding. They were on the same wavelength.

"Turn it on its end and two people can advance up the stairs behind it," Silas said.

He sensed victory as long as his quarry didn't possess any weapon more powerful than a revolver. "Get the body out of the way," he instructed. It was just a matter of time before he laid his hands on Jenny. Losing a man was the price of going to war.

45

"Use maximum aggression," Smithies had instructed. "I want Jenny, Sam and A-Ken back in one piece."

The words were ringing in Steve Jameson's ears as they bounced along the road through the heavy winds. The meaning was clear. He didn't need it spelling out. Surprise was your best friend. Protecting your own took priority. Payback was a two-way street.

He was trying to match too many imponderables against too few options. Clarity of thinking under pressure was usually his speciality. It was a prerequisite for passing SDU selection. Today it was taking longer than usual. He was missing something. He needed to re-think.

Working against the clock was a challenge. Deploying against two targets with the bare bones of a team was a headache. Something had to give. Getting to Jenny and Sam before Silas did was their first priority. They could leave A-Ken until later. Or to someone else.

He suddenly realised the solution was staring him in the face. He snatched the telephone list out of the glove box. He found the number. The ring tone was a relief. The cellular signal could be hit-and-miss in a storm.

"DVC. Quickly," he demanded.

He felt bad for his aggressive tone. It was sometimes necessary to get things done.

"Cheuk, DVC Sai Kung," came the voice after several moments. Jameson was thankful the DVC was still there.

"Terence, its Steve Jameson," he said. "We need to talk. ACP OPS has turned out SDU. We're on the way, but I need a favour. Are you up for it?" he asked.

Jameson was loath to delegate a difficult task, but he viewed this as lateral thinking to solve a problem, rather than abdicating responsibility. Whether Smithies would agree with him with the benefit of hindsight was debatable. He might not be so charitable in his judgement. For now, it was what Jameson had to do.

They'd never met but Jameson had heard the DVC was a solid bloke. Jameson hoped Cheuk had the balls to pull it off. There was no way he could refuse. His local knowledge would be a real advantage.

"No problem, Steve," said Cheuk. "Tell me what you need."

Their conversation was brief. After hanging up he turned to his men and began briefing them.

"Pass a message to the rest of the team," he said. "Forget Sai Kung town centre. I want the whole unit down to the house on the coast. Pronto."

The wide highway had given way to narrow rural roads. They were making good time considering the drenching rainfall and buffeting winds. The roads were emptying rapidly. Speed was critical so they kept the blue lights flashing and pushed the vehicles to their limit.

"ETA two minutes," the driver finally advised. The crew tensed at the prospect of imminent action. Kit was re-checked.

"Remember, we don't know where they are," Jameson said. "Go hard, assume they are nearby."

"Thirty seconds," said the driver.

"Ready weapons," ordered Jameson into the radio receiver. He heard the crew pulling back their MP5 cocking handles. He knew the other crew would be doing likewise. His own handle sprang home with a satisfying mechanical thud. He loved the sound. He loved the weapon. It was German engineering at its lethal best. Fingers re-checked safety switches. Hands went to door handles. They were silent, ready for action.

The two Land Cruisers skidded to a halt. The road was covered in muddy running water, draining down from the hillsides in ever growing torrents.

"Go, go, go," shouted Jameson.

They were out in seconds, doors slammed behind them. They dismounted into all round defence, six weapons searching for threats. They were covering their arcs, looking for targets. There were none.

The two Land Cruisers accelerated away into the night. He had ordered them to stand by nearby. Discreetly. Silence resumed. They were standing stock still. Like dark statues, ninja-like. The night enveloped them. The wind howled in welcome. His eyes adjusted to the darkness.

"On me," Jameson ordered quietly. He could see the start of the path. It looked dark but not impossible. They moved off in single file. He kept his underslung torch off. Stealth and speed were equally important. He felt a tap on his shoulder. A willing body took over on point. He fell in behind. The scout led them along the path at a fast paced walk, MP5s at the ready.

Jameson would have preferred to run the entire distance, but it was too risky. The path was uneven underfoot and at this pace they could still react if they had contact.

They were soon soaked. The rain was relentless. It dripped off noses and ears. It seeped into every crevice

Water pooled in their boots. Warm sweat and tepid rain mingled. Wet dog met mouldy cotton. Adrenaline overrode discomfort. The rain was an irritant but not the enemy. No one ever died from chafing.

Their concentration was total. Jameson dared not look behind him. He sensed his team as they followed. Occasional curses confirmed their presence. Unseen roots and slippery boulders attacked indiscriminately.

They were 25 minutes into their march. He knew their destination must be close. The pitch-black night retreated. A glow appeared over the hill. The light increased in intensity. It reflected on trees and low clouds, flickering and twisting as it grew into flames. There was a smell of smoke in the air.

The trees opened up. The fire was close by. The scout halted. Jameson joined him on one knee. He raised a hand. His crew spread out in a skirmish line to either side.

The top of the house was alight. The inferno illuminated trees around the clearing. Eerie shadows danced in the bushes. He could feel the heat on his skin.

Seeing no sign of life, Jameson feared the worst. Were they too late? There was no room for speculation, the situation required certainty. The time for caution was over. He signalled the team to advance. He headed for the front door as an entry point.

They advanced slowly. He had never felt more exposed. It was the longest thirty seconds of his life. They could hear it now. The crackle of flames pierced through the gale. Clouds of acrid smoke eddied in the wind. His eyes stung. They were almost there. Their luck held.

No shots or shouts announced their arrival. The door was splintered, the frame bent and marked. Two holdalls and breaking tools lay scattered on the grass.

Then shouting split the night. It was coming from the upper floors. Male voices. Threats and foul language. Fingers went to triggers. Muscle memory. Teamwork kicked in. It was automatic. That was why they trained so hard. An MP5 covered the nearest window. Another pointed upwards. A third covered their flank. Their luck held.

Jameson paused at the door. His eyes recovered their night vision, spoilt by the dancing fire. He entered silently. A dark shape in the corner caught his eye. The shape was deathly still. He crept closer. A prod with his boot confirmed his suspicions. The pool of blood told him all he needed to know.

He shifted his attention up the staircase. Swirls of smoke met his gaze. A whisper told him the ground floor was clear. He readied himself for action. Sodden gloves dropped to the floor. He wiped his hands. The moisture clung persistently. It was show time.

He climbed silently, one step at a time. He heard voices. Only Mandarin. Only male. The flickering glow above grew brighter and it drew him on seductively. The smoke became thicker. He was thankful for its cover.

A tangle of furniture caught his eye. They would need to be careful. He could only guess a route through it. He moved past it by feel. Hard wood brushed his leg. His passage was imperceptible. His confidence grew. He was past third base. He felt like a tiger patiently approaching his prey, inch by inch, one cautious step at a time.

Shadowy forms came into view. They were silhouetted by the blaze above, wraith-like in the smoke. A corridor lay between him and them. Smashed doors led off to the right. They were oblivious to his presence. Oblivious to the danger. He made himself small. He picked a target. He waited.

He heard noise on the staircase, a friendly presence approaching. Behind him a loop of twine caught a boot and claimed a victim. The figure crashed to the ground. He tensed. An MP5 clattered noisily on the hard floor.

He could wait no longer. He released the safety catch.

"Armed police, stop or I shoot," he bellowed the well-practised phrase in Cantonese. He heard it repeated over his shoulder. The figure on the floor scrambled to his feet. Their underslung torches kicked in. The shadows disappeared, like rabbits dodging headlights.

The response was instantaneous. Muzzle flashes erupted. A volley of shots rang out. He heard the sound of impacts on the hard walls. Clouds of dust and plaster filled the air.

Jameson switched to automatic. He fired a burst. It felt good. Another burst came from over his shoulder. He heard the tinkle of brass shell cases striking the floor. Time was standing still.

He shouted another warning. Nothing happened. The lull in the firing felt strange. He heard panicked voices. Banging and the sound of breaking glass reverberated along the corridor. The dust cleared. He saw an arm raised. An object came skidding towards them. An automatic weapon opened up on them. He could feel the power behind it. A dozen rounds whipped past him. He knew it must be an AK-47. He pulled in his head. It felt a futile gesture against a hail of steel. He heard a grunt behind him. He feared the worst. Their luck ended.

"Grenade," he shouted. Training kicked in. He dived for cover. It was every man for himself. The doorway to his right was closest. Feet together. Head away from the threat. Start counting. Wait for detonation. Go again.

It seemed like an age. It should have exploded by now. He risked a peep. The cylindrical shaped grenade lay in the doorway. He saw the pin still in place. They had struck lucky. It was amateur hour.

A shout brought him back. The voice sounded anxious.

"*Daai-lo*, A-Lap is hit. They're gone."

He stepped over the grenade. A dark figure passed in front of him. He followed him down the corridor. The figure entered the next room.

"Clear."

Jameson took back the lead. He checked the final room. He knew it was futile. It was empty. Only the staircase to the roof remained. The ferocity of the flames was diminishing. He feared what lay beyond.

"Clear," he shouted. Glass from the window crunched loudly underfoot. The window grille was missing. A discarded holdall lay to one side. A mess of clothing and personal items filled the room. A trail of blood led to an old bed. The mattress was missing.

He approached the window. Shadows disappeared into the trees, along the path.

"Outside, quick," he shouted. "They're heading for the road." He heard feet pounding down the staircase.

He glanced along the corridor. A-Lap was slumped against a wall. Blood oozed from a shoulder wound. His hand covered the wound, a bloody dressing clutched beneath. He managed a thumbs up and a weak smile.

"Target secure," Jameson reported into his radio. He thought of the two men left behind on the road. He prayed they could finish it. What happened next was out of his hands. It was time to check the roof.

46

Terence Cheuk's service had been remarkable only for the speed of his rise. He was on the verge of superintendent rank. In a Force where ten years to superintendent was impressive, he was looking at eight. He was considered a high-flyer.

He had been sent to Sai Kung Division for a reason. It was common knowledge. It was one of the few divisions led by a chief inspector. He held a rare opportunity in his hands. It was a test.

The post was a poisoned chalice.

Succeed, and his status as one to watch would be confirmed. Doors to a carefully managed path upwards would open. The odds of a glittering career and senior position at PHQ would shorten.

Screw up, and he would become infamous as a nearly-man. Someone who could and should have done better. A contender overtaken by more junior colleagues, peers who had delivered on their potential. A succession of dull posts in division and district would inevitably follow.

Eighteen months should do it, he had been told. A year and half of arguing with bolshy drunken *gweilos*, of negotiating with conniving village representatives, and of listening to *gweipohs* whining about parking, parties and pythons.

He was paying the price for a succession of cushy nine to five numbers. His police life had involved precious little frontline work since the early days. Question marks over his operational capabilities had been raised.

Undoubtedly bright and capable, with clear potential, the reports said. Reading between the lines, something was missing. Something that his peers had in spades. They had cut their teeth at the coal face, rather than closeting themselves in Personnel Wing.

No one knew this better than Cheuk. He was all too aware of the clock ticking. The days of his golden boy status were numbered. He needed something to distinguish himself. To prove the doubters wrong. That something had just dropped into his lap. This opportunity felt surreal. SDU had unexpectedly thrown him a bone.

He had accepted the challenge without hesitation. He surprised even himself. Careful preparation was his trade mark. He never rushed anything. Others had commented on his clinical approach. He was not embarrassed about that. Better safe than sorry, had always been his motto in the past.

This one was special. Nothing ventured, nothing gained. He had assessed the potential rewards as exceeding the obvious risks. *Carpe diem*.

Cheuk found his man in their small canteen. He had interrupted the constable's dinner. What he had in mind would not suit everyone, he told him. He would make it worth his while. Acceptance was immediate.

They were standing beside the armoury hatch. The pair had changed into plainclothes. Cheuk quickly briefed his new partner. He silently nodded his understanding. He appeared unfazed by the opportunity. His calmness was disconcerting.

They rapidly drew arms. A revolver and six rounds each. A plainclothes holster, beat radio and handcuffs. It was all they would need. Weapons loaded, they pulled up hoods on their black raincoats. They commenced the short walk.

The streets of Sai Kung were deserted. The glare of the orange streetlights gave the twilight scene a surreal, apocalyptic, look. The wind had picked up strength. It raced through the town, howling through gaps, searching for weakness. A tree here, a window there, nothing was safe from its tendrils. Shredded leaves and stripped branches covered the ground. Vegetation mixed with rubbish from blown over bins created a slippery mat underfoot. Parked vehicles were covered with the same filthy residue.

They walked slowly, bodies bent against the ferocity of the gale, faces averted from the stinging sheets of warm rain. They looked up as they turned the corner. They had made it in time. The driveway was empty. The vehicle they were expecting was nowhere in sight. A lone figure was visible in the window. The ceiling light silhouetted him. It was as they had arranged. The figure watched them approach. The door opened before they reached it. They entered.

"Thank you for coming yourself, A-sir," Billy said.

He quickly closed the door behind them. Cheuk welcomed the silence after the wind. He was relieved to be out of the rain. His trousers were soaked. He was pleased they'd made it before A-Ken returned.

"Just the two of you?" Billy asked. The constable said nothing. He just grinned, patting the bulge that the holstered weapon made under the raincoat.

"Don't worry," Cheuk replied. "We have it in hand," he said. "There are other teams deploying."

Cheuk had chosen his oppo carefully. The man was a product of the Police Cadet School. He was built like a brick outhouse. His reputation matched his physique. In six months, he had received more assault complaints than anyone in the entire district. He was the terror of Diamond Hill. His posting to Sai Kung was temporary, whilst his latest transgression was being investigated. He had arrived with an unusual back story.

"Best wait in the back," Billy suggested.

He ushered them through the kitchen into in a darkened room. Cheuk checked the floor. He noticed wet footprints in their wake.

"Best wipe those off before he returns," he suggested. "I wouldn't want to ruin the surprise."

The constable grabbed a tea towel that was hanging by the sink and with his foot wiped across the tiled floor, removing the prints.

They used the time to perfect their plan. Cheuk deferred to his partner. He knew a brawler when he saw one. Management 101, horses for courses. Brawler was happy to take the lead. Possible redemption was the reward. Cheuk would take the credit but take him under his future protection if things went well. They both knew the score.

The plan was simple but Cheuk remained concerned about the uncertainties. The entire gang returning unexpectedly would put them in serious danger. Billy anticipated the problem. Billy would warn them if A-Ken returned accompanied. The garden light dimming would be the signal to slip out of the back. Taking on all of them was unthinkable. Leaving them for SDU was sensible.

Cheuk was concerned whether A-Ken was armed. Billy couldn't remember seeing a gun. Cheuk remembered A-Ken had absconded with his personal issue Detective Special. They assumed he must be carrying it. Cheuk's partner seemed unfazed. Brawler's confidence was starting to be infectious. Cheuk thought he might even be enjoying himself. He reminded himself to be patient. To remember his training. To act like a man. He hoped his nervousness was not showing.

The room where they sat was modern. A floor to ceiling glass window and aluminium-framed door overlooked a small garden. The desk was cluttered with files and papers. The walls were covered with holiday photos of Billy and his deceased wife. The policemen's escape route lay beyond the vegetable garden. A wooden gate led to a rear lane.

They only had to wait for ten minutes. The sound of a diesel engine on the road announced the arrival of A-Ken's truck. It reversed noisily into the drive and then fell silent.

The wooden door to the kitchen was ajar. Two fingers' width of light was enough, better than any periscope. They could see and hear any arrivals. They waited patiently, ears straining, revolvers in hand. Cheuk felt his heart pumping furiously. He worried he might faint. They heard the cab door slam. Billy was standing in the doorway. He greeted A-Ken warmly.

"Everything okay?"

"So far so good," said A-Ken. He sounded happy. Comfortable. Cheuk heard another voice. It was beside him, whispering quietly.

"Relax, leave this to me, boss," his constable said.

Cheuk nodded his agreement. He took a step back from the door. He knew a professional when he saw one. Delegation did nothing to help his heart rate.

Billy continued his charade. "That's good to hear. Time for food?" He was playing his part well.

"Sure. I'm always hungry," A-Ken said. "You know me, cousin."

"I've got snacks in here."

The door opened and Billy entered. A-Ken was close behind. The strike came with unexpected speed and ferocity. Even Cheuk was taken aback. The timing was immaculate. The door slammed shut the moment A-Ken entered. The revolver struck A-Ken violently on the side of the head. Cheuk could feel the power and venom of the impact. A-Ken grunted as he reeled from the blow. Cheuk made his move. He deserved a share of the glory.

"Don't move motherfucker. I'll blow your head off," he shouted and jammed his revolver into the back of A-Ken's neck. Brawler's hands were lightning quick. A-Ken was slammed against the door. A flurry of punches mangled his face. His revolver was snatched out of the holster at his waist. Strong hands pulled him down. Handcuffs appeared. He was cuffed roughly. Violently. Expertly. First one wrist and then another. He was face down on the gleaming tiled floor. Smudges of blood marked the floor. It had taken seconds.

A-Ken had been bested by a gorilla-like foe. Resistance was futile. He said nothing.

"You're under arrest," Cheuk said.

He looked at his partner. He was sitting triumphantly astride the prone figure. He had not broken sweat. They locked eyes. Cheuk nodded in appreciation. The brawler smiled in victory. The message was unspoken. Cheuk owed him and the debt would be paid when the time came.

Billy was standing in the doorway. He approached cautiously now. "Sorry, A-Ken," he said. "This is for your own good. It's what's your mother would have wanted."

Blood dripped from a deep wound over A-Ken's eye. He faced the wall to avoid eye contact and remained silent. Cheuk switched on his beat radio.

"Console, DVC Sai Kung, over."

"Send," came the instant response. They all knew the DVC had been out on an operation.

"Inform SDU, one bird detained in the nest," he reported. "Please arrange transport. Over."

Cheuk replaced brawler kneeling on A-Ken's back. Brawler stood and re-arranged his jacket. He smiled and picked up A-Ken's keys from the floor. He winked at Cheuk.

"Well done, A-sir, good arrest," he said. They had delivered the turkey. It was time to cook it.

47

Silas smiled, their plan was coming together. With him and Dragon supervising, the other two gang members patiently manoeuvred the chunky table up the staircase. Piece by piece they dismantled the crude barricade and deftly cleared a route through the chairs. Silas hung back. His role was illuminating the top of the staircase. Someone had to do it.

The plan to use the heavy table to shield their ascent worked like a dream. The thick wood easily absorbed shots fired down the staircase by their unseen enemy. He had only counted three more rounds. That was encouraging. It indicated their foes had limited ammunition. Or just a single weapon. Or both.

Dragon had a bloodlust. Nothing could hold him back. The AK-47 would be his means of revenge. He directed the assault enthusiastically and countered sporadic shots with vicious bursts of fire. He aimed pot shots at anything that moved. Not much had. The blood trail they found at the top of the staircase explained why.

Silas was heartened by the bloodstains. They led along the corridor. He wondered which one was hurt. He hoped it was the *gweilo*. That would make things easier. They would make him watch the fun. If he lived that long.

The doors on the corridor were locked. It was child's play to break in, they kicked in the doors one by one. Only the third room, the largest, held any interest. Belongings were scattered around the bed. Blood covered the floor. He could smell Jenny's scent. A frisson of lust and excitement surged through his body. They were close.

He smelled smoke. It came from above. The staircase to the roof was alight. A discarded bottle of kitchen oil lay at the foot of the stairs. Three mattresses had been dragged halfway up. The fire had quickly taken hold. Two gas canisters sat amongst the flames.

It was another amateur booby trap. It seemed more of a danger to the defenders than anyone else. All they had to do was wait. The fire would burn itself out and the canisters would cool. Then they would make their final assault.

"I'm coming for you, bitch," he shouted up the staircase. The others joined in with jeers and insults that echoed around the walls. He caught Dragon's eye and laughed as they competed to launch their foulest insults up towards their waiting foe. There was no response. Silas did not expect one. She would be talking soon enough he thought grimly.

The tension had evaporated. Silas gathered his team in the large bedroom, away from the smoke and the flames. Nobody said anything as they marked time. The glow reflecting from the corridor illuminated their faces, their confident grins orc-like amongst the prancing shadows.

He took the opportunity to search the room. A beat radio lay next to the bed. Silas pushed the test button and heard a familiar sound: it was switched on. A momentary panic set in as he wondered if they had used it to call for help. It seemed odd that they had not taken it up to the roof with them.

He forced himself to calm down and think. They were in the middle of nowhere in a typhoon, any assistance would be slow to arrive even if they had called for help. Beat radios were notoriously unreliable. It would be surprising if they could a get a signal in such a remote location. He needed to find out.

"Console, over," he said, as he pressed the send button and heard a musical tone.

Dragon and the others were staring at him intently, like he had gone mad. He waited ten seconds, but the radio remained stubbornly silent.

"Console, over," he repeated. Again no response. He had his answer. He grinned with relief and tossed the radio into the corner of the room.

"No signal," he announced jubilantly. "The gods are with us."

"Perfect," Dragon agreed. "Let's check the staircase," he said, and they followed him out.

The fire was still burning fiercely. The heat kept them pinned close to the doorway but already the inferno was past its peak. The thin old mattresses were rapidly being consumed by the flames. Silas watched with satisfaction, oblivious to the heat and smoke.

A clattering sound came suddenly. It was behind them, along the corridor. Loud and metallic, they all heard it. They turned and pointed their weapons towards the source of the noise, fingers on triggers.

"Armed police, stop or I shoot," came the shouted warning. Silas felt sick. Dragon was first to respond. He pushed Silas through the doorway, the others followed. Dragon sprayed a burst from his AK-47 along the corridor. The sound was deafening. The bright muzzle flashes illuminated two dark figures at the far end of the narrow space. A cry of pain indicated a bullet had found its mark. A burst of machine gun fire was returned just as Dragon ducked back into the room.

Silas cursed their bad luck. Another fifteen minutes, that was all they had needed. The cops had arrived moments too soon. They must be SDU, he realised. The weaponry and tactics were distinctive. The chances of success against them ranged from slim to zero. Disengaging was the only option, they needed to make a run for it. Better to live another day than stand and fight. It was hopeless.

Silas looked around at his team. Panic seemed to be setting in. Dragon's two assistants were whispering conspiratorially close to the window. It looked like they were considering escape options.

Dragon was blinded by rage. He still had fight in him and engaged the cops fearlessly. The crazed grin on Dragon's face told Silas he was enjoying himself.

Dragon paused and reloaded, the empty magazine dropped at his feet with a hollow metallic sound. Dragon tossed Silas a grenade. He told him to throw it. Silas did as he was instructed. As it left his hand he realised the pin remained in it. His face burned with embarrassment. It was the final straw. Pressure sorted men from boys. He was not in Dragon's league. It was time to leave, they all knew it.

They faced a choice. SDU assault on one side. Burning staircase on the other. The window was the only alternative. Silas ordered the metal grille to be kicked out. It came away easily. Thirty years of corroding sea air helped their cause.

The ten foot drop to the grass was the least worst option. Silas went first. It didn't end well. He was limping badly. His ankle was either broken or sprained. Every step was agony. He knew he couldn't get far.

He hobbled to the trees. The others joined him. SDU would not be far behind. He was surprised by the lack of a police cordon. Luck was with them.

They were looking back at the building. Its roof was glowing red, flames were bursting from the staircase. They could see no one. He slumped to the ground and Dragon came over.

"My ankle is screwed. I can't go on. Just leave me," Silas said between gasps.

They had seconds to decide, pursuit was imminent. Dragon grasped his hand and said his farewells. It was the right decision. They agreed to meet back at the Mong Kok safe house.

"Get into the trees and hide. We'll lead them away from you, good luck," Dragon said.

Silas didn't hesitate. Without uttering a word, he limped off the path into the trees. Dragon fired a long burst towards the house. It was deliberate, he was attracting their attention. He was loyal to the end. Silas saw the three of them turn and jog up the track towards the road.

48

Jameson could smell the salt in the winds blowing in off the sea. It tasted fresh and reinvigorating after the smoke-filled air downstairs. He was standing next to Sam on the roof. The flames were gone but smoke lingered in the air. A voice came from below.

"*Daai lo*. Three birds down on the road. No survivors. Chu-sir is missing."

"Roger," Jameson shouted.

There were just the four of them remaining at the house. A-Lap was downstairs. He was sitting in the same position where he had been shot. They had stabilised him but it would be a while before they could get a stretcher to him. He was as comfortable as could be expected with a shoulder wound like that. His partner was outside, on guard. Jameson was taking no chances.

The other three had chased the gang up the path. He knew they wouldn't catch them. That wasn't the point. They were briefed not to. They only needed to push them onwards and block their return path. They were sheepdogs herding sheep. The Grim Reaper awaited.

"Three dead," Jameson said. "Silas is not among them."

Sam gave no reaction. He was standing silently. His elbows were on the parapet. He was staring blankly out towards the dark sea. White capped waves foamed and roiled. The flashing blue light of a police launch could be seen approaching in the distance. It was bucking and heaving in the heavy seas. The crew were earning their money for once. Jameson rebuked himself for the uncharitable thought. Rather them than me in weather like this.

Sam wore only a tee-shirt and shorts. He was drenched but seemed oblivious to the rain. He was shaking his head and muttering. Jameson wondered if he was going into shock.

"I remembered your advice," Sam said quietly.

Jameson moved closer to hear his words. They were standing side by side. The wall felt cold to his touch. After an hour, the novelty of the incessant rain was wearing off. Warm rain had become cold damp and he felt himself flinch as a drop went down his neck. He wiped irritating drops of water off his nose. They were instantly replaced.

"I took the shot," he continued. "It wasn't enough."

Jameson thought he saw a single tear run down Sam's face. It was instantly obliterated by the pelting rain.

"Tell me what happened," Jameson requested.

"We were just waiting and hoping," said Sam. "It was Jenny's idea to delay them by barricading the doors and staircases. It was the best we could do."

Jameson said nothing. He tried to imagine what it must have been like for them as the gang came ever closer. A sudden shiver went through him. He put it down to the cold and the wet.

"She was just unlucky," he continued. "I took a shot down the stairs and they fired back. She wasn't even close to the staircase. It was a freak ricochet. It could just as easily have been me instead of her."

Jameson thought of the vicious neck wound that he had just seen on the woman's body. Even with immediate medical assistance it would have been fatal nine times out of ten. He felt nauseous at the thought of what it must have been like for Sam to deal with it alone.

"I carried her along the corridor and tried to stem the bleeding," he explained. "She was unconscious. Once I heard Silas's men coming up the stairs I carried her to the roof and started the fire. I just held her close and waited. I don't know how long it was before the shooting started. She died a few minutes before you arrived on the roof."

Jameson saw tears streaming down Sam's face. He decided he had heard enough. He could feel his own anger rising. It didn't matter how many of the gang SDU killed, he had failed in his mission of keeping both Jenny and Sam alive. He didn't relish the inevitable conversations with Smithies and McClintock.

"You did your best Sam. That's all anyone could have asked of you," he said.

He glanced at the bloodstains covering Sam's tee-shirt and hands. There was more red than white. Diluted blood was dripping down his legs. Even his white socks were stained red.

"Come on," he said gently. "Let's get you back. This is no place to be in a typhoon."

Jameson saw Sam take a lingering look at the body lying peacefully in the corner. The flames had consumed anything they could have covered her with. She lay exposed to the elements. It was one final indignity. Sam wiped his eyes and headed for the stairs. It was over. She was at peace.

Their walk to the road was unhurried. They remained silent. In any case, attempts at conversation were hopeless in the face of the gale howling around their ears. Jameson was content to leave Sam with his thoughts. He trudged behind, head down. He was a man wrestling with demons.

Half way along the path they passed a team of a dozen SDU lads running in the opposite direction. Both groups were using lights, a blue on blue precaution. Friendly fire was the last thing they needed. Not on a day like today. The team waved an acknowledgement as they jogged past. They carried four collapsible stretchers between them. Three for the bodies and the casualty. One spare, in case they found Silas.

It was a slow journey. Jameson was in no hurry. He saw the lights from distance, flashes of blue reflecting off clouds. Like a beacon, they were visible for miles around.

As they approached the road, Jameson was surprised by a sentry emerging wraith-like from the shadows of a bush. He welcomed them warmly. The dark of the path was replaced with the bright headlights of a dozen vehicles. The road was packed with unmarked Land Cruisers and high-sided Mercedes vans. The SDU vehicles surrounded a battered white lorry. Three bodies lay on the road close to the lorry, where they had died. Exposed to the elements, the pounding rain was washing them clean of blood and gore. Streams of diluted blood followed the camber of the road and seeped mournfully into the grass verge. The gang's guns lay beside the cadavers, awaiting CID investigators and crime scene photographers and all the rest of the circus.

Jameson guided Sam to the back seat of a Land Cruiser and wrapped him in a blanket. Two sugary black teas in polystyrene cups appeared from nowhere. Jameson accepted them gratefully. He left Sam to reflect alone, in silence.

Jameson noticed the cab of the lorry was pockmarked with puncture wounds and the windscreen shattered by gunshots. The road was littered with shell casings. The team were beaming at their success. Using A-Ken's truck to lure the gang in as they emerged from the bushes had been a masterstroke. They didn't stand a chance against two dozen MP5s. It was a textbook ambush. The gang had foolishly taken on the unit head to head and lost. Big boys' rules. Five down, one to go.

Jameson recognised a familiar face nearby and was puzzled. It was an old colleague, he wondered why he was here. Jameson returned the high five he was offered nonetheless. The visitor was grinning mischievously. Jameson was suspicious, he was a well-known troublemaker. He bore the gift of being able to start a fight in an empty room. It was the reason he had left SDU after one indiscretion too many, despite his undoubted talents.

"Long time, no see, A-sir. Good arrest," Brawler said, laughing uproariously.

49

It was four weeks later. The *baai kwan daai* was a major event. The Regional Commander had stood by his rash offer to pay the beer costs. That alone was incentive to attend for many.

The Tsim Sha Tsui station compound had been cleared. Trestle tables replaced vehicles. Large plastic tubs of iced water, cooled shiny cans of San Miguel and Carlsberg. Hundreds of station staff and visitors milled around in the shade. Most were drinking beer. Others were demolishing industrial quantities of roast pig, duck and chicken. Stories of derring-do and disaster were *de rigeur*. Laughter was in the air. Despite everything, it was a joyful occasion.

This *baai kwan daai* was the largest held in the station for many years. Three assistant commissioners were present. It was unprecedented. They were here to celebrate a case study in teamwork and cooperation.

It was intended as a police-only affair but a few guests from other services had also been invited. ICAC were not amongst them. Three RAF flight crew attended in tweed jackets. They were led by a portly moustachioed Flight Lieutenant. He seemed determined to drink his bodyweight in beer. A 28 Squadron plaque had been donated to the Officers' Mess to mark the occasion.

Steve Jameson and his team from SDU were leading the charge. They had donated several roast pigs. Chunky chopping boards bedecked folding wooden tables covered with plastic sheets. Grubby-looking caterers enthusiastically hacked pigs into pieces. It was serious work. Armed with shiny steel meat cleavers, they worked at lightning speed. One dangled a half-smoked cigarette from the corner of his mouth. No one cared.

ICAC and *O-Gei* investigations were still underway. They anticipated it might take twelve months to complete the paperwork. Convictions would conclude the matter. A-Ken was singing like a bird in custody. Silas's assets and safe houses were gradually being uncovered. His network had been dismantled.

All shots fired by police had been justified, there was no stewards' enquiry. A slew of compliment letters had been distributed to the players. There was talk of Commissioner's and Governor's Commendations. Possibly even Gallantry Medals.

It had been the bloodiest ten days in Hong Kong's recent history. The body count was skewed in favour of the police. They had been lucky. More could have been killed and injured. Public gratitude and sympathy were noticeable. It wasn't always that way.

Silas was still missing. The hunt to find him continued. Speculation was that he had drowned in the midst of the raging typhoon, washed away as he tried to evade police.

Stories describing mayhem and murder had flashed worldwide. It was rumoured privately that the Commissioner was sceptical of the tactics employed. He said nothing publicly. He was content to accept the plaudits. He and the Governor saw the bigger picture. The forces of law and order had prevailed. Public confidence in the authorities had been upheld at a critical juncture. The masters in London were happy.

Sam took another swig from his Carlberg. He scanned the crowd for familiar faces. He had felt a bit more relaxed these last few days. He could start to enjoy the glow of accomplishment. It was a memorable case. He was either famous or infamous, depending on who was telling the tale. Most people were still keeping their distance. He understood why. The locals knew a *haak jai* when they saw one, someone who brought bad luck with him where ever he went.

Sam wondered if his luck would improve after the ceremony. It was his first time bowing before *Gwan Daai*. It seemed worth a try. All the *gweilos* had already done it. If nothing else, it made the locals feels better.

He could hear McClintock's voice. He was loudly regaling an audience with his recollection of events. A gaggle of senior officers were watching nearby. They looked on disdainfully. Sam smiled at the scene. McClintock revelled in his reputation as a rule breaker. He was cleverer than most people knew. The obnoxious Scottish loudmouth, who flirted with disaster and came up smelling of roses, was a fabrication. It was his own creation, a marketing masterclass. He was constructing his own legend, a proven tool for climbing the Force's greasy promotion pole. He knew the power of imagery. There was only one thing worse than people talking about him. That was people not talking about him.

Only Jenny was missing. He was struggling with her loss. He knew it would take time. His head told him he was not responsible. His heart was telling him something else. The grief he felt was unlike anything else in his life to date.

He shuddered at an image of her body lying cold on the windswept rooftop. He remembered how he had cradled Jenny in his arms as they waited for salvation. She had grasped his hand tightly until the moment she quietly slipped away just after the gun battle below ended. The familiar feeling of nausea had returned.

He pulled himself away from the scene. Re-living that moment was his daily reality. But today was not a day to be sad. There would be plenty of those to come.

Sam saw Liu talking to a film crew. Their vests said Police Public Relations. He was dismayed to see The Harlot. It was an encounter he was keen to avoid, on this of all days.

Sam caught Liu's eye. He was wearing an ear-to-ear grin. Liu was a star of the show and he was enjoying himself. A return to SDU was rumoured to be imminent. For him, Inspector Sam had not been a '*haak jai*'. They touched cans to toast health and success.

"*Yam booi*, A-sir," said Liu.

"*Yam booi*," Sam replied. He threw back his head and finished off the last of his Carlsberg, crumpling the empty can. He squashed it mercilessly, ready for the next one, and wiped his greasy mouth with the back of his hand. A stocky SDU-type walked past. He subtly nodded an acknowledgement to both of them. What they had done meant something.

"I've got a question for you Mr. Liu," he said.

"Go ahead, A-sir", Liu said. He was looking puzzled.

"Now this is all over, what exactly is your relationship with the DVC?" There was a dynamic that he could still not work out. It was starting to bug him.

"Oh, that," said Liu laughing. "I thought you knew. He's my brother-in-law. Capiche?"

Epilogue

They were sitting in the 'Chin Chin' bar of The Hyatt Hotel at the foot of Nathan Road. It overlooked the scene of the recent shootout. They were the first to arrive. McClintock had invited the others for a 1 p.m. start but arranged to meet Sam an hour earlier. It was an opportunity to talk through recent events in peace.

It was Friday. The bar was still quiet. A smattering of local merchants were entertaining visiting American businessmen. The Western restaurant next door was reputed to be one of the most expensive in Kowloon. A few well-heeled tourists had sought respite from the midday sun.

"Beer?" McClintock asked.

The cheerful waiter looked immaculate in his plain black suit and white shirt and tie. He wore a small golden badge over the breast pocket. The service was no less impressive.

"Good afternoon, Mr. McClintock. Nice to see you again." He welcomed them in flawless English. "What can I get you today?" he asked.

"Just two beers for the moment, thank you, Jonathan," McClintock responded. "We've booked a table for 'Hugo's'. Add this to the bill, will you?"

They were sitting in a corner. They were well away from the highly polished wooden bar. Its mirrored shelves and rows of glasses and expensive-looking liquor bottles were spotless. Sam guessed that the table had been specially requested by McClintock. No other guests were in earshot. Sam faced the window. McClintock sat opposite. He was complying with Lofty's maxim of always sitting with your back to the wall. They could have been twins. So similar in many ways. So different in others.

They sat in silence until the beers arrived.

"Cheers. So how was your leave?" McClintock asked amiably. Sam could feel piercing eyes interrogating him.

"It was good to see the folks," he said, and he meant it. Their brief reunion after ten months apart had been emotional. He had not realised how much he missed them.

"Wonderful," McClintock said. "We thought a week away might do you some good. After all that's happened," he ended more quietly. A week in the UK had been McClintock's idea. He had been correct. A change of scenery had helped Sam come to terms with recent events.

He thought about the last few weeks. Time had passed by almost unaccountably, like an out of body experience. He felt disorientated. Being dragged away from the comfortable routine of sub-unit duties had been unsettling. He felt like a part-timer, having spent so little time at work in recent weeks.

With so few possessions, moving to a higher floor in the Hermitage had not been difficult. It was one more irritant in a seemingly endless round of distractions. Changing apartment had felt as if a further link to Jenny's memory had been surgically removed.

Sam had hated Jenny's funeral service. It had been a painful experience. It was all the worse because of his prominent role. He abhorred the scrutiny that came with it. He felt like a small goldfish in a large public bowl. With sharks circling.

The Force had rallied around after Jenny's death. She had been granted a Force funeral with full honours. It was as though suggestions of impropriety had never existed. Sam marvelled at the efficiency of the well-oiled machine. It had swung into action almost as soon as the typhoon dissipated. Welfare officers fussed over every detail of the arrangements.

Nothing could have prepared him for the alien spectacle at Hung Hom Funeral Parlour. The gaudy funeral decorations, strange incantations, and raw displays of emotion were overwhelming. Attendance was in the hundreds. He knew few of them. Many had never met Jenny. They had been touched by her story. Others attended out of ghoulish fascination.

Only Jenny's father attended from her family. A welfare officer introduced them after the service. He looked equally shattered by the experience. He thanked Sam for his efforts in trying to protect Jenny. To Sam it was the worst thing that happened to him all day. He could only mumble a response.

He had been discomfited by the whole experience. He was like an actor playing the big stage in his first role. He knew he could not walk away. Not yet. Not until he had played it through to its melancholy conclusion. Only then could he allow the light to shine on his feelings. His head was warning him to disarm the things he had buried so deep. Before they exploded. He needed to let Jenny go.

He felt adrift. He suspected it was to do with the sense of unfinished business. The nagging thought that he should be somewhere else. That he was missing something. That he was somehow letting Jenny down.

"It's been a rough few weeks," McClintock said kindly. "Try not to blame yourself. You did your best. Jenny was just plain unlucky. That's the fact of the matter."

Sam knew all that. His heart was rebelling against his head. It didn't matter how many times he was told the same thing by McClintock, Ralph or his parents. He felt directly responsible. He felt guilt for him living and her dying. It was down to a stroke of bad fortune that could not be accounted for. The ricochet that had killed Jenny could barely be replicated in ballistics tests, never mind anticipated and avoided.

Sam said nothing. McClintock did not rush to fill the silence. He felt sad, flat, and directionless. He knew that his lack of energy was only partly down to sleep-deprivation in recent weeks. The malaise went deeper. They both knew it.

"It's not been an easy thing to come to terms with," Sam said eventually. He was finally being forced to confront the issue. It was something he had become adept at avoiding in everyday conversation.

"I've been questioning myself and everything else since it happened. I guess that's normal?" he asked.

"Absolutely. Completely normal."

Sam paused again. He was staring blankly out of the window.

"I've got a decision to make," he explained. "That's part of the problem. I'm under pressure to go home. Back to my parents, maybe even to Alice. To put all this behind me and make a fresh start," he said with a sigh.

"Or?" asked McClintock pointedly.

"Or," Sam replied, "dig in and carry on."

"You should stay," McClintock said quickly. "You have a bright future in the Force. You should know that. Jenny would have wanted you to stay," he added.

Sam caught his eye. It was a low blow. He knew it was the truth.

"Is it that simple?" Sam asked.

It was McClintock's turn to be silent. Sam could see that he was building up to something.

"What is it?" he asked.

"I know you did everything you could for Jenny. I was just wondering why you only fired four shots when they attacked you in the house. Anyone else would have fired all six. What stopped you?" he asked.

There was a long pause.

"Jenny stopped me. We were alone. The radios couldn't pick up a signal due to the storm. We were trapped. We both knew it was only a matter of time. She made me promise that I wouldn't let them take her alive. The last two bullets were meant for us." He had told no one. It had been their final secret.

"Jesus," said McClintock. The shock and revulsion was obvious. "Why didn't you tell anyone?"

Sam had shifted his gaze away from McClintock's face. He was staring aimlessly at the building opposite. Memories of that night were distracting him. The image of Jenny's head in his lap as her life ebbed away kept endlessly re-appearing. The sounds of gunfire still echoed in his ears.

"I'm sorry we let you down," McClintock said solemnly. "You deserved better."

Another silence followed before Sam plucked up courage to tell McClintock the truth.

"Would it surprise you if I told you I've been obsessing about Silas? In my dreams I hunt him down and kill him."

"Not at all, laddie. I would have been more surprised if you weren't."

"If I stay, will you help me find him?" Sam asked the question coolly. His arms were folded across his chest. The seriousness and menace of the challenge was unmistakeable.

McClintock said nothing. He had been offered a Faustian pact. A smile appeared. He slowly nodded his acceptance. He grasped Sam's hand and shook it firmly. He held it longer than normal and squeezed.

"Too fucking right son, don't get mad, get even. Me and you are going to get on just fine and dandy. Mark my words. Finish your drink, it's time for lunch." He stood and drained his glass. "Welcome to the team."

If you enjoyed reading this book, look out for the further adventures of Inspector Sam Steadings. Coming in 2023:

THE DISTRICT

You may also enjoy similar 'Asian Thrillers' set in the 1980s and 90s available from Thaumasios Publishing Ltd.

The Reliable Man Series
by Valerie Goldsilk & Julian Stagg

The Inspector Scrimple Series
by Valerie Goldsilk

Further details at:

www.thereliableman.com

Printed in Great Britain
by Amazon

82825896R00200